case. Kick back in your stilettos to find out who knocked off a mogul's wife: the supermodel, the designer, or her own hubby!"

—*Us Weekly* on *Live at 10:00, Dead at 10:15*

"Entertaining and fast-paced."

—*Romantic Times BOOKreviews* on *Shooting Script*

"Only Elsa could fashion such a lively murderous tale."

—Calvin Klein on *Live at 10:00, Dead at 10:15*

"It's impossible not to wonder who the real-life models for her characters were. A fun and fast-paced read, with l⎯ of dish on an industry that can be as ugly as it is beautiful."

—*Calgar⎯ ⎯ 10:00, Dead at 10:15*

"The mystery's protago⎯ ⎯rson, an attractive television pr⎯ world of fashion and society. As ⎯and, of course, fashion—I couldn't w⎯ ⎯o, Dead at 10:15]. Klensch pulled it off, with th⎯ ⎯ that kept me awake and guessing till the end."

⎯⎯yn Theiss, *The Cleveland Plain Dealer*

"No one communicates with more style or more authority than Elsa Klensch. She's the ultimate insider."

—Donna Karan

"Elsa proved that television cover of fashion could be successful. Now she proves that she is as good at writing fiction as she is in front of a camera."

—Oscar de la Renta on *Live at 10:00, Dead at 10:15*

"If Mickey Spillane dealt in dress patterns and couture instead of lead and vengeance, this is the kind of book he'd write. Brisk and sharp, building to a satisfying and hilarious payoff."

—*New York Post* on *Live at 10:00, Dead at 10:15*

"I enjoyed this novel. An interesting series that bears watching."

—*Mystery News* on *Shooting Script*

"The illicit sex, gorgeous clothes, and filthy-rich guests should appeal to Danielle Steel fans."

—*Booklist* on *Shooting Script*

"A tale of deadly intrigue at one of America's top design houses. Fast-paced and funny—a debut with style."

—*Kirkus Reviews* on *Live at 10:00, Dead at 10:15*

BOOKS BY ELSA KLENSCH

Style

Live at 10:00, Dead at 10:15

Shooting Script

Take Two

TAKE TWO

A Sonya Iverson Novel

Elsa Klensch

A TOM DOHERTY ASSOCIATES BOOK

New York

TAKE TWO

Copyright © 2007 by Elsa Klensch

A Forge Book
Published by Tom Doherty Associates, LLC
175 Fifth Avenue
New York, NY 10010

www.tor-forge.com

Forge® is a registered trademark of Tom Doherty Associates, LLC.

Library of Congress Cataloging-in-Publication Data

Klensch, Elsa.
    Take two : a Sonya Iverson novel / Elsa Klensch.—1st ed.
        p. cm.
    "A Tom Doherty Associates Book."
    ISBN-13: 978-0-7653-1445-1
    ISBN-10: 0-7653-1445-2
    1. Iverson, Sonya (Fictitious character)—Fiction.   2. Women television producers and directors—Fiction.   3. Women publishers—New York (State)—New York—Fiction.   4. Sisters—Fiction.   5. Family secrets—Fiction.   6. Inheritance and succession—Fiction. 7. New York (N.Y.)—Fiction.   I. Title.

PS3611.L46T35 2007
813'.6—dc22

                                                            2007028849

First Edition: November 2007

Printed in the United States of America

0   9   8   7   6   5   4   3   2   1

To the unsung thousands of volunteers across America
who so generously give their time and energy.
Thrift shops would not survive without them.

Acknowledgments

Many thanks to my longtime advisor and friend, Jerry Krone, to my ever-supportive editor, Melissa Singer, to my agent, Kay McCauley, and my husband, Charles.

TAKE TWO

Chapter 1

"Thank you for everything, Marta," Kathryn said with genuine feeling. "I couldn't have gotten through it without you."

Marta's hand shook as she poured scotch into crystal glasses. She put a couple of ice cubes into one tumbler and handed it to Kathryn.

"I need a strong drink and so do you," she said.

Kathryn didn't want the scotch. She was desperate to go home, take a sleeping pill, and escape for a few hours. But she took the glass and sat on the sofa.

Marta sat beside her and took a long swallow. "I loved Zoe as a sister, but . . ." Her voice trailed off.

Kathryn closed her eyes. What was coming now? For God's sake, they had just said a final good-bye to her mother at the funeral home. How strong Marta, her godmother, had been at the funeral service, standing at the podium in her stylish yellow suit. She'd worn it, she said in her tribute, as her way of thanking Zoe Pettibone for being a "constant ray of sunshine in my life."

Now Marta's energy had dissipated and she looked exhausted, distraught. Kathryn felt she should hold her, but something about Marta's manner held her back.

"Marta, what do you mean you 'loved her as a sister, but'?" she asked. "What do you want to say?"

Marta didn't answer. She gulped down the rest of her drink, then poured another. Clutching the glass, she turned to face Kathryn.

"I'd never have called Zoe a coward, but at times she just couldn't face the truth," she said. "Now, as I realize what I have to tell you today, I know I'll never forgive her for that."

Kathryn rose and walked toward her as Marta sank into a chair.

"Marta," Kathryn said, "if anyone knew my mother, I did. She had faults, but she wasn't a liar. She worked hard at her job as a fund-raiser. She got out there and fought for what she believed in. I'm proud of her. Nothing you can say will change that."

Marta snorted. "Be proud. But you have to accept the fact that she lied to the person who mattered most to her."

Kathryn's chest tightened. She didn't want to talk about her mother's weaknesses, now or ever. Marta knew how she'd suffered through her parents' unhappy marriage and bitter divorce. Now both were dead. What could be left to discuss? She knelt by Marta's chair.

"What are you talking about?"

Marta put her hand on Kathryn's shoulder. "Do you remember how your parents fought? How they were never at peace with each other?"

"How could I forget? It was one ceaseless battle for the seventeen years before I went to college and Dad left."

"You were the problem between them."

"Marta," she protested, "what are you talking about? I don't believe that. Both of them loved me, and I loved them. It was the differences between them, their ages, their backgrounds, even their political views, that caused their problems. Not me."

Marta shook her head.

"No. You were the problem. Not you as a person, but the fact that they had so much trouble having a child. That's why your mother could never summon the courage to tell you this herself." She paused, then gave a short laugh. "Now I understand why."

Kathryn sat back on her heels to hide her frustration. She just wanted Marta to get on with her story, whatever it was.

"Marta, out with it. You know you can tell me anything."

"Your mother was terrified of losing you. Remember that, Kathryn. It will help you understand."

"Marta, tell me. Please."

Marta leaned back and closed her eyes.

"Kathryn, you're adopted. You're not your mother's birth child."

Kathryn looked at her blankly. "Adopted? What do you mean?"

"I mean adopted. When we were stationed at the Embassy in Paris. I helped your mother make the arrangements."

Kathryn fought the disbelief that was sweeping over her.

"Why didn't she tell me?"

"Your father wanted to, but your mother was against it. She told me she'd tried many times, but never had the courage." Seeing the horror on Kathryn's face, she added, "Kathryn, she loved you as much as any mother could love a child."

Kathryn struggled to her feet and walked to the sofa. Sitting, she ran her hand over the brocade on the seat to reassure herself where she was.

Suddenly she was filled with anger at Marta. "Why tell me now, and on this of all days? Couldn't you have waited?"

Marta's answer was quick. "No, I couldn't wait. I knew if I didn't tell you today I never would. Try to understand, I promised Zoe and I couldn't break my promise." She paused. "Anyway, I always believed you had a right to know, and I'm glad that I'm the one to finally tell you."

Kathryn sat in silence. She might have known her mother, but she thought, as she had so often in the past, that she had never completely understood her. Zoe Pettibone had been a full-bodied, temperamental woman whose sudden bursts of anger were followed by unexpected treats. How robust, how full of life she'd been. And then she died, still and shrunken on the hospital bed, stripped of her strength by two crippling strokes.

Kathryn looked at her godmother. Marta put her hand to her eyes and wiped away the tears. "When I made the promise, I did it so lightly. I didn't for a moment think she'd go before I did. She was a year or two older, but physically she was always stronger." The horror of what she was saying crept into her voice. "I didn't dream I'd ever have to do this. Never. Kathryn, please, I've tried to do it with compassion."

Kathryn wasn't listening. Resentment surged through her. "It was cruel of her not to tell me as a child, but it was brutal to have you tell me after she died."

Marta sat beside her.

"Don't judge her now. You'll understand in time. Zoe couldn't admit to herself, let alone to you, that she wasn't your birth mother. As wrong as it may seem, having to adopt a child made her feel she wasn't a complete woman. What's more, your father didn't make it easy for her."

Marta leaned over and took Kathryn's hands in hers, rubbing them as if to warm them. "When Zoe married your father, he was over forty and desperate to have an heir. He was the last of the Pettibone line and he wanted it to continue. But Zoe had miscarriage after miscarriage. It seemed impossible that she would carry a child to full term. She blamed herself and became deeply depressed. We were afraid she was suicidal.

"Then she became pregnant again. She stayed in bed for months and only when the doctor told her the baby was fine did she go shopping. Just for a few hours, to buy baby clothes. I'll never forget it. She was deliriously happy. She knew the baby was a boy and that he would fulfill her husband's dream."

"This all happened in Paris?"

"Yes. But the baby was premature and lived for just a few hours. Lewis blamed her, shouting that she should never have left her bed, that she had killed his son. Zoe nearly went mad. Eventually, Lewis agreed to adopt a child. But he wouldn't consider a son; he insisted a Pettibone male had to have Pettibone blood. I looked for a little girl and I found you."

Kathryn sat silent, overwhelmed with sadness, struggling to understand everything Marta had told her. Then she asked quietly, "Do you know anything about my birth parents?"

"Yes. Your mother was so young—just a teenager at an American school in Switzerland. As for your father, I know nothing."

"What was her name?"

"She was a Woodruff, from the New York publishing family. But let's not go into that now. You need time to absorb all this. Be gentle with yourself. I'll tell you everything I know later."

Kathryn got up and walked to the window. In the courtyard below, a father tossed a ball to three children, a boy and two girls. They laughed as the boy missed the catch and the smaller girl ran after it. A family, playing together, Kathryn thought. They hadn't a care in the world. She bit her lip.

"I feel empty," she said.

Marta came and stood by her.

"Your mother loved you as no one ever will again. Remember that." She put her arm around Kathryn's shoulder. "You need time to deal with this. Please don't judge me harshly. I had to keep my promise to tell you."

"I don't judge you at all. I know how much telling me must have cost you. And you know how much I love you."

Marta pulled her close and they stood for a moment holding each other. Then Kathryn broke free.

"I'm going to walk home. You said I need time to think, and I do."

"Kathryn, please stay with me. You shouldn't be alone."

"No," Kathryn said. "I must be by myself."

Marta kissed her on the forehead. "I'll let you go then, and with my love. This has been a dreadful day for you. But it's over, and you're young and strong enough to put it into the past."

Kathryn nodded, blinking back the tears.

"Call me the minute you get home. I must know you're safe. I won't stop thinking of you and what I've done."

Kathryn kissed her good-bye and walked blindly out of the building. The sun was bright on her face. She pushed past people without seeing them. Tears ran down her face.

"Mother, Mother, Mother," she cried out loud, "I want you back so we can talk. Why didn't you tell me? Why did you leave me to face it alone?"

Chapter 2

Hilda Woodruff Fowler's Fifth Avenue apartment, Manhattan
Thursday, 6:30 P.M., one month later

The private elevator slid to a stop at the penthouse floor. Sonya Iverson, senior producer for the top-rated *Donna Fuller Show,* stepped out, and collided with a man standing in the entrance hall.

"Sorry," he said as he moved back. Sonya recognized him by his smile, a flash of white teeth in a tanned face. Steve Pendleton. As usual, he was dressed in the East Side personal trainer's uniform, a black workout T-shirt and pants. Sonya had met him while working on a story about a new fitness craze.

"Working late, Steve?" she asked.

"I take it as it comes." He grinned.

"So you train Hilda Woodruff?"

"You could say that," he said with another grin. "How's life with you?"

"Fine," Sonya said. "I'm working too. But I hope it won't be too late an evening, I have an early morning meeting."

"Hilda will be on time," he said. "We didn't do a full workout. I just massaged her foot. She won't need to shower."

Sonya looked at him with interest. "She hurt her foot?"

"It's nothing," he said, and paused. Sonya sensed he was holding something back.

Then he added, "Hilda told me you were coming and that you're doing a story on the Woodruffs." He paused again and looked away for a moment. "Sonya, I know you're fair, so I'm asking you to ignore the rumor that's going around about her. It's not true. Hilda would never do that. It's just talk—jealousy about her power and her money."

Sonya raised her eyebrows and gestured her ignorance. "*The Donna Fuller Show* is not about gossip. I don't know what the rumor is and I'm not interested." But she guessed what it was. Hilda, whose husband was dead, had a lover. And probably one who was married.

"Don't tell me that." She heard the irritation in his voice. "You're a journalist; you must have heard something. All I'm asking you to do is to ignore it." He walked into the elevator.

Sonya watched him go. What was that about? He knew something about Hilda and was doing damage control.

Steve Pendleton worked with bored wives in Manhattan. He trained women whose husbands were too busy making money to pay attention to them. To many of them, trainers were like psychiatrists. The odds were Steve Pendleton knew all there was to know about Hilda Woodruff.

Sonya turned to the wall opposite the elevator where a gilt mirror hung over an ornate commode. On the commode's top stood an urn filled with dozens of white and pale yellow orchids. Pure luxury. Just what she expected. She was here to talk to three of the richest women in New York, heirs to the Woodruff magazine empire. The subject was a story about the fortieth anniversary of the Woodruff thrift shop, Woody's, which was almost as famous as their fashion magazines. She had been invited to dinner to meet the Woodruff sisters and to discuss the benefit party they planned.

Sonya took advantage of the mirror to check her appearance. She'd wanted to look sophisticated and professional, so she had caught her red curly hair back from her face and added dark green shadow to bring out the color in her eyes. It worked. She smoothed the deep green satin of her dress over her body with satisfaction.

A maid in a snappy black-and-white uniform appeared in the doorway and led her to Hilda Woodruff's cool beige library. At first glance it suggested old money. Bookcases filled with finely bound books lined the walls. The armchairs, with their beige-and-white-striped satin upholstery, were wide and comfortable, and the pile on the carpet was deep enough to quiet any private conversation. Yet the room was like a stage set. Little if any reading was done there, and it was likely that the only time those books came off the shelf was when they were dusted.

As Sonya entered the room, she saw two women sitting on a sofa. They turned, smiled, and stood up to greet her. The taller of the two held out her hand.

"I'm Julia Jenkins, the middle Woodruff sister," she said. "And this is Gussie Ford, who runs our famous Woody's." Julia's voice was strong, almost theatrical in tone. She stood tall and dignified, with dark blond hair framing her face.

"You'll remember me from your visit to Woody's last week," the small, plump woman said as she shook Sonya's hand firmly. "I'm so happy to see you again. And I think it's wonderful you're considering doing a story about our shop. I'll set up everything you want. You can count on me."

"You certainly can count on Gussie. We all do," Julia broke in. "She's run Woody's for forty years, and she's the reason for its success."

Sonya liked Julia immediately. Her manner was down-to-earth and at the same time warm and gracious. "Well, I certainly was impressed with Woody's when I looked it over last week with your press director. And I hear you have some interesting customers for me to meet."

"Real characters," Gussie said. "Some even buy things from us and then sell them on eBay for triple the price. I've told a few that *The Donna Fuller Show* might do a story on us and they can't wait to be interviewed. You know how people are. They all enjoy boasting how smart they are at finding bargains."

Julia motioned them to the sofa and pulled up a chair to be near them. After the maid had served each of them a glass of champagne, Sonya turned to Julia. "Tell me how and why your mother started the thrift shop."

"Well, as you know, my mother and father were from Maine and moved here a few years after they were married. My mother had been involved in charitable work in Maine and wanted to continue here, but she found it difficult. In those days, in the fifties, New York society was pretty much closed to newcomers.

"My father, who was a no-nonsense man, told her to start her own charity. He came up with the idea of a high-end designer thrift shop and he helped her find a good location on Madison Avenue. At first, they raised money to educate children whose fathers had been killed in World War II, but our list of charities has changed over the years."

Gussie thumped the arm of the sofa defiantly. "Julia, dear," she said. "Give credit where it's due. It was Anthea, your mother, who was the force behind Woody's."

Julia laughed. "Yes, Gussie, you and Mother were a team. No one ever expected Woody's to grow into such a success."

Sonya thought Gussie's round, corseted body would burst with pride. Her eyes gleamed and her whole body shook, including the tight ginger curls on her head.

"Well," Sonya said, getting back to the focus of her story, "I guess being connected to the Woodruff family and its powerful fashion magazines didn't exactly hurt."

"Of course not," Gussie said. "Anthea decided to take full advantage of it. We never pressured them, but designers and manufacturers realized what we were trying to do. They wanted their fashions to appear in the Woodruff magazines and we wanted their leftover clothes to sell in our thrift shop."

She laughed out loud. "Of course, James wouldn't let us have any influence on the contents of his magazines. Those decisions were up to the editors. But who could refuse, especially when Anthea called?"

Sonya nodded, then said, "And you still get designer clothes?"

"Yes, and I'll save some of the best for you to photograph. Let's see, Thursday is always furniture day. That's the day we bring the new pieces in from the warehouse. That would be great to photograph too. Often we have customers waiting to see what comes in and, if they find something they like, they hold on to it until I come and price it. Last week I had two women fighting over the same set of chairs." She dropped her voice confidentially. "That was an uncomfortable hour or two. But I simply upped the price until one woman backed out."

Gussie's enthusiasm was infectious, but underneath it, Sonya surmised, was a shrewd business mind. Woody's might make good television, but Sonya still had to have it approved by her executive producer, Matt Richards.

She smiled at Gussie. "You know things aren't quite definite, so don't plan too far ahead yet. We'll make the final decision tomorrow at our morning meeting."

She turned to Julia. "What part do the Woodruff sisters play in running the shop?"

"Hilda heads our family foundation, so she is technically in charge of the shop and has a small office there. Ellin and I help out when needed. I'm there a lot. It's fun."

At that moment, Hilda swept into the room, dressed to kill and obviously determined to dominate her two younger sisters. Her red silk caftan dipped to a deep V, revealing much of her thin, bony chest.

Her high-heeled gold mules sank into the deep pile of the carpet. Sonya got up to shake her hand.

"I'm so sorry I wasn't here to greet you," Hilda said. "I had an urgent call from Paris and I didn't want to wait till the morning to solve the problem. Have Julia and Gussie told you about our benefit party?"

"Not yet," Sonya replied. "I'm getting some background on Woody's. It's fascinating."

The maid refilled their glasses and poured a drink for Hilda. The oldest Woodruff took a delicate sip and said, "The party will be sensational. We'll make the shop look like an extravagant bazaar filled with the most charming wonderful things for people to buy."

"You'll sell things at the party?"

"Of course, that's what Woody's is about. We've been collecting unique pieces for months. We want our celebrity guests to go away with treasures and say to their friends, 'I bought it at Woody's.' It will be a first-of-its-kind party and chic fun. Tell me, what would be the point of having a party in a thrift shop unless the guests get a bargain?" She didn't wait for an answer. "I want to upgrade Woody's image. After all, it's a showcase for the Woodruff Foundation—"

Julia interrupted, "Mother wasn't concerned about image. She cared about helping the unfortunate."

Gussie turned to Sonya. "Yes. That's what was always important to her."

Hilda snorted in irritation. "Don't be so dumb. That's exactly what raising the image will do. It'll attract more customers, and that means we'll increase earnings—and donations." She turned to Sonya. "We'll do our own documentary. I want a record of everything for our family museum in Maine. Father built it, in Portland, where my great-grandfather started in business. We are one of the great old New England families. Everyone knows that."

Sonya shifted uncomfortably. "Tell me about the guests," she asked. "Who will you invite?"

"Everyone of importance. Name a celebrity and you'll find them on our list. And believe me, they'll come. When the Woodruffs throw a party, people are afraid not to come. Everyone will be here. Just everyone."

She looked around the room and drew a sharp breath. "Everyone that is, except my baby sister, Ellin. She's not here tonight and she probably won't make the party—"

"Please, Hilda," Julia interjected, "not now."

But Hilda wouldn't stop. "Oh, Sonya. I don't want to burden you with our problems, but there's one in every family. The relative who always comes late with no consideration for anyone else."

"Hilda, why don't you call Ellin? That will put your mind at rest," Julia said, attempting to smooth things over. "I'm sure she's coming."

Hilda left the room abruptly, with a dramatic sweep of her caftan. No one spoke. Julia sat back in her chair, sipped her champagne, and finally said, "You must excuse Hilda. She's always impatient with Ellin."

Gussie sat up. "I think I hear the elevator opening. Ellin's arrived."

Ellin Woodruff Shelby was a slight, pretty woman who was dressed in a trim beige suit with a double row of pearls—the conservative style of an Upper East Side matron.

"It was the cats, wasn't it, that kept you late?" Gussie asked. Ellin stood at the door looking around the room, as if she didn't want to enter.

"Yes, it was the cats," Ellin replied softly. "I'm glad to have them, but they are a lot of work." She walked to Sonya and held out her hand. "I'm Ellin, the youngest sister. My husband is a vet, and a few years ago he became interested in Bengals. They're a mix of an Asian leopard and a domestic cat. He started breeding them, but it took up so much time that I took over. Now it's taking too much of my time. That's why I'm often late, as I suppose Hilda told you."

"Not exactly," Sonya replied, then added quickly, "I've seen your Bengal cats on your Web site and they're adorable. I'm a cat lover and I found each one more appealing than the last."

Ellin's face lit up. "Then you must come and see them. Let's arrange a date. Saturday afternoons are always great for me."

"Thank you," Sonya said. "That sounds fine."

"Ellin, you're here at last." Hilda's voice came from the hall.

"Yes, and I'm sorry I'm late, but feeding and putting the Bengals down for the night takes time, particularly as I've just had a new litter."

"Enough about your cats." Hilda moved ungraciously to Ellin and let her place an apologetic kiss on her cheek. "Come girls, bring your champagne to the table and let's eat," she commanded. "We have a lot to discuss this evening."

Hilda stepped forward and waved to Sonya to come with her. As she did, her mule caught on the carpet and she stumbled. She would have fallen if Ellin hadn't reached out and caught her. Sonya glimpsed her ankle. It was bound in an Ace bandage.

She looked up and saw Julia and Gussie exchange alarmed looks. Hilda saw them too.

"Julia, don't look like that. There's nothing the matter with my foot," she snapped as she bent and pushed her mule back on. Sonya was surprised at the strength of her reaction to a simple stumble. What was wrong with her foot?

Hilda's tone changed in a flash as she smiled at Sonya. "Come, Sonya, you must be hungry."

They all walked toward the dining room in silence. Sonya could feel the tension among the sisters.

Chapter 3

Sonya poured herself a mug of coffee from the machine in the conference room and went to her usual seat in the middle of the table. The overstewed brew was always bitter, but the caffeine would give her a needed jolt to start the day.

She was the first to arrive for the regular eight thirty Monday morning staff conference. She wanted to check her notes on the Woodruff story so she was ready for the questions her executive producer, Matt Richards, would fire at her.

She had learned a lot about the three sisters during last night's dinner. Hilda, the eldest, was so arrogant it made Sonya wonder just how much control she had over her sisters' money. Julia was the peacemaker, but there was more to her than that. She'd shown she knew how to confront Hilda. And Ellin? Was she really as timid as she seemed? Her late arrival for dinner hinted that she played a passive-aggressive game with her eldest sister. She resented Hilda, a feeling that probably went back to childhood. Hilda must have been a bossy elder sister. Sonya shrugged. She'd find out more about Ellin when she visited her to see the Bengal cats on Saturday afternoon.

The shock of the evening was Hilda's treatment of Gussie. After dinner, they sat in the library discussing the story until eleven. Then Hilda ordered her car and driver to take Sonya home. Sonya had suggested that she give Gussie a lift, but Hilda had insisted the doorman get Gussie a cab. It'd been a tense moment. Sonya's only consolation was that as she left, Gussie patted her on the arm and said, "Don't be concerned. That's Hilda."

At first she had thought Hilda was demeaning Gussie, putting her in her place as an employee. But now Sonya felt that there was a deeper reason. She thought back to her chance meeting with Hilda's trainer, Steve Pendleton. He said there was a rumor going around about Hilda. Gussie undoubtedly knew what it was, and Hilda didn't want Gussie gossiping to Sonya.

She put the thought out of her mind and reread her notes, deciding how to organize the story.

Hilda would be the spokesperson for the family. She was the oldest sister, the head of the Woodruff Charitable Foundation and the person who managed the controlling interest in Woodruff Publishing. Hilda had a presence that would come through well on camera. She was attractive, with a clear, low voice. Sonya couldn't ask for more. Neither would Matt.

Gussie was the trump card. With her plump face, shrewd, knowing eyes, and bouncy curls, she was a good contrast to the Woodruff sisters. Besides, she had a million stories to tell about the shoppers at Woody's—both sad and funny. At dinner last night she told one that showed the kind of person she was, about a woman seeking a wedding dress.

"She was in her forties, tiny, and sad," she said. "She appeared every Saturday looking for a wedding dress. She wanted it to be simple. Few women send their wedding dresses to thrift shops, so I told her to rent one and gave her the names of some of the places she could go."

Gussie paused and glanced at each of the sisters for their reaction. Only Julia smiled at her. Gussie continued, "Still, she came back, looking. I felt sorry for her, and put in a few calls to designers who might have something in their sample rooms. It wasn't easy because most brides wear revealing dresses these days. Then at last, one came in. I put it aside for her. It looked beautiful on her, and when I told her so, she burst into tears. She said her fiancé had been killed in a car crash.

"For a second I believed her. Then as she stood nervously waiting for my reaction, I realized she was lying, the wedding was a fantasy. She dreamed of being a bride, and spent her Saturdays searching for a wedding dress. It was her way of coping with feeling lonely in a big city."

Sonya underlined the story in her notebook. Yes, Gussie was a winner. And while the Woodruff sisters, with their money and power, would form the basis of the story, Gussie would provide the human touch.

She was smiling at the thought of Gussie's warmth when Rick Carlton, the show's other senior producer, came in.

"You look pleased with yourself," he said. "Have you got a murder lined up this week? It's been months since you solved the last one."

Sonya forced a laugh. Rick was referring to the murder of Errol Swanson, the former network chairman, who had been shot just before the opening of his wife's spa in Hawaii.

Solving that murder and getting the story on air, with exclusive footage, had brought her a lot of attention—more than she liked or wanted. She'd become the butt of some friendly teasing at the network.

"Stop it, Rick," she said. "Enough is enough. I'm fed up with the whole business."

Rick glanced at the door. "Sorry. It just tickles me that you got the story, and the killer, by ignoring Matt's directions."

Sonya nodded. Executive producer Matt Richards had been at the spa in Hawaii and he and Sonya had argued about the direction the story should take. Sonya had followed her instincts and solved the murder. Matt resented it.

Sonya signaled to Rick to change the subject as three other members of the staff took their places at the table.

"Is Donna coming to the meeting?" one of them asked.

Sonya shrugged. "I hope so," she said. She knew Donna had much to offer.

Since the problems with Matt in Hawaii, Donna had been coming more frequently to the production meetings. Her insight often gave a story an unexpected twist and she had a calming effect on Matt's abrasive manner.

Sonya had disliked Matt from the moment he'd joined the show two years ago. Okay, the ratings had soared. *The Donna Fuller Show* was one of the network's most popular shows. Matt was only thirty-two and quick to point out that he'd soon be in line to head programming for the network. And maybe he would.

The rest of the junior producers had joined them at the table by the time Donna walked in, gave them a smile, and a brisk, "Good morning." Sonya smiled in return. Donna was as immaculate as always in her blue suit and matching top. Matt walked in behind her, threw down a pile of papers, and sat next to her at the head of the table.

"Let's start with you, Sonya," Matt said. "You can't imagine how surprised I was when I saw your story summary on the worksheet for today's meeting. I couldn't believe that Sonya Iverson was asking to do a puff piece on the anniversary of a thrift shop."

Sonya felt her cheeks flush as a nervous round of laughter broke out around the table. Encouraged by the reaction, Matt pressed the point.

"I thought you only wanted to do 'important' pieces. Why is this little old lady who runs Woody's worth the time of one of our top producers?"

"Enough, Matt," Donna broke in. "The Woodruff sisters—from the publishing company—run the thrift shop. Let's hear what Sonya has to say."

Sonya gave Donna a grateful glance and began. "Yes, you're missing the point, Matt. This story is about the three Woodruff sisters. Their mother started the shop forty years ago. And they're having an anniversary benefit."

"Right," Donna agreed. "Give us some background on them."

Sonya turned to the others around the table and continued, "Their mother, Anthea, who was the wife of the publishing magnate James Woodruff, started it. The shop has been an amazing success and one of the reasons is that they ask designers to donate clothes. They have the power because of the fashion magazines the Woodruff Publishing Company owns—"

"And the sisters don't mind admitting to blackmail? Send me some of your cast-off samples and I'll see you get a credit in the magazine," Matt cut in.

"Well, you could put it that way, but that's not how they do things," Sonya snapped back. "My guess is that the Woodruffs were never involved with the editorial staff. I would say that Hilda, the eldest sister, is too snobbish to even socialize with them. The other two sisters have other interests."

She took a deep breath. "Anyway they cut the labels out, so the shoppers don't see the designer names."

Donna smiled. "Of course, Matt, any woman worth her salt can recognize a designer outfit from the expensive fabric, if not the cut. That's the truth, isn't it, Sonya?"

Before she could reply, Matt interrupted. "How do the designers react to this so-called setup?"

"I talked to several, and they all laughed at the question," Sonya replied. "They said that the magazine editors decide what outfits to photograph."

She looked through her notes to check the facts. "The designers had nothing but praise for Gussie Ford—the one you call 'that old lady.' They say she's an industry character." Sonya read from her notes. "Here's a direct quote from James Curtis, the grand old man of New York fashion. He said, 'She knows as much about fashion as any editor.' He considers her a good luck charm and invites her to his shows. He also said that donating unwanted samples and other odds and ends was quite a handy tax write-off."

Matt cocked his head to one side and leaned on his hand. It was his usual position, a gesture of disbelief or disinterest.

"So you expect some of the designers to come to this benefit sale?" he asked.

Donna laughed. "Matt, please. They'll all come to a party given by the Woodruff sisters. They may not stay for long, but they'll come."

Sonya looked gratefully at Donna. "And it won't just be to show face," she added. "Gussie's been collecting special items that will be sold at the benefit, so it will be like a treasure hunt."

"Special items? Like what?"

"There's no list, but the word is that the Woodruff sisters have been housecleaning. They'll be donating a lot of things, and so will their friends."

"What about the Woodruff sisters, apart from their housecleaning? Hilda's the one who's always in the society pages, isn't she? She's the sister Donna would interview about the shop."

Sonya was glad to have his interest, if not yet his approval. "Yes, definitely. Hilda wouldn't have it any other way. I went to her home for dinner last night. Hilda was married to George Fowler, the hotelier who died in a car crash about a year ago. She is by far the most glamorous of the sisters. She inherited millions from her husband as well as from her father. She now calls herself Hilda Woodruff. She heads the Woodruff Foundation and oversees Woody's. She says the shop makes quite a lot of money for charity."

"Do you believe it?" Matt challenged.

"Yes, I do. I don't know if you've ever seen the shop, Matt, but it's huge, made up of three stores on Madison Avenue. It stocks everything imaginable, not just designer clothes but furniture and electronics. All sorts of things that the rich want to get rid of for a tax break. It's a big operation, and all supervised by your 'little old lady.' "

She turned to Donna for confirmation.

"It's true," she said. "The shop is famous across the country, and so are the sisters. I'm surprised you don't know about them, Matt."

"I know Hilda from photos. She's good-looking."

"Yes, she's attractive," Sonya said tartly. "She's in her fifties."

"Oh," said Matt, disappointed. "That old, huh?"

"She's thin and well maintained. From the portrait of her mother that hung in the dining room, she looks very much like her."

"And the other sisters?" Matt asked.

"Julia and Ellin. Julia is more interesting. She supports several theater groups. You'll see her at the opening of many avant-garde plays. Ellin is married to an East Side veterinarian, Derek Shelby, and dedicates her life to breeding Bengal cats in their penthouse apartment."

"I know Derek Shelby," Matt said. "I've seen him several times at Foxwoods, the Indian gambling casino. He likes poker. Ellin must be a generous wife."

Sonya knew Matt liked to gamble, but she wasn't interested in the details. He went on, "Come to think of it, I saw him there last Friday."

"Oh," she said, her interest aroused. "I'm going to their apartment on Saturday. Ellin invited me to see her Bengals. Maybe I'll meet him there."

Donna broke in. It was obvious she'd made up her mind. "Matt, Sonya should go ahead with the story and take it wherever it leads her."

"Okay," said Matt reluctantly. He was annoyed to have Donna give the approval. "At the very least," he admonished, "make it an 'only in New York' piece. Three society sisters giving a fancy benefit in a rag shop." He laughed. "We'll give it ten minutes at the most. That'll be plenty. The party's on Friday, so we'll run it the following Tuesday."

Sonya knew the piece deserved more than ten minutes of airtime. But she wasn't arguing. She'd do exactly as Donna said—go wherever the story led her, and fight for more time when she'd finished the piece. But first she had to call the Woodruff sisters to tell them the story had been approved, and then call Gussie to arrange the shoot of the shop early Monday morning.

Chapter 4

Kathryn Pettibone put her hands over her ears, buried her face in the pillow, and screamed. New York was too much to bear. The noise: the thunder of the traffic, the screeching sirens, the insistent beat of the bass in the next apartment where partying went on all night. Worse, the joylessness of living in a rented place where nothing was hers. Just looking around the room made her depressed.

She had to pull herself together. Make a new life in this over-crowded city. To re-create what she'd once had in Washington. She'd had a career there, before her mother's illness. As a photographic styl-ist for magazines, she put together outfits for fashion layouts and arranged rooms for decorating shoots. Now she had to get it together again. But she was in New York for another reason, and she must put up with this dreary apartment for a few months.

She knew New York was not the reason she was depressed. She missed her mother. She wanted the security of being able to turn to someone who loved her. Even in the worse of the worst of times, Zoe's strength had been her anchor.

She closed her eyes, forcing herself to forget.

She'd left Washington compulsively, as if by getting away fast she could escape the memory of her mother's death and the shock of learning she was adopted.

Moving to New York had been her immediate thought when she'd learned that her birth mother, Hilda Woodruff Fowler, was living there. A reunion with her had become the most important thing in Kathryn's life. She had to be here, in the same city, and subletting this furnished apartment was the fastest way.

Perhaps she had acted too quickly. But when she made her plans, she hadn't expected Hilda to reject her completely. The letter she'd received from the attorney was cold and impersonal: "Mrs. Fowler will not have her life disturbed in any way by something that was settled thirty-eight years ago."

The letter made her feel more unloved than ever. She bit the pillow. She had a right to know her mother, to know who her father was. She had a half brother. She had aunts and a cousin. If Hilda refused to have anything to do with her, then she would find a way to approach the others. She shivered; it sounded easy, but she would need all the courage she could muster to do it.

Kathryn grabbed the bottle of tranquilizers on her bedside table. She'd take two, double the dose, wait half an hour, and then call Marta. By then she'd be able to speak calmly.

But when she called Marta, there was no answer. Where was she? Kathryn started to panic. Why didn't she answer? Hadn't Marta insisted that Kathryn report to her every day?

Then she remembered it was Friday. Marta was at the Kennedy Center. She had season tickets. Kathryn felt a pang of envy. In Washington she had had an organized life. Outings she planned and looked forward to. She should have been with Marta. They had subscription tickets to the ballet. Who had Marta taken instead? "Stop it," she told herself firmly, "this is ridiculous." It was just that she was lonely.

When the phone rang at eleven, Kathryn hardly heard it. She had turned up the TV to deaden the noise of the party next door, and the tranquilizers had made her drowsy.

"Are you all right?" Marta asked. "You called my cell, but didn't leave a message. Why?"

"Oh, Marta, I'm sorry." Kathryn sighed with relief. "I'm fine now. I had a bad moment, longing to be back in Washington and at the ballet with you. But I took a tranquilizer and now it's working. How was the ballet?"

"The ballet's not important. How are you?"

"I'm okay. Marta, I'm now a volunteer at the Woodruff family's thrift shop."

"How did you manage that?"

"Let me tell you what an experience it was. I felt as if I were being interviewed for a job at the CIA. An old woman, Gussie Ford, runs the shop. She's got to be over seventy, and she's a tyrant. I felt she wouldn't accept me until I'd proved I wouldn't steal any of the secondhand clothes.

"I followed your advice and didn't tell her my real name. I said I was Kathryn Petite. You know that's the name I often used as a stylist."

"Yes, I remember."

"She wanted to know everything about me. Who my mother and father were, where were they living when I was born, did I have any brothers or sisters."

"What did you say to her?"

"I joked a bit. I asked if she needed my fingerprints. Then she said it was necessary to be careful about who worked in the shop. I guessed it must be because of the Woodruff sisters. Apparently they visit the shop quite frequently."

"Did she say anything about them?"

"Not much. She gave me a rundown of the history of the shop. I knew it all anyway. Then she told me about the party they're having next Friday to celebrate the shop's fortieth anniversary. Gussie's pretty desperate for an extra pair of hands as she wants the place to look fantastic. She asked if I could come for a few hours each day."

"Tell me more about the party," Marta asked eagerly.

"There'll be a lot of great items on sale. Gussie hopes the store will get publicity on what the celebrities buy at the party. You know, 'Nicole Kidman bought a 1930s hat,' that sort of thing. That would help them raise more money."

"Are you going to be there?"

"I hope so; it would give me a chance to meet the family."

"When do you start?"

"Well, I've already helped out for a few hours. Gussie wanted some clothes organized, so I put them together the way I would for a fashion shoot. It was fun getting back to work after all the time I spent caring for Mother."

"Do you think she was testing you?"

"Maybe, but anyway I passed. She asked me to come back Monday morning and work from eleven until three. Then as I was leaving she asked me if I could come in tomorrow and I said yes. So everything is working out fine."

"Are you sure?" Marta's voice rose with concern. "You wouldn't lie to me?"

"Of course I'm not okay. At least not yet. But I'm determined to get to know Hilda Woodruff Fowler. When I've done that, I'll get on with my life, I promise you."

"What about your life here?"

"Marta, you know the year before Mother died, I dropped everything to care for her. I have to start over wherever I am, in Washington or in New York. I'll be okay."

"I'm going to hold you to that. I've got the feeling that this whole thing is more traumatic than you're letting on."

Kathryn drew in a sharp breath. "I can handle it," she said firmly.

"Very well," Marta said. "You know I'm here if you want to talk. And if you need me, I'll catch the next shuttle. Just be easy on yourself."

After they said good night, Kathryn looked at her watch. Eleven thirty and she was wide awake. No more tranquilizers. She had to read, to concentrate on something outside of herself before she could sleep.

She went into the living room of the tiny apartment. At the end of the room, next to the kitchen, was the dining table, and on it was the scrapbook she'd made of the Woodruff family.

She started it after she learned Hilda Woodruff was her birth mother. She spent hours on the Internet and at the public library, checking old newspapers, between visits to the attorney who handled her mother's estate.

She opened the book to the first page. Her grandfather James Woodruff had been a public figure. He had a nose for a deal and proved it from the moment he joined his father in the family business in Maine. James also had a ruthless determination to succeed. When he was forty-five, he moved his family to New York and started building the company that would make him one of the richest men in the country. Tracking down this history had been easy. Although James had disliked publicity, there were profiles on him in many magazines. Most were far from flattering.

The photographs showed him to be a heavy man with a square face and small, wide-spaced blue eyes. He was bald and his ears stuck out. Kathryn ran her fingers over one of the glossy photos. What kind of grandfather would he have been?

Anthea, her grandmother, had come from an old Maine family.

Reading between the lines in the stories, Kathryn had gathered that many felt that Anthea had married beneath her. Anthea was the belle of Portland and had many suitors. In one of the articles James joked that it took him five years to win her. They married when she was twenty-three, so he must have begun courting her when she was eighteen.

Anthea, with her blue eyes and classic features, had been a beauty. Kathryn picked up a magnifying glass and studied her grandmother's image. There was no doubt about it, in her coloring, Kathryn resembled her grandmother. She sat back and smiled. She was connected to the family.

She turned the pages, looking at the photos. Anthea's style never changed. Decades passed, but Anthea kept her fine blond hair brushed up from her face, swept down, and then curled up at the ends.

Anthea's favorite color had been pink. She wore bare pink evening dresses to show off her slim figure, strings of pink pearls to emphasize her long neck, and wide-brimmed pink hats to protect her complexion. When she died, James covered her coffin with a blanket of pink roses.

It was ironic that she had worked so hard for cancer research charities, and then fell victim to the disease. It had moved quickly; treatment was useless. She'd barely been seventy when she died—too young, Kathryn thought.

Together, James and Anthea produced three daughters, Hilda, Julia, and Ellin. One article Kathryn had found said James was disappointed in not having a son.

Kathryn thought ruefully that she, the first of his grandchildren, was also a girl. What would James Woodruff have thought? What about Anthea?

She doubted they would have put a grandson up for adoption.

Hilda had married George Fowler, the heir to a chain of hotels, and they had a son, Kathryn's half brother. What a happy moment the arrival of Wells Fowler must have been. Wells looked nothing like the Woodruffs—he must have taken after his father. She had studied his photographs so often she was sure she would recognize him immediately when she saw him. But would she ever have the courage to speak to him? And what would she say?

The tranquilizers had made her mouth dry. She went into the kitchen and poured a glass of water. Setting it on the table, Kathryn resumed studying the book.

Julia had married while she was still at college, had a son, King, and then a divorce. She was the daughter who looked most like her father. She had James's square face and was developing his double chin.

Kathryn turned the pages of the scrapbook until she found the bio of Julia she had compiled. She wanted to check if Julia was pregnant before she married.

Looking at the dates, she saw that it was true—Julia was four months pregnant on her wedding day. That meant James and Anthea must have known about the baby and given their approval.

Maybe Julia had been tested to find out the baby's sex. Maybe James was so delighted when it was a boy that he arranged for the marriage. Or maybe Julia had simply demanded to keep her child.

Kathryn pushed the book away. It didn't matter how it had come about. Julia had kept her baby. Hilda had not. Someday soon, Kathryn would know why.

If Hilda wouldn't speak to her, Kathryn would find another way. She'd bide her time, wait for the right moment. She'd start with Julia. Julia understood the importance of a mother's bond with her child, a child's ties with its mother.

Julia would help her.

All she had to do was be patient and keep her courage high.

Chapter 5

Hilda Woodruff lay on the massage table in her dressing room, eyes closed in relief as Steve Pendleton's firm fingers massaged her ankle.

"There's magic in your touch," she said. "I don't know how I managed before I found you."

"Well, you don't have to worry anymore. I know how you've suffered, and I'll always be here to help."

Hilda opened her eyes and smiled at him. "Thank you," she said. "You make my life bearable." It was the truth. The clubfoot she was born with had scarred her life. It had been mostly corrected over the years by surgery and long periods in plaster casts. Eventually the doctors told her she could live a near-normal life, but the slightest twist to her ankle filled her with dread. Just the thought of more surgery could overwhelm her and leave her sleepless at night.

Steve had given her confidence. He had taught her to cope with the anxiety.

A string quartet played softly in the background. Hilda watched Steve's strong, muscular body reflected in the mirrors that lined the walls.

"I know I did no real damage. I had put on the support bandage but I was wearing those stupid high-heeled mules."

"Just relax and let me work," Steve said. "I'll ice it and then put the bandage back on. Then you can rest. And don't forget what I keep telling you; even though your foot has been corrected, it still needs care. I'm afraid you have a problem that will never go away."

Hilda grimaced. "Every doctor who's ever treated it has told me to rest it when I'm tired. But I wasn't tired or careless; I was angry. The whole thing was Ellin's fault. It's always Ellin's fault. She was late, as usual. I know she does it on purpose to irritate me. I can't stop myself from getting angry. She makes me furious."

Steve calmed her. "I know it's hard, but you need to keep relaxed and take care of yourself."

Steve was always so encouraging, a real friend. The one person she could trust.

"I had Sonya Iverson from *The Donna Fuller Show* over, to discuss doing a piece for the show. Did I tell you that they've decided to go ahead with it?"

"Yes, you mentioned it last night, when you called and asked me to come this morning. You must be pleased."

"I am. But having Sonya there put me under a lot of stress. That's why I got so angry. You know I can usually control myself. Julia suggested I track her down. I left the room to phone her. Before I could call, I heard her arrive. When I got back to the library, she was there, telling stories about her hideous Bengal cats. She's so proud of them; you'd think they were her children. Imagine a Woodruff breeding cats—in an apartment. It's disgusting. The minute you walk into the foyer you can smell them." She grunted with revulsion.

Steve lifted her foot, gently testing it, turning it to each side and then flexing it. "Do you feel any pain now?" he asked.

"No," she said, "none at all." She smiled. Steve was an attractive man, but it was his skill and knowledge that meant everything to her.

She remembered how grateful she'd been the first time he came to work on her foot. It was just after her husband, George, was killed in a car accident. She was exhausted from dealing with the lawyers about George's estate, and her problems with her son, Wells. Steve had come to the apartment to massage her foot every night so she could sleep. Yes, Steve had saved her sanity. She had needed to talk to someone about her problems, and he had been there to listen. There was little he didn't know about her.

She looked at him, bent over her foot, working with total concentration. There was something about his hands moving over her body that created a bond between them.

"You know Ellin and I have never got on," she continued. "She was the baby of the family, born seven years after me. Our lives as children were so different. You know, Steve, my parents were ashamed of me."

"I can't imagine that."

"It's true. I was deformed, and that wasn't supposed to happen in the Woodruff family. My mother couldn't face the difficulties of caring for me, so she hired nurses to do it."

"That must've been hard."

"Yes, I felt so lonely. After my operations she would visit me in the hospital, but I can't remember my father ever being there, or even sending me a present."

Steve was sympathetic, as always. "And you were in so much pain."

"Yes, but it wasn't just the pain. I was afraid that I would never be normal like other children. Never be able to walk or run or play games. I cried myself to sleep night after night."

"It couldn't have been easy."

"Ellin had everything. She never understood what I had suffered.

She never even tried." Hilda fought back tears of self-pity. "And now she has the audacity to accuse me of ruining her life with what she calls my constant criticism."

Steve nodded his understanding. "Hilda, you must ignore all that."

"But she does everything to upset me, like being late on Thursday. Steve, I was so embarrassed."

"I can understand that. There's nothing more aggravating than someone who's always late."

"And it's so rude. I avoid seeing her as much as I can, but on Thursday I felt we had to act as a family. I could have met Sonya by myself, but I thought it was better for us to do it together."

Steve crossed the room to a small refrigerator and took an ice pack from the freezer.

"I'll put this on your ankle for twenty minutes. That will calm it down." Hilda watched as his tanned, deft fingers wrapped the pad in a hand towel and then fastened it about her ankle.

"Now tell me more about your dinner party."

"Well, I told Julia I might be late as I had an appointment with you." Hilda laughed. "I had the courtesy to warn her. Julia came early, so there'd be someone to greet Sonya Iverson. Gussie was with her, as usual."

Steve placed a pillow under Hilda's foot.

"You've always gotten along better with Julia."

"Yes, it's always been that way; she saw what I went through. I guess it's because our nanny would bring her to visit me in the hospital. We played together as kids and we built a close relationship."

"Of course," Steve murmured.

"That sort of relationship stays with you through life. Of course, nothing's perfect. We have different views on how the company should be run."

She closed her eyes for a second.

Steve took a Diet Coke from the fridge and sat on the stool near Hilda's dressing table to drink it. "How did you get along with Sonya Iverson?"

"Sonya seems bright enough, and she was extremely interested in Woody's. She asked question after question. Who donates the things we sell, who buys them, do we give tax valuations. She even asked how long we keep pieces before we reduce the price." Hilda laughed. "It was a challenge to keep up with her, but we managed."

Hilda turned her foot slowly, looked at Steve, and smiled. "That's good, not an ache, not a twinge of pain."

"I told you to keep that foot still." Steve grinned. "Don't you ever listen to me?"

"You know I hang on every word," she said sweetly. Then she laughed again. "Of course Donna Fuller will interview me herself. I am Hilda Woodruff, after all." She studied Steve for a moment. "Do you know Sonya?"

"Yes, I do. I've been interviewed by her once or twice on health stories."

"What do you think of her? Do you trust her?"

Steve hesitated, then answered carefully. "She has an excellent reputation as a journalist."

"Do you think *I* can trust her?"

He paused again. "As I left your apartment Thursday night, I had a few words with her. She didn't say anything outright, but I think she may have heard some rumors about you. My guess is that she thinks you have a lover and that he may be married."

"What makes you believe that?"

"When Sonya Iverson is on a story, she digs deep. She has a lot of contacts. Sonya can start with a rumor and track down whatever truth there is. I don't want to alarm you, but just be careful what you say to her. She's smarter than you think."

"Oh, Steve, don't worry. What I do is my business and mine only. Hilda Woodruff knows how to take care of herself, you can count on that." She laughed. "If I want to keep something hidden—even from you, Steve—it will never come out.

"I'll see to that."

Chapter 6

Sonya sensed the presence of the cat the moment she was shown into the large, dimly lit room. She let her eyes get accustomed to the gloom and then searched for the animal, glancing over the heavy furniture, the sofas and chairs, with their untidy covering of books and magazines. Ellin Woodruff Shelby dressed neatly and conservatively, at least when she visited her sister, but her home was a mess. Perhaps the reason she had been late for Hilda's dinner was not because of the cats, but she had made an effort to dress to please her sister.

A swift movement caught Sonya's eye. The cat had leapt from the top of one bookcase to another. Now it stood alert, its back arched. It had to be a male, it was so big, so arrogant in its strength. Sonya knew it was bred from a wild animal. She was a cat lover, but she preferred ones that sat in her lap and purred. It seemed unlikely that this beast would stoop to such domestic intimacy. It must be only a few short years since its ancestors stalked through the jungle.

The cat confirmed her verdict with a quick, short bark. Startled, Sonya jerked back, then turned as Ellin entered the room. "Raj is magnificent, isn't he?" Ellin said. "He's happy to welcome you, and so am

I." She held out her hand in greeting. "So it's decided, you're doing the piece about Woody's. I'm glad. Maybe we should use Raj in it."

Ellin laughed, and her enthusiasm lit up her face. Sonya smiled, relieved that she was so relaxed. This Ellin would be easier to interview than the uptight one she met at her sister's apartment.

"Raj is more than magnificent. He's majestic," Sonya said, gazing up at the cat. Raj was looking at her with huge green eyes. She felt an urge to stroke him, to win him over.

"He gave me a strange welcome," she said. "It didn't sound like a meow. It was more like a grunt or a bark."

"Yes, I heard it. Believe me, it was special. That bark is his welcome. Bengals don't talk much. The most affection I get from Raj is a low, guttural purr that sounds like a motorbike."

She motioned Sonya to a comfortable chair and offered coffee.

"I keep it fresh. Derek is addicted to it. He drinks ten or twelve cups a day. More if he's busy or has been out late." Then she added, almost to herself, "And he is often out late."

Sonya accepted the coffee. While Ellin was gone, Raj watched Sonya and she watched him. His uncompromising stare was a bit unnerving.

"How long have you been breeding Bengals?" she asked when Ellin returned with the drinks and settled in the chair beside her. Raj jumped to the floor and stalked over to sit beside Ellin.

"It must be five years or more. It was Derek's idea. I only took over when he became too busy at his veterinary practice to look after them. Bring him a sick kitten or puppy and he'll worry about it for the rest of its life." She bent down and stroked Raj. "Sometimes I think he loves animals more than people. Perhaps that's the way a vet should be. Anyway, that's how he is, and nothing will change him now."

She smiled, but Sonya saw that the smile didn't reach her eyes. She wondered how happy Ellin's marriage really was.

"With all his work, I guess you don't get to spend as much time to-gether as you'd like."

"He's a busy man."

Sonya put her mug on the table. At Hilda's dinner party, Ellin had been the most withdrawn of the three sisters. Sonya had put it down to shyness. But now Ellin seemed reluctant to talk at all. Perhaps she regretted her invitation to show Sonya the Bengals.

Sonya said, as lightly as she could, "Well, Ellin, you must have loved animals to marry a vet."

"Oh, yes, I did, and indeed I do."

"How did you two meet?"

"We met at school at Cornell. We planned to open a joint practice somewhere in the country, so we could treat many different animals, but things change."

"You don't like living in New York?"

Ellin ignored the question as she reached down and picked up the cat. "Sweet, sweet Raj," she said, "you are the best kitty I've ever bred." She tried to cuddle him, but after a moment Raj struggled, jumped down, and ran out of the room.

"That's his real nature," she said. "I think it was the Bengal's touch of wildness that appealed to Derek. It certainly did to me. The last thing I wanted was to care for the spoiled cats and dogs of rich people."

There was an awkward silence. Sonya waited for a moment, then asked, "Why did you settle in New York?"

Ellin bent forward and straightened the books on the coffee table. Sonya said nothing, wanting an answer.

Ellin took her time. "It was my dad," she said. "He insisted his daughters live here in the city, where he could watch out for them. He was a rich man and a public figure. Both he and Mother were fright-ened we might be kidnapped. And then Dad bought Derek a partner-ship in a clinic, and that was that."

Sonya thought of her own childhood, growing up with only a mother, and longing for a father to run to when she had a problem. But having a controlling father like James Woodruff couldn't have been a bed of roses either. She suspected that Ellin had told her only part of the story. Perhaps she resented her father's interference? Sonya made a mental note to ask more about it when she interviewed her on tape.

Derek appeared at the doorway with Raj nestled against his shoulder. Ellin stood up, reaching for the cat. Raj drew back, then leapt to the floor and sped off.

"Please excuse Raj," Derek said, turning to Sonya. "He has a strong personality and is extremely active. But if Raj doesn't want to talk to you, I certainly do. We've been discussing Woody's anniversary for months. And all of us in the family are happy you're doing a story about it." He shook Sonya's hand with a strength that surprised her. He was not tall, but he moved his slim, compact body with an easy grace. She could understand why the young Ellin Woodruff had fallen for him.

"Well, whether or not Raj approves of me, I'm happy to be doing the story." She gave a quick laugh. "It's fascinating."

"Fascinating it may be," Derek agreed, "but as usual, Gussie has laid down the law; she told us Woody's has to be full of treasures for the party. We've had to dig into our closets to see what valuables we can come up with. Now I've got some sorting to do before I start packing.

"Why don't you both come and see what has to be done before you start on your cat tour?"

Ellin gave him a small smile. "Okay, anything to keep the peace, and anything to finish packing the last of the stuff and getting it out of here."

As they walked toward the dining room, Ellin explained, "I've been sorting out all week. Last night I asked Derek to put aside anything he wants to keep, and pack the rest. It has to be finished right now, as I promised Gussie we'd get it to her this afternoon."

On the dining-room table was an assembly of china, picture frames, silverware, and glasses, as well as sweaters and some small rugs, neatly rolled.

Ellin gasped in anger. "You haven't packed a thing, Derek. You've left it all for me."

"You told me to go over the things and put aside anything I thought we should keep. That's what I did. See that pile? That's what I thought we should consider."

Ellin's face went red. "I spent last night packing the four boxes in the hall while you enjoyed your poker night. You could have done your part."

Derek said nothing, just moved to the things he'd set aside and picked up a tartan blanket. "You may remember I had this in college. I'd like to keep it and these Japanese Imari plates that belonged to my mother."

He picked up a box of fondue forks, took one out and examined it. "Remember these? I won them for you at that Las Vegas night party."

Sonya looked at them. "They're beautiful," she said. "I can't imagine why you would want to give them away."

The forks had long rods of polished steel, and had obviously never been used. The handles were mother-of-pearl. Each one was lavishly studded with a different semiprecious stone—turquoise, coral, jade, lapis, onyx, and rose quartz.

Derek put the fork back in its box.

"They cost a lot, but they were worth it. Ellin's father loved to gamble and he took us to the party. He staked us. Because it was a charity-do, we had to spend our winnings on prizes. These forks were the only prize that Ellin admired, so I played until I won enough to get them for her." He turned to his wife.

"Remember how pleased you were, Ellin?"

Ellin put her hand up and wiped a strand of hair from her face. Sonya glimpsed the anger lingering in her eyes. "Yes, I remember," she said, "but we don't use them. What's the point in keeping them?"

"Oh, come on, Ellin. We had such fun that night. Let's keep them as a remembrance."

"You had fun playing poker and so did Dad. I didn't," Ellin said. "*I* want to get rid of them. I want them packed with everything else and taken to Gussie this afternoon, as I promised," she said.

He put the box on the table. "Fine. Give them away. I don't want any mementos either."

Ellin took a deep breath. "Why don't you take Sonya on the cat tour, as you call it, while I finish packing," she said.

Derek hesitated. After an awkward pause, he said, "Okay. As soon as you're ready, we'll pack the car and get the boxes to the store."

Sonya looked from one to the other, wondering what had happened at the Las Vegas party to make Ellin's memories so sour. For that matter, what kept their marriage together—the Woodruff money?

As he guided Sonya down a long corridor, past the kitchen and laundry, Derek said, "This is a huge old apartment, with four servants' rooms. As we don't have live-in help, we use those rooms for the cats.

"Bengals are extraordinary. They love climbing and they love heights." He opened a door and pointed to the ceiling. "See the high platforms we built? That's how they get their exercise. Raj is our dominant tom, and he likes to sit up there, posing regally, while he surveys his estate."

Sonya's mind was not on the cats; she was thinking of Ellin and Derek and their relationship. But as they entered the room, she summoned up a question. "How long have Bengals been bred?"

"Pure Asian leopards were sold in pet shops until the late sixties. When that became illegal, breeders began crossing them with domestic cats. It took about four generations to breed the Bengal. I make it sound easy, but it was a difficult and time-consuming task. The first breeders had to try several kinds of spotted cats, like the Burmese and the Abyssinian, until we got the Bengal we wanted."

He picked up a kitten and smoothed its fur, then handed it to Sonya and smiled as she cuddled it to her cheek.

"I work long hours," she said. "Would it be hard to look after?"

"No, Bengals are just like any other cat. There's just one thing you have to worry about. Keep the lid of the toilet down. Bengals love water. They'll jump into it and have to be fished out when you find them."

Sonya rubbed her cheek against the soft fur. "It's an adorable little kitten; I'm very tempted." Then she put it back on the shelf. "No, it's not possible. I travel a lot and I wouldn't want to leave it."

"Well, if you change your mind, let Ellin know," Derek said. He showed Sonya the rooms where the breeding queens were kept, then walked her back to the dining room.

Ellin was still packing. She looked up, frowning. "I'm not finished. I need help," she said to Derek.

He glanced at his watch. "I've got phone calls I have to make. Give me half an hour."

"Phone calls?" Ellin's voice rose.

"To clients who are worried about their pets. Nothing serious."

She sighed. "Oh, Derek, Derek."

Sonya touched her arm.

"I'll help," she said. "Between us, we can do it in a few minutes." She picked up a sheet of newspaper, wrapped it around a bowl, and added it to the stack in the box beside Ellin.

"You've obviously done this before."

"Yes," said Sonya, "I've moved several times since I left home in Minnesota."

Ellin turned away and gathered an armful of sweaters. She was upset, and Sonya decided not to press her with further questions. There would be time for that when she was on camera.

They finished the packing in silence.

By the time Derek returned, with Raj draped on his shoulder, six more boxes had joined the first four in the hall. A pile of clothes on hangers lay draped over them, waiting to be loaded into the car.

"Come with us," Ellin said.

Sonya nodded. She might learn something for her story.

Derek joined in, "Yes, do. You'll see just how Gussie bosses us around."

When they arrived at Woody's, Gussie had two volunteers waiting, and Derek began to help them unload.

Gussie ushered Sonya and Ellin through the store to Hilda's office at the back. "It's small, but there's no space in my office. It's piled high. So let's sit here for a moment while they get the things out of the car."

The office could barely hold its furnishings: a table, one comfortable leather chair, and two folding chairs. Ellin sat down, then picked up a heavy brass vase from the table and sniffed the top. "I might have guessed. Hilda comes here to smoke and uses this for the ashes. I can smell them." She handed the vase to Gussie. "You know it's illegal to smoke in here."

"Stop it," Gussie said. "Hilda comes here for business. She has to make calls and here, by the window, is the only place her cell phone works. I make sure she keeps the door closed when she's smoking, and as soon as she's gone I wash out the vase and spray the room. How can the smoke harm anyone else?"

Ellin glared at Gussie. "Oh, Gussie, why do you justify everything Hilda does?" Gussie gave her a quick look that suggested there was more to this than was being said.

"What's all this about Hilda?" Derek was at the door, holding the bunch of hangers with clothes drooping off them.

"Nothing you don't know about," Gussie said. "Put those on the rack over there, then you can be on your way."

"Okay, whatever you say." Derek tried to hide his annoyance at the dismissal. "Gussie, I've got to tell you, those volunteers are really something. You ought to be training Marines. The blonde—Kathryn?—has already unpacked one of our boxes."

Gussie glared at him. "Keep your eyes off my volunteers. You are in enough trouble as it is."

Derek turned to Ellin. "Take a look at her, Ellin. She reminds me of someone, but I can't think who it is."

"Oh, Derek, she looks like any one of your blond clients. One of those women who insists that you call her on Saturday afternoon."

"Ellin, that's enough. Let's go."

Gussie spoke quickly, "Yes, go. We have a lot of work to do here."

Sonya confirmed the arrangements she'd made with Gussie to start shooting at the shop on Monday morning, then followed Ellin and Derek out of the store. As she did, she took stock of the volunteer Derek had mentioned, Kathryn. She was tall and blond, but she was too thin.

As she got into the car for a lift home, Sonya tried to remember where she'd seen Kathryn before. Maybe she had been in the shop when Sonya had first visited, with the Woodruff press director.

Neither Derek nor Ellin spoke until they reached Sonya's apartment. They gave her a quick good-bye and drove off.

Sonya stood on the sidewalk watching the car move away. There was no doubt about it. That was one unhappy couple.

Chapter 7

Hilda's apartment
Sunday, 11:30 A.M.

Hilda Woodruff struggled to hide her annoyance with her son, Wells, as he entered the foyer of her apartment house. She stretched up to give him a welcoming kiss even though she disliked brushing against his bristly, two-day beard. His baggy, low-slung jeans and old black sweatshirt disgusted her. He managed a classy hotel, and she knew he would never dress like this at work. He did it to annoy her.

"You said we'd eat at a good restaurant, but where can we go with you looking like that?"

Wells laughed. "Mother, with your money we can go to any restaurant no matter how I look. I know it and so do you, so stop complaining."

"Wells, it's not a matter of money, or the show of money. It's a matter of respect. I want to have a pleasant time with you and I would like you shaved and in clean clothes."

Wells sighed.

"I don't see you often and I certainly don't ask much," she continued. "Surely you could consider my feelings for once."

Wells didn't answer, and Hilda forced herself to stop. If she went on, she would lose her temper. And then Wells would lose his temper too. Wells was sometimes hotheaded, and never seemed able to control it with her. If they argued now, their whole time together would be ruined, and worse, she would accomplish nothing.

Wells turned away from her. "Mother, I do consider your feelings. If I didn't, I wouldn't be here. Now, can we stop this discussion about my faults and go? I've got a taxi double-parked outside."

Hilda smiled at the doorman as he opened the taxi door.

"Where are we going?" she asked as Wells climbed in beside her. How she hated riding in New York taxis! The front seats were set so far back that there was no legroom. It was ridiculous that the driver had so much space while the passengers were cramped in the back. It was also absurd that Wells had not booked a limousine and driver.

"Where are we going?" he repeated. "Why, to Crown's, of course. Where else would I take you? It's your favorite restaurant."

"They'll never let you in dressed like that."

"It's Sunday, the rules are relaxed. I run a hotel, remember. I know what's what."

"Well, whatever you know, I'm embarrassed by the way you look."

"Oh, Mother, you should have had a daughter. The two of you could have spent all day fretting about how you looked."

Hilda ignored him and pretended to be engrossed in the slow-moving traffic. Was that a chance remark, or did he know about her daughter? The daughter she had given away thirty-eight years ago, who had recently, suddenly, reappeared.

Her heart raced.

Wells couldn't know. The woman had tried to reach Hilda and no one else. She knew that from her daughter's letter. And the letter Hilda's attorney had sent in reply was worded in a way that guaranteed that the woman would be in trouble if she tried to contact the rest of the family. And if Wells did know, he would be only too eager to confront his mother, to berate her for what she had done.

Hilda had no misgivings about having let that red-faced, squalling baby go. Her one regret was that her mother had not arranged for her to have contraceptives before she had gone to Switzerland. It would have spared her so much.

Hilda shook her head, remembering. When she'd asked to go to a finishing school in Switzerland, she'd been surprised that her parents unexpectedly agreed. They said it was to compensate her for the problems she'd had with her foot. But Hilda knew that her request had been an act of defiance. She'd wanted to show her father that she could manage by herself.

Hilda closed her eyes and sank back into the seat. It was pointless to agonize about the problems she'd had with her father. He was dead, and she was now head of the Woodruff Foundation, chair of Woodruff Publishing's board of directors, and administrator of the family trust funds. He might never have loved her, as he did Julia and Ellin, but she'd won in the end.

"What's the matter? Why are you so silent?" Wells asked.

"I was just thinking about your comment. What my life would have been like if I had had a daughter."

After a moment, Wells laughed. "Think of the competition she would have given you with Dad. On the other hand, it might have been fun to have a sister around."

She tried to laugh, but no sound came out. His response made it obvious that he knew nothing about his half sister.

The waiter ushered them through the crowded room to a corner banquette, the most sought-after position in the room. From there they had a full view of the restaurant and in turn could be seen by everyone. It was Hilda's regular seat, but she wished she could refuse it. She needed to have a serious talk with Wells and she didn't want to be seen arguing with him. She'd have to keep her voice low and keep smiling.

The waiter took her order, then waited patiently while Wells perused the menu.

"You know what I feel like," he said, "pancakes and maple syrup. But I guess that's not served in a French restaurant."

"Oh, Wells, you're being impossible." Hilda smiled at the waiter. "Bring him eggs Benedict. I know he loves them."

Wells ordered a vodka and tonic, handed the menu to the waiter, and watched him walk away.

"You don't have to order for me, Mother," he said. "I'm perfectly capable of selecting a meal from a French menu. All I did was say what my favorite Sunday morning breakfast is."

"Please, Wells, the last thing I wanted to do is upset you. I apologize if you think I humiliated you." Hilda's tone was low and calm. Wells's voice could shake walls, and she didn't want him to blast off here. But to expect pancakes and maple syrup at Crown's was ridiculous, and he knew it.

She picked up her glass of water and sipped it. "I want to talk to you seriously about a number of things."

"Okay, let's get on with it."

"First of all, there's the party at Woody's on Friday night. It starts at seven, but Gussie would like all of us to be there at six."

"Why?"

"Gussie's having a special little reception for the volunteers. She thinks the Woodruff family should show our appreciation for their hard work. The volunteers never get any attention in the press, while the family gets a great deal of publicity for our charitable work."

"Fine. What does Gussie want me to do?"

"She'd like you to give a little speech to thank them, shake a few hands, pose for some photos. Of course, Sonya Iverson will be there, shooting everything for *The Donna Fuller Show*."

"Well, I suppose I can thank the volunteers. I just wonder if it's appropriate. After all, you three sisters know them. Wouldn't the thanks be more meaningful coming from one of you?"

"I think it's important that a member of the next generation of Woodruffs speak up. It will indicate that you will continue the shop your grandmother started."

The waiter brought their food. Placing the dishes on the table, he said quietly to Wells, "If you don't like these eggs Benedict, sir, please choose something else and I'll bring it immediately."

"Thanks," Wells replied, "I'm sure they'll be fine."

He picked up his fork, tasted the eggs, then said sarcastically, "Delicious. I should always take your advice about food, Mother."

He dipped his fork, took another mouthful, and wiped his mouth with his napkin. "Tell me more about the party."

"As it's to celebrate the shop's forty successful years, I think it is time we thank Gussie publicly for all her efforts. We are giving her a gold pendant with her name and the date of the anniversary engraved on it. It really is quite beautiful. Julia ordered it at Tiffany's. It is small, but as she'll wear it every day, she wouldn't want it to be too ostentatious."

Hilda took a bread roll from the basket, broke it open, and rolled a bit between her fingers.

"We would like you, as the next head of the family, to present it to her. What do you think?"

Wells stared at her in disbelief.

"To start with, I'm not the next head of the family. My cousin King is older than I am. Ask him."

"Oh, for goodness' sake, stop it." Hilda fought back her frustration. "Why must you always argue? I'm the head of the family now, and you are my son. That makes you the head of the next generation."

He laughed. "Well then, if seniority is so important, why don't you present Gussie with her gift?"

"Because this will be a good opportunity to introduce you to the press. We expect a lot to come."

Wells shook his head. "No way, Mother. If I present the gift, it will raise Gussie's hopes of continuing indefinitely at the store. How old is she? Seventy-five, eighty? I want her phased out and someone younger brought in."

Hilda looked at him, and shook her head.

"Wells, we could never force her into retirement. Your grandmother would turn in her grave. Do you know how close they were?"

"Of course I know. I've heard the family stories a million times."

"My mother's dying wish was that we should look after her."

"That's exactly what I want to do." He scooped up the last mouthful of eggs, then pushed his plate away.

"Let's spend some money to hire a qualified woman to help Gussie. It would be better for her not to have the stress of the day-to-day problems of the shop. Then she can leave when she wants to."

Hilda panicked. Gussie would never voluntarily give up her position at Woody's. If she were forced out, she could cause endless trouble. She knew too much about the family, going back to James Woodruff's dubious business practices.

"Gussie will never accept anyone coming in to help her," she said, "Woody's is her life."

Wells ignored her. "How much does Gussie earn? Where does she live? How would she manage if she retires? What have the Woodruff sisters done about that?"

"I'm sure you would say what she gets is not much, but Mother left her something in her will. And of course she has her apartment. The Woodruff Foundation owns it. It's small but comfortable, and it's hers rent-free for life."

"Have you ever been there?"

"No, but Julia has, and she said it's nice and quiet. A decent size for one person. Gussie has several cats, and Julia said the place was a bit of a mess. But Gussie has everything she needs. You can't make me feel guilty about her. She and Julia are really close and I'm sure if Gussie needed anything, she would tell Julia, Julia would tell me, and the family would provide it."

Wells drained his vodka and tonic and signaled to the waiter for the check.

"The speeches and the pendant are okay, but what counts is money. Give Gussie a raise, move her into a bigger apartment, make sure her medical coverage is the best, and when she does decide to retire, give her a good pension. That's gratitude."

Hilda looked up at the waiter as he approached and said, "More coffee, please."

She smiled at her son. Things had gone relatively well so far; she could afford to be gracious. "Okay, Wells, I'll think about it."

She fell silent as the waiter refilled her cup. It was time to broach a more serious topic.

It was hard to know how to begin. She had never been close to Wells. He had been a difficult child, had wanted always to be with his father. Since George's death, Wells had become secretive. Hilda knew little about his private life, who he dated or even if he dated. However he spent his time, he was discreet enough to stay out of the gossip columns. She gave a little cough to clear her throat.

"What I really wanted to say, Wells, is that it is time for you to come and work at Woodruff Publishing. I insist—"

"You *insist*?" Wells interrupted. "How can you insist?"

"I'm your mother. I'm getting rid of King. He's not executive material and I won't have him in charge of Woodruff Publishing. He'll be out of the company in a few months and I want you to take his place.

"It's the Woodruff family business. It will bring you more prestige, more money, more satisfaction than working at any hotel. Wells, believe me, it will open the world for you." She darted a quick look at him to gauge his response.

She could see that he was furious, but his voice was ice-cold. "So that's what all this is about. You're starting a new campaign to get me to work at Woodruff Publishing. You want me under your control. Well, it's not going to work. I'm staying where I am."

He picked up the bill, glanced at it, and then slammed down a credit card.

"I'm in a family business. My father's. I intend to stay there."

Hilda pulled back from him as the waiter stepped close to retrieve the bill and credit card.

"And think about this," he continued. "You believe you're in complete control of the Woodruff money, but you are only head of the board. There are nine other members, and we can vote you out. Believe me, it wouldn't be hard to do."

"Wells, you don't need to get nasty—"

He ignored her and continued, "Come to think of it, it's about time both you and Gussie retired."

Hilda froze. She hadn't expected such a strong reaction. But she wasn't going to let him get the better of her. She patted his hand and smiled at him. "Wells, I know you. You don't mean everything you've said. We can talk again another time."

"Just try me, Mother." The waiter had returned with the credit card slip. Wells signed the check, took his copy, and put it and the card in his wallet.

Without a word, Hilda reached for her handbag, stood up, and headed toward the door.

Wells was fearless. He always had been. But she was still his mother.

Chapter 8

The sun was shining on the front windows of Woody's when Sonya and her cameraman, Perry Dalton, drove up Madison Avenue. The light was perfect for shooting and Perry worked fast. He parked the van and quickly unloaded the equipment onto the sidewalk, leaving Sonya to guard it while he got the shots he wanted.

It was the midmorning lull in the heart of Manhattan's Upper East Side. People had gone to work, children had gone to school, and the women who were at home were preparing for their days. There were few people on the street, but everyone who passed stopped to look at Woody's windows.

Gussie had told Sonya how important "theme" windows were to a thrift shop. "A good theme lures buyers like nothing else," she said. "But they're not easy to do. The perfect window is seasonal, glamorous, and fun. Fashionable, but not too much so. The clothes must be wearable. Some people shop at Woody's for crazy fashions, but not many."

For the anniversary party Gussie had gone all-out. The main window was designed to look like the corner of a romantic bedroom. A mannequin stood in front of a small dressing table, her makeup strewn in front of her. She wore a bikini patterned with tiny fish plunging through foaming waves. Filmy dresses were flung over a love seat, high-heeled sandals were scattered across the rug, and piled on the dressing table, beside the makeup, were strings of colorful beads. Placed in the corner was a sign: SUMMER IS PARTY TIME, SO COME IN AND GET READY.

The window was amusing and sexy. When Perry finished shooting, Sonya pressed the buzzer, preparing to compliment Gussie. But it was a younger blond woman, not Gussie, who opened the door. Sonya recognized her as the volunteer who'd helped unpack the Shelby boxes on Saturday afternoon. Derek Shelby had commented on her efficiency.

"Gussie's on the phone," the woman said in a low voice. "She won't be long. I'm Kathryn, one of the volunteers. I'm helping get things ready for the party. Gussie asked me to take care of you."

Sonya studied Kathryn as she led the way to the counter. In the clear morning light she was beautiful, with pale skin and amazing blue eyes. But she seemed tense, and Sonya wondered why. Her left hand was bare—no wedding ring. She was in her thirties, perhaps a divorce was the problem. But whatever it was, she had a lot of free time to devote to the thrift shop.

"You must be one of the regular volunteers," Sonya said, testing her. "Every time I'm here, you're working."

"No, I'm not a regular, at least not yet. I've just moved to New York. I'm an extra hand helping prepare for the party," Kathryn said.

Sonya's interest was roused. "Oh," she said, "the party. Do you know the Woodruff sisters?"

Kathryn gave her a quick look. "No," she said, "I don't." She turned to Perry and asked where he would like to set up.

"The sun is shining right on the entrance and casting shadows through the front of the shop. It's better if we start at the back and work there for an hour or so. It'll be easier to light. Of course, if Sonya prefers, I'll set up for the interview in Gussie's office. Sonya's the boss, she makes the decisions." He gave Sonya a wicked grin.

Kathryn looked apologetically at Sonya. "Whatever you say. I worked as a stylist on magazines, and I'd like to help if I can."

"Which magazines?" Sonya asked.

Before Kathryn could answer, Gussie came bustling out of her office, full of anticipation, her ginger curls bobbing.

"Now you must tell us what you need," she said. "We want to make it perfect for you." She shook Sonya's hand. "We are so proud to have Woody's on *The Donna Fuller Show.* We're the thrift shop that started the fashion for antique clothing. We consider ourselves big business. And we make a great effort to stay current."

Sonya looked critically at the older woman. Gussie was dressed in beige, a shapeless sweater set and matching pants. If she wanted to present the store as having a designer image, this was the wrong outfit. Gussie read her thoughts.

"These are my work clothes," she said. "I put them on at six this morning. I've brought a blue suit and a white lace blouse for the interview. I can change in a jiffy."

"Okay," Sonya said. "We'll shoot the back of the shop, then do the interview, and finish with the fashion."

"Fine." Gussie took her arm. "I'll show you around. And then, while you work, I'll get on the phone. Companies have been offering to supply drinks for the anniversary party. I have to finalize that. And then there is the party bag that we'll give each guest. We're getting lots of goodies for that. I hope my old friend Anthea Woodruff is looking down at me and thinking I'm doing well." She beamed at Sonya. "Let me show you the room we named after her. Anthea's Room is where we display the best of the designer fashions."

Anthea's Room took up a good third of the front of the shop. It was partitioned off from the rest of the store, with a large sign over the wide, open entrance. The space was filled with carefully arranged clothes, handbags, shoes, and scarves. The artful arrangement of the garments and accessories was impressive. "You must have worked so hard to put all this together for us," Sonya said.

"Well, Kathryn did a lot of it. She's only been here a few days, but when I realized how good she was at making things look beautiful, I asked her to come in over the weekend and get things ready for you and the party. It's a great coincidence. She couldn't have arrived at a better time."

Sonya touched the embroidered ruffle on a red silk dress. Then she lifted the skirt and watched as the ruffles moved gracefully in her hand.

"Didn't I tell you," Gussie said, unable to hide her pride. "It's the best place in the city to shop for something special at a great price.

"That's vintage Oscar de la Renta. Isn't it beautiful? At least ten years old and in perfect condition. It will be bought by some young woman who will wear it to a New York gala and look sensational."

Gussie turned the skirt to show Sonya the stitching. "With these pieces, there is a lot of unseen work inside. It's that detailing that makes them what they are. It's quality. Quality makes clothes look great for years."

Sonya let the skirt fall. "Vintage fashions are quite the rage."

"Yes, Julia Roberts gave the trend a big boost when she wore a vintage Valentino dress to the Oscars the night she won for best actress. She looked magnificent. And everyone was reminded of the beauty of older clothes."

Sonya nodded and pointed to a portrait of a blond woman hanging on the wall at the end of the room. "Is that Anthea Woodruff?"

"Yes, I had an artist paint it from a photograph of her, but it doesn't do her justice. Anthea was ravishing."

Sonya stepped closer to take a better look at the painting. "She seems a bit like Hilda," she joked.

"No, no, no." Gussie was fierce. "Anthea's eyes were the most startling blue. She could have been a film star. Hilda will never be the beauty her mother was, no matter how many face-lifts she has." She looked meaningfully at Sonya. "Anthea was a good woman. It was a pity her marriage wasn't happier and it was a tragedy she died so young." Her lip quivered and tears filled her eyes. "If only she were here with us today. Everything would be so much easier."

Sonya was surprised at Gussie's distress. She put her hand on the older woman's shoulder, felt it shaking, and moved her toward the door. "Gussie, you must be tired from the pressure of the party," she said. "Why don't you make those phone calls and get ready for the interview, while I work with Perry."

"Thank you for understanding. Kathryn will help you with the shoot." Gussie went into her office and shut the door.

Perry was adjusting the tripod when Sonya sank into a chair he'd placed for her. "How's it going?" she asked.

"So-so. Kathryn says they cleared out a lot, but there's still too much furniture. It's hard to get a good shot of any one thing."

"Just get what you can," Sonya answered, pulling her notebook out of her bag. "It's the high fashion I'm more interested in, that and Gussie. She was in tears a moment ago. The family must be getting at her." She shook her head. She had to concentrate on the shoot. "Anyway, let's get a lot of shots of her working in the store."

Why had Gussie become upset so quickly? When they'd arrived, she had been full of energy. But just minutes later, she had seemed almost defeated. Was it Sonya's mention of Anthea? Reminding Gussie of her lost friend? Or was it Hilda?

With Sonya guiding the shots, Perry quickly finished taping the furniture. They had decided to interview Gussie in her office. It was small and shabby, but when Kathryn placed a vase of white flowers and a large Delft plate in the background, the scene came to life. Gussie had collected herself.

"Wow, I see you changed into a blue suit for me," Perry said as he focused the camera on her. "I like that."

"Well, you're not the only man in my life," Gussie retorted. "I just got a call from one of the costume designers on Broadway. He said the boys want to give me a private party to celebrate the anniversary."

Sonya signaled to Perry to roll the camera.

"Tell me about the boys," she said.

Gussie smiled at her. "Well, the boys are set and costume designers. They come here quite often. Say, for instance, they are doing a play that's set in the sixties, then they want prints and colors of the period. And often we find something that's perfect to inspire them."

"Do the actors wear clothes from Woody's onstage?" Sonya was incredulous.

"No. The designers just want to get ideas for the costumes, but they often buy furniture and use that onstage. Many of them send me tickets to their shows so I can see what they've done. That's part of what makes running a thrift shop so fascinating."

Sonya smiled at her. "What's been the best part of it?"

"Well, the fact that the thrift shop idea worked. When we started it, all of us except Anthea doubted that it would make much money for the Woodruff charities. But it's turned out to be a gold mine."

Gussie clasped her hands together. "There's no shame in wearing secondhand clothes. It's good that good things are used again. Selling rubbish went against Anthea Woodruff's grain, and it goes against mine. Last year, I had a young couple, who had very little money, furnish their apartment from Woody's. They invited me up to see it and I was amazed at what they'd done. It was classy, comfortable, and spotlessly clean."

Sonya flipped slowly through her notebook. She'd seen that Gussie was perspiring, and she wanted to give her a moment to collect herself.

"Is there a particular type of woman who comes into the store, maybe looking for a dress for a special occasion?" she asked.

"No, no, many different sorts of women shop here. All ages, all sizes," she said. "Some come with friends, but mostly they come alone. The rich women are the worst. They bring their seamstresses." At Sonya's look of astonishment Gussie laughed, then continued, "Yes, that's right. They want to make sure that anything they buy can be altered to fit them. Sometimes they can take over our single fitting room for hours. It can be a real problem if we get busy."

Sonya checked her list of questions. "How about setting aside pieces for a particular customer? Say I wanted a vintage lace dress, would you keep an eye out for it?"

"Yes, of course," Gussie said with a gentle smile. "But I'd charge you extra for it and I would only keep it for forty-eight hours. Vintage lace is very much in demand."

"What's the strangest request you've ever had?"

"Well, last spring, a smartly dressed woman came in and asked me to collect oversized jackets from the eighties. You know, the ones with wide shoulders and brass buttons. She wanted thirty of them in different sizes and colors."

"Thirty jackets?"

"Yes, she was having a reunion party for her graduating class. Harvard Law '83, I think it was. She planned to ask each of the women to wear a jacket. Apparently the party was a wild success. And then she

had all the jackets dry-cleaned and sent them back to me for resale!"
Gussie's pleasure was obvious.

After a few more anecdotes about clothes and customers, Sonya carefully moved on to her final topic. Not wanting to upset the older woman,
she'd kept the questions easy. But now it was time to talk about the family.

"What role do the Woodruff sisters play at Woody's?"

"They are all busy women. I take care of most things on a day-to-
day basis."

"And Hilda Woodruff?"

"As I said, she's a busy woman."

It was clear Gussie wasn't about to say anything more. She closed
her mouth tightly at the mention of Hilda's name. Her opinions were
not going to be recorded on camera.

All that was left to do was shoot the front section of the store. Perry
set the lights, and Kathryn stood waiting to arrange the objects she had
set aside for different shots. Her skill was amazing. She always had the
right piece at the right moment. Sonya wondered why she was volunteering at a thrift shop when she could be earning money as a stylist.

Another hour of work and it was a wrap.

Sonya was waiting for Perry to pack the gear when the buzzer rang
frantically. Kathryn opened the door. "Sorry, we are closed for business this morning," she said.

But the woman on the street pushed open the door. "Don't you
know me?" she said. "I'm Julia Jenkins, one of the Woodruff sisters. I
want to see Gussie."

She pushed past Perry's tripod, stumbled over a cable, and started
to fall. Perry grabbed her and steadied her. She looked at him in be-
wilderment. "Where's Gussie?"

Before anyone could speak, Gussie came running out of her office.
"Julia, Julia, what's the matter?"

Julia sank, panting, into a chair. "Oh, Gussie, I have to talk to you.

Hilda's at it again. She's all but fired King. You know King's temper—he could do anything. I'm frightened."

"Stop it, Julia, you're being ridiculous." Gussie bent down and whispered into her ear. Julia glanced at Sonya and Perry.

"I forgot you were going to be here," she said.

Gussie helped her to her feet. "Let's go into my office. You must have something to drink. Some hot tea?"

"Water, cold water, would be fine."

Gussie shot a look at Kathryn, who headed for the kitchen. As she moved away, Sonya signaled to Perry to shoot the two women as they made their way across the shop to the office.

Julia's hair was disheveled at the back where she had rested it on the chair and Sonya could see gray roots. She wore black trousers and a loose casual shirt; Sonya guessed she'd left home in a hurry.

"King called me from his office at ten o'clock and insisted that I go down there." Julia was almost weeping. She clutched Gussie's arm for support. She made no attempt to lower her increasingly shrill voice even though she knew Sonya was present. "She's had his name taken down from his office door and all his things packed."

"Why?" Gussie asked.

"She left a memo on his desk. It said that the board had decided to reduce his responsibilities and move him to a lower-level office. King demanded that I confront her. I tried, but she wasn't in her office, probably deliberately avoiding a scene. She knew how angry King would be. Oh, Gussie, this is too much. Something has to be done about Hilda. She can't be allowed to destroy the family."

As the two women reached the office door, Kathryn came up to them with a glass of water. Julia took it with a trembling hand and managed a thin smile of thanks. Kathryn moved away; Julia and

Gussie went into Gussie's office. The door closed behind them with a click—had Gussie locked it?

Perry lowered the camera and he and Sonya shared a look. Sonya raised an eyebrow. Was there a way to work some of the family tension into the story on the charity shop?

Chapter 9

Gussie pushed open the street door and paused, listening. Yes, that was Kathryn's voice. She was using the phone.

"I'm going crazy. I don't think I can stand it much longer," Kathryn said. "You have to do something for me, and do it fast." She looked up and saw Gussie. "Thank you," she added quickly. "I'll call back later."

She put down the phone and walked to greet Gussie. "I'm sorry, I was talking to a real estate agent. I'm just in a sublet, and I'm looking for a permanent apartment. I used the shop phone and I'll pay for the call. I couldn't get a connection on my cell."

"That's okay, Kathryn," Gussie replied. "We all have that problem with cell phones. The only place to get a connection is at the back of the shop, near Hilda's office. There's a window there, and it helps."

Gussie tilted her head to get a good look at Kathryn. "Thanks for coming early and opening the shop for me. Many of my other volunteers have children to get to school or other family needs, and I hoped you would be free." She looked around the shop. Everything was in order.

"I really needed the help this morning. I had to take my sick cat to

Derek Shelby's clinic. He couldn't find what was wrong with her, so he's keeping her to do some tests. I hope I can pick her up tomorrow."

"Good. The vet will find what's wrong. You can put your mind at rest."

"Yes, I must stop worrying." She hesitated. "Derek's a good vet. A good vet with a lot of charm." She felt a sudden surge of annoyance, thinking of his easy manner, which hid the faults that made Ellin miserable. Gussie didn't like taking her cat to Derek, but she knew Ellin would be upset if she went to another vet.

In her office, Gussie put her handbag in the bottom drawer of the desk and hung her coat on the hanger behind the door. She sighed and sank into her chair. She had to make a start on the phone calls and tackle the paperwork. But she couldn't concentrate. Not with Kathryn just outside, in the shop.

Everything about Kathryn reminded Gussie of Anthea Woodruff. Not just the shape of her face and the cornflower blue of her eyes, but her body and the way she moved. Even the tone of her voice. Gussie had gone through old photographs and spent time recalling memories of Anthea. The resemblance was uncanny. It was as if Anthea had been born again.

Kathryn Petite had to be Anthea's granddaughter.

She was the child Hilda had given birth to, so many years ago in Switzerland. Anthea had hesitated about placing her for adoption, but Hilda had insisted.

How ironic that the baby had grown up to be the image of her grandmother. If only Anthea were alive to see her.

What did Kathryn want? It seemed likely that there was only one reason she would volunteer at Woody's. She probably wanted to get close to Hilda and eventually claim her place in the family.

But perhaps Kathryn wanted a share of the Woodruff Trust. Gussie decided she had to discover what it was that she desired.

She lifted the volunteer time sheet from the desktop file. Three women were coming in to work the afternoon shift. They could cover the shop. Afternoon coffee at the local café was the answer. She would invite Kathryn out for a break. She had known the manager for years. He would leave them undisturbed. There they could thrash it out with no one listening. If things really got bad between them, the manager was likely to intervene.

Everything went according to plan. Kathryn accepted Gussie's invitation and they headed around the corner. The café was warm and welcoming, with dim lights and wood paneling. The manager greeted Gussie by name and showed the two women to a booth at the back. Kathryn ordered a long black and Gussie her favorite double cappuccino. As they waited, Gussie looked about, glad to see that she had correctly guessed that the place would be nearly empty at this hour, the lunch rush over and the bulk of the late-afternoon crowd yet to come. The manager was ruffling through papers near the cash register. The waitresses were tidying up and seeing to the needs of the few customers.

"Kathryn," said Gussie, leaning across the table. "Are you enjoying working in the thrift shop?"

"Well, yes," she replied defensively. "It's a new experience. I'm lucky that this is such an important time at Woody's."

Gussie sat back as the waitress put the coffees in front of them, then picked up her spoon and stirred the froth on her cappuccino. "Did you know about the anniversary party before you came to the store to volunteer?"

"No, it was a coincidence. As I said, when my mother died, I decided to put Washington behind me and start fresh in New York."

"And until you find a job, there's nothing you want to do but work at Woody's?"

Kathryn was ready to work at the store every day. She couldn't be looking very hard, Gussie thought.

Kathryn reached out and touched Gussie's hand. "Yes, Gussie. Don't be concerned. I'll be there when you need me."

Gussie looked down, avoiding Kathryn's eyes as she pulled her hand away. "Kathryn, I'm going to level with you. I don't believe you're interested in charity work. I believe you're connected with the Woodruffs."

Kathryn sat back against the leather booth, looking shocked. "What do you mean?"

"Well," said Gussie, leaning forward, pressing her argument, "I suppose your motive is money."

"Money," Kathryn said shortly. "I'm not interested in money. My parents provided for me. It's nothing compared to the Woodruff millions, but it is enough. And, I've supported myself for years, working as a stylist."

Gussie noticed that Kathryn did not deny the connection with the family. She leaned forward, her voice low. "What do you want from the Woodruffs?"

Kathryn said nothing.

Gussie said insistently, "Your looks give you away. You are related to the Woodruff family, aren't you? Tell me who you are."

Kathryn laughed awkwardly. "What do you mean, my looks?"

"Everything about you, the way you walk, the way you talk, every movement you make, reminds me of Anthea Woodruff. I believe you're her granddaughter. The baby Hilda had when she was sixteen and who was adopted in Paris."

Kathryn sat frozen. At last she whispered, "She doesn't want to have anything to do with me. Her attorney sent me a letter, saying she wouldn't see me, not even once."

"Then why are you here?"

"Because I feel I have a right to know my background, and if Hilda won't help me, I'll appeal to other members of the Woodruff family."

A wave of fear gripped Gussie. "When did you get this letter?" she asked.

Kathryn looked at her blankly for a moment. "The letter." She shook her head as if forcing herself back to reality. "A week or so ago."

"A week or so ago," repeated Gussie. "When did you find out that you were adopted?"

"About a month ago." Kathryn's voice was unsteady. "My god-mother told me after my mother's funeral." She shuddered. "It was a dreadful shock."

The waitress came to the table, and Gussie asked her to clear away the dirty cups and bring fresh coffee.

"Tell me the story from the beginning. Who were your adoptive parents? Weren't you happy enough with them?"

Kathryn paused. Gussie could see her pain.

"My adoptive parents were Lewis and Zoe Pettibone," she said in a flat voice. "My passport says I was born in Switzerland, but at the time, my parents were living in Paris. My father worked in the American Embassy there. He came from a good, solid, Midwestern family. My mother was an American of Greek origin and she was studying archeology at the Sorbonne when they met."

"They had no children of their own?"

"No. My godmother told me my adoptive mother had a number of miscarriages and then a stillborn son. She became depressed, and the doctors recommended she adopt. My father didn't want to, and only agreed if the baby was a girl."

"And they never told you that you were adopted?" Gussie asked in disbelief.

Kathryn shook her head again. "No, Mother was proud and wanted me to see her as my mother. She didn't want me to know I was adopted. It wasn't a happy marriage. My father was nineteen years older than my mother and they came from completely different backgrounds. They stuck it out until I went to college and then divorced. My father retired and went back to Europe to live. He died in Italy ten years ago."

Kathryn was struggling to control herself.

"My mother had dark, curly hair; my father was tall and big-boned, with gray hair and brown eyes. I'm a natural blonde with blue eyes. I never felt I belonged to them."

She reached into her handbag, drew out a tissue, and blew her nose.

"Gussie," she went on, "they loved me but they fought all the time. I was glad when my father left home and I only had my mother to cope with. It got more difficult when she got sick. She had a series of strokes, and she hated being handicapped."

"Haven't you any aunts, uncles, cousins?" Gussie waved her hands in frustration. "Surely there was someone there to help you?"

"I have no family, only my godmother, Marta Sayles. She arranged for the adoption and knew Hilda was my birth mother."

"So after your mother's death, you came to New York to try to meet Hilda?"

"Yes, but first I did research about the Woodruffs. That's how I learned about Woody's. I thought if I worked in the shop, I would at least see Hilda from time to time, and maybe develop some sort of relationship."

Gussie shook her head. "You will never have any relationship with Hilda. She is a powerful woman who is interested only in controlling the Woodruff empire. Go back to Washington."

Kathryn leaned forward angrily. "She would never relent and recognize her own daughter? That is ridiculous. She must realize I have rights. The Woodruffs are my family. I want to know my half brother, my aunts, my cousin. And I also want to know who my birth father was. Tell me, what right does Hilda have to cut me off?"

"With Hilda, it is not a matter of rights. It is a matter of her position. She is a rich, prominent woman and the press would tear her apart once the story came out."

"Gussie, the last thing I want to do is fight with her. Have some compassion. You can't imagine what it's like not to have a family."

Gussie closed her eyes. She did know what it was like. Her mother had died when Gussie was in her teens and she had been forced to care for her alcoholic father. When he'd passed on leaving her with nothing, she had been suicidal. Anthea Woodruff's friendship had saved her. Anthea had made Gussie part of the family and given her a purpose in life.

"Gussie, please, aren't I entitled to some recognition?"

Gussie nodded. "Yes, yes, but I'm trying to think about how I can protect you."

Kathryn's voice rose. "I don't want protection, I want my family." She took a key ring out of her handbag. "Here are the keys to the shop you gave me last night. Take them. I'm not coming back. If I can't get close to the Woodruffs through Woody's, I'll find another way." She tried to hand the keys to Gussie.

"Keep your voice down," Gussie said, pushing Kathryn's hand away. "This is private business, just between us." The manager was staring at them. He'd half-risen from his seat. Gussie smiled at him and he sank down again.

She studied Kathryn. She is not just Hilda's daughter, she told herself, but Anthea's granddaughter. What would Anthea want? She knew at once.

"Kathryn," she sighed, "I'll help you. But you must let me have time to find a way. I am the only member of the family who knows about you. If you went to Julia or Ellin, they wouldn't believe you. No one else knows about Hilda's first child. The others would say that you are an impostor who wants some of the Woodruff money. Neither Julia nor Ellin are fond of Hilda, but they would accept her word before yours."

She looked at Kathryn's hand, clenched around the keys. "Put those away. I need you and I want you to work in the shop, to help me prepare for the party. But you must promise to wait and not say anything to the family about being a Woodruff. When the celebration is over, I'll figure out a way to deal with Hilda and get you the recognition you deserve."

Kathryn hesitated, then put the keys in her bag. "Why should I trust you, Gussie? One minute you tell me to have nothing to do with Hilda, the next you say you'll help me get to know her."

"I thought of Anthea, your grandmother, and what she would want me to do," Gussie said, feeling tears welling up in her eyes. "The answer was simple—help you in any way I can. So that's what I'll do."

Gussie struggled out of her seat, picked up the bill, and walked toward the door. As they stopped by the cashier, she said, "You must be patient. This will take time. But leave it to me. I know the Woodruff sisters." She forced a smile at the manager, who stood watching them.

Kathryn shrugged her shoulders and said, "Tomorrow." Then she walked away quickly. Gussie sensed she was crying.

Chapter 10

Derek and Ellin's apartment
Tuesday, 6:30 P.M.

Raj jumped down from the shelf and rubbed against Ellin's leg, his harsh purr rumbling deep in his throat.

"Good boy," Ellin said as she picked him up and put him on her shoulder. "So you do love me. It's just that you can't resist Derek's charm." She nestled her face into his fur. "I know all about Derek's charm. After all, I married him. The question is, dear Raj, why do I stay with him?"

Derek could charm anyone, even her notoriously hard-to-impress father. He would have preferred her marrying into a wealthy family, but when Derek came to New York, James Woodruff had accepted him immediately. He'd even offered Derek a job in the publishing company.

Ellin cuddled Raj closer. "But if I hadn't married Derek, I wouldn't have you and my other Bengal babies to care for. Derek may take the credit but you know you're mine." She kissed the top of his head. "Dear Raj, you are the true love of my life."

Her cell phone vibrated against her hip. She took it out of her jeans pocket and glanced at the number. Julia.

"Hi. What's up now? Has King summoned the courage to attack Hilda?" She laughed.

"Ellin, this isn't the time to joke. I'm so worried about him I don't know which way to turn."

"Okay, tell me."

"But I'm not calling about King. I think I did something terrible."

"What do you mean?"

"After I left King at the office yesterday, raging about his demotion, I went to Woody's. I was so angry at Hilda; I had to talk to someone. I told Gussie the whole story—I called Hilda evil." Julia paused for breath, then wailed, "Sonya Iverson, the TV producer, was there. She must have heard everything I said."

As Julia talked, Ellin walked to the big bay window and sat, looking down on Central Park. The view calmed her. The people looked like ants, the cars like toys.

"If Hilda finds out, she'll be furious," Ellin said, "but then she is furious about most things." She hesitated as she thought. "But I doubt Sonya would listen to a private conversation. And even if she did hear what you said, how could she use it in a story about our party?"

"You're being naïve," Julia objected. "King says a reporter can always use a family fight to beef up a story. The fact that we're having a family battle would be a juicy scandal. King believes Gussie is a devious old woman who's made Woody's the center for gossip on the Upper East Side. He claims that Gussie will tell Sonya everything. He expects to hear it on the business news tonight. He says Gussie's got too much say-so and has to retire." Julia took a deep breath. "I know he can be unreasonable. But there's some truth in what he says."

Ellin thought of the pain Gussie had caused her. It was true—she knew too much. Life without her would be easier for all of them.

"But getting rid of Gussie won't solve King's problem with Hilda," she said.

"No, I realize that, but remember, Hilda hates King because Dad was so fond of him. After all, he brought King into the business while he was still at school. King's angry, and this time his anger is justified. Hilda demoted him without giving a good reason and he says that's against the company rules. She refuses to speak with him or even see him. It's degrading. If she doesn't change her mind, he says he'll insist we call a board meeting and vote her out. After all, we own close to two-thirds of the family shares."

There was a long silence. Ellin knew what her sister wanted.

"Julia, are you asking me to come with you to confront Hilda? I can't. Don't ask me. I can't do it." Even the thought made Ellin's heart pound.

"Ellin." Julia grew more insistent. "Hilda has to be stopped. King says if we don't act he'll hire an attorney. I don't want our family affairs dragged through the courts and neither do you. I've arranged to meet her after dinner at her apartment. Please come."

Ellin felt sweat beading on her forehead. She knew she had no choice. "Okay, I'll come. But you'll have to do the talking. You know I can barely speak to her. What time do you want me to be there?"

"She's going to a cocktail party, so she'll be home about eight thirty. Say I meet you in the foyer at eight forty-five."

"Okay." Ellin hung up without saying good-bye and sat looking down at the park. When they were children, Hilda had criticized her constantly and destroyed her self-confidence. It had set a pattern for life. Ellin knew that tonight would be no different.

Raj jumped from her shoulder, darted across the room, and raced down the hall toward the front door. Derek must be home. "Is that you?" she called.

"Yes," he replied. "It's me."

Derek walked into the room and sat down. "Fix me a scotch, will you? I'm bushed." Ellin went to the bar and poured them both a drink.

"Thanks," he said as she handed him a glass. "Gussie's pussycat, as she calls it, was in a coma when she carried it into the clinic this morning. It was old, sixteen or seventeen years. I told her I'd run some tests, but I knew it was hopeless. I tried everything, but it died about an hour ago. Now I have to tell her."

"Gussie will understand; it can't be the first time she's lost a pet, and Julia told me she has at least three more at home. But if you tell her tonight, she won't sleep. Do it tomorrow. It won't upset her half as much if she's busy working."

"Okay, if that's what you think. I'll tell her tomorrow." Ellin's husband looked at her over his glass. "I have to go back to the clinic as soon as I've had dinner. I wasted the day looking after that damned cat. Now I have to catch up with my other patients."

"That's fine. I've got an after-dinner date with my sisters."

"What's it about?" Derek got up and poured himself another drink.

"King. Hilda demoted him and moved him off the executive floor. She gave him no reason and he's threatening, among other things, to hire a law firm to fight her."

"Hilda won't let it come to court. She couldn't stand the publicity."

"You're right, as you so often are about Hilda." Ellin drained her glass and got up. "I'd better see to dinner."

Julia was waiting on the sofa in the lobby of Hilda's apartment house when Ellin arrived. "Don't tell me. I'm late again," Ellin said, trying to lighten the mood.

"No, you're on time. Hilda's the one who's late. The doorman says he hasn't seen her. And once she gets here, she'll still keep us waiting.

She'll have to freshen up, as she calls it. That can take half an hour. And for what? We're her sisters; she doesn't have to impress us."

"Hilda has to impress everyone." Ellin gave a hard laugh.

Julia stood up, her back straight, ready to fight for her son. She held out her hand to Ellin. "Let's go up; the maid will let us in. We can have something to drink and discuss how to tackle Hilda." She told the doorman to tell Hilda they were waiting for her upstairs. A few minutes later they were seated in Hilda's library with drinks in their hands.

"Here's to dear old Dad and the mess he made of our lives by giving so much to Hilda." Ellin raised her wineglass.

"We were fools, not to realize what was going on," Julia said. "He was a sick man and she was at his bedside every day for months. He was a brilliant businessman but in the end, it was Hilda who made the decisions. And here we are, paying the price." Julia's voice was unsteady. "She was the daughter he liked the least, but in the end he turned to her."

Ellin sipped her wine. "He didn't like any of us much. I don't think he ever forgave Mother for not having a son. The wonder is that he didn't give her a divorce and let her take us back to Portland. He could have easily remarried and started another family."

Julia agreed. "Mother was a trophy wife. He didn't love her. Dad wooed and won the belle of Portland, Maine, and he wasn't going to admit that their marriage was a disaster. His reputation in Portland mattered more to him than almost anything. That's why he built that stupid museum there." She laughed. "Yes, he had the museum and Mother had Gussie."

Ellin looked hard at her sister. "Julia, do you trust Gussie?"

Julia said nothing.

Ellin repeated the question. "Julia, do you trust Gussie?"

"No, I don't, not completely. But I believe that whatever she does, she does with the best interests of the family at heart," she said slowly. "King is wrong to accuse her of being a gossip. I can understand his fury, but the story about his demotion would have spread anyway. What really matters is Hilda's plan to get rid of him. She wants him out of the company so Wells can move in and take over."

"I know, but Wells is happy where he is."

Ellin went to pour them more wine, then turned, bottle in hand, as she heard the elevator door slide open.

Moments later, Hilda stepped into the room, clad in a neat black suit. "That's okay. Go ahead, help yourself to my wine."

Ellin kept her voice low. "Thanks," she said calmly.

Hilda walked into the hall. "I'll be out to talk to you in a few minutes."

Julia accepted her refilled glass from Ellin. "She is so impossible; I can hardly bear to be in the same room with her."

Ellin's eyes glittered. "King is not the only Woodruff who wants revenge. She is so rude to me and always has been, since we were kids. I used to plan how I could kill her."

The sisters laughed and then sat, waiting, comforted by each other's presence.

When Hilda appeared, she had on the brief lace top and black skirt she'd worn under her dinner jacket. Black flats replaced her high-heeled sandals.

"I won't pretend I don't know what this is about," she said, sitting in an armchair. "You're here on King's behalf. You want me to reinstate him and give him back his office. Well, I have no intention of doing that. King is not a productive member of the Woodruff Publishing Company and he doesn't deserve to work there. If I had my way, I would have fired him."

"What stopped you?" Julia's voice was rough with anger.

"The other directors stopped me. They said it would be bad publicity for the company. The press would have a field day with it—"

"You don't have the right to fire King," Julia interrupted. "Father gave him the job. He said he wanted King to watch over the company. You can't defy his wishes, and you can't destroy my son's career. Ellin and I will do everything in our power to stop you. You agree, Ellin, don't you, Ellin?"

Ellin nodded. "Yes, I'm with King."

"And what about the legal side of it?" Julia sat forward in her chair. "King is a Woodruff heir. Have you considered that?"

Hilda's voice was scornful. "A minor heir, if you don't mind my saying."

She stood up and looked down on them, a typical maneuver since they were children. As usual, Hilda ignored Ellin and turned to Julia.

"Julia, you always take things too personally," she said. "You must try to be more objective. Let me tell you the facts about your son. First of all, his name is King Jenkins, yet he calls himself King Woodruff."

Julia snarled at her, "His name is King Woodruff Jenkins. He has every right to call himself King Woodruff."

"That's true," Hilda scoffed, "but it's also true he made himself the laughingstock of the company when he had a sign made for his door with that name on it. King is not executive material. I have the figures to prove how few sales he's brought in during the past year. He's not only incompetent, but incapable of dealing with staff, and erratic in his behavior. If it weren't for you, he would never have survived at the company."

Julia stood up, her fists clenched. "He'll make you the laughing-stock of the city when he hires a law firm and sues. Have you thought about that?"

"Yes, I have." Hilda moved closer to her. "And I've consulted my attorneys. I'll buy him off. But there'll be one condition to the settlement. He has to live in another country. I want him out of my way."

Ellin got up. "Stop it. This isn't just a matter of money, it's family. Father would never want this. Never in a million years."

"Father has been dead for six years," Hilda spat at her. "I head the Woodruff empire. That's something you should know, Ellin. You come around begging for money often enough."

Ellin held her breath. She looked at her glass of wine, then, resisting the urge to throw it into Hilda's face, put it down.

"There's nothing more to say," she said. "Julia, let's go."

Together they walked to the elevator.

"I'm glad we've got that settled," Hilda called after them. "Now we can all look forward to the party."

Chapter 11

The array of items atop the glass case looked more like a display at Sotheby's than a counter in a thrift shop. Gussie wasn't surprised to find such beautiful and valuable objects in the boxes Ellin and Derek had delivered. Gussie was only beginning to sort through the Shelbys' donations and she'd already found several treasures. The silver tray was delicately engraved. The eight champagne glasses were crystal and the set of fondue forks had mother-of-pearl handles studded with semiprecious stones.

Gussie lifted one of the forks out of the silk-lined box and felt the tip. It was so sharp it almost pierced her skin. Probably Ellin had never used them. Gussie ran her fingers over the smoothly polished cabochon stones on the handle. The gems had been rimmed in gold before being embedded in the mother-of-pearl. She wondered where the set of forks had come from and how much they had cost. She hoped Ellin wouldn't regret giving away these precious things. Sighing, she put the fork back in the box.

Maybe they were wedding gifts. Perhaps, after more than twenty-five years, Ellin's unhappy marriage was breaking up. Gussie had heard gossip that Hilda was having an affair with Derek, but she hadn't taken it seriously. Derek's passion was for gambling, not women. But who knew what Hilda would do to hurt Ellin. She'd been jealous of her sister since the day Anthea announced she was having her third baby.

Gussie shook her head in sorrow. The Woodruff sisters had had every chance to do something important with their lives but none of them succeeded. None had a happy marriage and none contributed to society the way their mother had.

The old woman picked up the silver tray and turned it over to see the markings. As she thought, it was sterling silver. What price should she put on it? How much would it bring to the shop? She reminded herself that the party wasn't only about raising money; it was also about making the new young celebrities aware of Woody's. The guests had to find bargains they could boast about. Maybe they would come back and buy, or more important, maybe they'd donate their castoffs to the store. If only Anthea were here to advise her. Even after all these years, at times like these Gussie missed her friend the most.

It was getting late, and she was hungry. She would eat before she started pricing. That would make it easier.

She went to the kitchen, where a chicken casserole was defrosting in the fridge. She took it out and wiped the container carefully before putting it into the microwave oven. Julia had brought the casserole, as she often did, and Gussie didn't want to break the fancy ceramic dish. While it heated, she sat at the table and looked around the small, bright room. When she and Anthea first planned Woody's, she'd said a kitchen wasn't necessary. All she needed was a kettle to boil water to make a cup of instant coffee. But Anthea had insisted, and she had been right. The clean bright kitchen, with the yellow-and-blue Italian tiles they'd picked out together, was a comfort. It made her feel closer to Anthea.

She closed her eyes and saw her friend as a child—a gangly young girl running along the beach in Maine, her blond hair a tangled mess, the taste of salt on her skin. The radiant bride walking down the aisle of the lovely old weatherboard church to the altar where James Woodruff waited for her.

Gussie had thought she'd lose Anthea after the wedding, but instead they'd grown closer. Anthea was desperate to have someone to confide in, and Gussie was happy to listen.

"I should never have married James," Anthea told her soon after the honeymoon. "He is a rough, crude man who is happiest playing poker with his friends. When we go to a party he boasts endlessly about how smart he is, the deals he makes, and how important he will be."

When Hilda was born nine months after the wedding, Anthea had sobbed in Gussie's arms. James had wanted a son and she had given birth to a girl with a deformed foot. He was disappointed and angry and he let it show. "That child is a cripple and will be trouble all her life."

Together, Gussie and Anthea had set about ensuring that Hilda got the best treatment for her foot. It meant long visits to doctors and long stays in bed with her foot in plaster. They gave her everything they could except her father's love. Hilda was an unhappy baby and James built a soundproof study so he could work and rest without hearing her cries.

Two years later, when Julia arrived, Gussie moved into the Woodruff home to help care for her. She was an appealing and uncomplicated child who ran to her father with open arms. He'd pick her up and twirl her around while Gussie watched and wondered how he could show such favoritism. Didn't he ever consider how Hilda felt?

When Hilda demanded to go to finishing school in Switzerland, Gussie had argued against it. She understood why the girl wanted to get away from the family and have a life of her own, but James's prophecy had come true. Hilda was a difficult, willful teenager who needed supervision and Gussie doubted she would get it in a finishing school. But she dropped her opposition when she realized what a relief it would be for Anthea to be free of her daughter for nine months.

She was not surprised when, one evening when she was working late at Woody's, a distraught Anthea came in with a letter from the headmistress of the school.

Hilda was pregnant and refused to say who the father was. She must be sent home.

"She wants an abortion, but I won't let her murder her child. She must stay in Switzerland and have the baby," Anthea said. "If I have my way, we will keep it. It's wrong to give a child away as if it were some sort of commodity."

"What does James say?" Gussie had asked, already knowing the answer.

"He keeps saying that Hilda is nothing but trouble. If it's a boy he might accept it, if it's a girl, there's no chance."

Anthea flew to Switzerland to care for Hilda while she waited for the birth. In her first letter after the baby was born, she said Hilda was set on having the infant adopted. "She is a beautiful, perfect little girl, but Hilda turned her head and wouldn't look at her."

Gussie understood Hilda's reluctance to keep her child, her fear that being an unwed mother at sixteen would be the straw that broke the camel's back after years of treatment for her foot and the difficult emotional path the teenager walked between her parents. But she also understood Anthea's sorrow at losing her first grandchild.

Gussie wrote to Hilda, to comfort her, but Hilda never answered.

When Hilda came back to New York, she was a different person. Her naïveté was gone and in its place was a hardness, a desire to lead her own life and ignore her parents.

Gussie sighed; Hilda would never accept Kathryn. The younger woman represented a past—and a future—that she had rejected long ago. It would not be possible to break down Hilda's resistance. Gussie began to regret having promised to help Kathryn get closer to the Woodruffs. What did she really know about Kathryn? Was she set on helping her because the younger woman reminded her so much of Anthea?

The oven zinged. The food was ready. She took it to the table and ate slowly, chewing every bite thoroughly. It was hard to swallow; her worry about Kathryn was like a lump in her throat. She sighed, got up, put the half-eaten meal in the sink and watched the water fill up the bowl.

She needed an outsider's view of Kathryn. Someone worldly, who knew a lot of people and would be a good judge of character. Perhaps Sonya Iverson? She was smart, with a cool head, but at the same time compassionate. Her judgment would be sound. And, despite the fact that Sonya was a reporter, Gussie felt that she was the kind of woman who would keep their conversation secret.

Gussie decided that she would call Sonya, ostensibly to thank her for the shoot. Then she could ask, casually, what Sonya thought of Kathryn. Gussie went to her office, switched on the light, and found Sonya's card on her desk. It wouldn't be right to call the cell and disturb Sonya's evening, so she dialed the office number.

The sound of Sonya's voice on the answering machine encouraged her. "Sonya, oh, Sonya, I feel so happy about everything you did yesterday. Thank you. And thank Perry." Gussie hesitated, then spoke in a rush. "I must talk to you. Please call me as soon as you can in the morning."

As soon as she hung up she felt foolish. What would Sonya think, hearing that?

Gussie sighed. Perhaps it was time to go home after all. Her cats would be missing her. As Gussie switched off the light, the door buzzer echoed through the empty shop.

She turned slowly and walked toward the entrance. It wasn't unusual to be disturbed even at this late hour. It could be anyone—kids playing on the street, someone with a bundle of clothes to donate, a volunteer wondering if she were all right. She stood on tiptoe to look through the peephole in the front door.

Immediately she began to struggle to undo the bolt. "Why are you here so late? What's happened?" Her hands were shaking and it seemed an eternity until at last she opened the door.

"Come in, let's go to my office." She tried to keep her voice from trembling. She led the way back through the dappled pattern of light from the streetlamp on the wooden floor.

Her heart was pounding and she couldn't catch her breath. She paused to rest for a moment, leaning on the display counter. An arm slid around her neck and jerked her head back hard. She struggled against it, but the arm was too strong. She bent her head and tried to bite the hand that held her, but the hand was gloved.

She couldn't breathe and she couldn't scream, but she fought as hard as she could, kicking with all her strength. She heard her attacker's heavy breathing, heard a hand groping about on the counter. She heard the fondue forks rattling in their box.

A moment later Gussie jerked in agony as something sharp pierced her skin and slid up under her ribs. The old woman collapsed without a sound, pain twisting her features.

About her, Woody's faded into complete darkness.

Chapter 12

Sonya dialed the number again. Still busy. She put the phone back on the dressing table. It was her habit to check her office voice mail first thing each morning, in case Matt or Donna had left a message there. She'd been trying to reach Gussie since hearing the older woman's message. Gussie had sounded so upset.

Her home number was unlisted, so all Sonya could do was call Woody's. Gussie was an early starter, but who could she be talking to for so long so early in the morning?

Sonya picked up a triangular sponge, poured a little foundation on it, and dabbed it on her cheeks. Then she smoothed it over the sides of her face. The skin there needed particular care; it was still tight from the face-lift she had last year. She studied the result in the mirror and smiled. She had thought long and hard before having the surgery, but now she had no doubt it was the right decision. Looking young was important in television.

She picked up her cell and dialed Woody's again. Busy. The phone had to be off the hook. She shrugged. It was pointless worrying. Gussie probably wanted to discuss something about the way they'd photographed the shop. But Gussie had praised their work at the beginning of the message. No, whatever the problem was, it wasn't about the shoot. If Gussie was troubled, most likely it was something to do with the Woodruff sisters. And that almost surely meant Hilda.

Sonya looked at her face in the magnifying mirror. Just a touch of shine on her eyelids and lips and she was ready. She pulled a golden brown sweater over her head and tucked it into her matching brown jeans. She looked good in that shade; it highlighted the red in her curls and made her pale skin come alive. She slipped on brown zip-up boots and grabbed her handbag. She was ready, but where to go?

She decided before she reached her front door. Woody's. She wouldn't be able to concentrate on anything at the office until she'd talked to the old woman. She caught a cab almost immediately, but Madison Avenue was clogged with traffic. Each time she waited for the lights to change, she pushed down her frustration and anxiety. When, at last, the cab stopped at Woody's, Sonya shoved money at the driver and, without waiting for change, got out and pressed the buzzer.

The door swung open immediately. Kathryn stood there, pale and shaken, her hand tight on the knob.

"What's wrong?" Sonya asked.

Kathryn's lips trembled.

"What are you doing here? I called the police." Her voice was shrill.

Sonya moved to step into the shop, but Kathryn pushed her away and tried to close the door. Sonya pushed back and stepped inside.

"What on earth is the matter with you, Kathryn?" she demanded. "Gussie left me a message. I want to see her."

"You can't. The police told me not to touch anything or to let anyone in. I was waiting by the door for them when you buzzed. I thought it was them."

Sonya looked at her. Kathryn's face was drained of color, and she clutched her handbag to her chest as if to protect herself.

"The police? What's happened?"

"It's Gussie, she's on the floor over there. Murdered." She pointed to the counter that stood in front of Gussie's office. "On my way here I stopped and bought her a cappuccino from the café around the corner. It's her favorite. When I came into the shop I found her."

Sonya went toward the counter. To the side of it, one of Gussie's short plump legs, clad in support hose and a black orthopedic shoe, stuck out at an awkward angle. Kathryn was right. One glance told Sonya that Gussie was dead.

Sonya stepped forward cautiously. Gussie lay on her back behind the counter. The killer had used what appeared to be one of the sharp steel fondue forks from the set on display to stab her. Gussie's chest and outstretched arm were covered with blood; there was a dry pool of blood on the floor. She must have been dead for hours. Her head was twisted to one side, and her once shrewd yet kindly eyes stared as if she were begging her killer to stop.

Sonya stepped back and took a deep breath to calm herself. Gussie must have let in someone she knew and been taken by surprise. She must have struggled; she was the type of woman who would. She was strong for her age, but she was old. It wouldn't have taken much to overcome her.

Sonya turned away and walked back to the door. She opened it and stood, breathing in the fresh air. Then she turned to Kathryn, who was looking at her wide-eyed. "I'm sorry if I was tough on you," she said. "Finding Gussie's body like that must have been a terrible shock. Please sit down and rest. The police are going to want to question you, and that will be exhausting."

Kathryn didn't move. She whispered, "I just thought—what if the murderer is still here?"

"I don't think so," Sonya said calmly. "My guess is that Gussie has been dead for some time. The murderer must be long gone."

Kathryn shivered. "I'm frightened."

"I understand," Sonya replied. "I'll stay with you. But I must call the office and report what happened."

She dialed the number, hoping her executive producer Matt Richards hadn't arrived yet. She didn't want to spend time answering his irrelevant questions. Her luck was in. Rick Carlton answered.

"Rick," she said, "I need Perry at Woody's thrift shop on Madison Avenue. Sign the job roster for me and get him on his way." Sonya realized her heart was racing, her breath coming fast.

"What's going on? Are you okay?"

"Yes," she gasped. "Rick, there's a body here at Woody's. Gussie Ford, the woman who manages the shop, has been stabbed. I'd like Perry to get here, camera rolling, before the police."

"Hang on, Sonya; I'll see where he is."

Sonya waited, leaning on the door jamb, cell phone pressed to her ear. She watched the people passing; they seemed to be in another world. She wanted to bring them into her reality. To shout at them that Gussie had been murdered. That her blood-soaked body lay on the floor a few feet away.

She visualized the scene. Had she missed anything? If there had been something there to show who the killer was, it would have been hard to see in the few moments she'd allowed herself to look.

Then Rick's voice said, "Perry's on his way. He said to tell you the Midtown traffic is horrendous so he'll come through the park. He'll call you if he gets stuck."

"Thanks, Rick. I owe you one."

"Hang on," said Rick. "What do I say to Matt?"

Sonya spoke quickly. "I interviewed Gussie yesterday. Last night she left me an urgent message on the office phone. I couldn't get back to her, so I stopped by the shop on my way to work. One of the volunteers had come in, found the body, and called the police. Got it? The police are on the way. I'll call when I've got more. Bye."

Sonya closed her phone, turned to Kathryn, and put her arm around her shoulders. "Stop worrying. It's going to be okay. We won't be alone for long. Perry's on the way as well as the police. Let's sit on the sofa in Anthea's Room. We can see the police arrive from there, and it's a long way from the body."

For a moment Kathryn didn't move. "I'm not telling anyone about it. Not you or anyone else," she said.

Sonya was puzzled. "Come on, Kathryn," she said. "You will have to tell the police what happened. It would be extremely foolish not to. They'll think you're hiding something."

She led her to the sofa and half closed the door of the room. "There," she said. "We'll still hear the buzzer, but we can't see the counter."

Kathryn collapsed onto the sofa, breathing in quick, short gasps.

"Stop it." Sonya kept her voice low. "You'll be all right. You've got nothing to worry about."

"I don't want to talk to anyone. You can't force me."

"What is it?" Sonya asked. "Do you know something about the murder?"

Kathryn shook her head violently. "No, no. That's not it. I know nothing about the murder. I just let myself into the store and found her. Then I called the police."

Sonya reached out and gripped Kathryn's hands. "Kathryn, at least tell me when you last saw Gussie."

Kathryn swallowed hard and began. "Yesterday afternoon. She took me out for coffee." She hesitated. "She wanted to thank me for coming in so often, because it's such a busy time."

"Did you come back to the store with her?"

"No. There were other volunteers here. I told her I'd come back in the morning, then left her at the café."

Sonya felt Kathryn was not telling her the whole story.

"Did you know Gussie before you came to Woody's?"

"No."

"What about the other members of the Woodruff family?"

"No."

"Why did you decide to volunteer here?"

"I told you, I worked as a magazine stylist in Washington. I knew about Woody's long before I decided to come to New York. I wanted to see how it operated, what the clothes were really like." Her voice was sincere, and Sonya wanted to believe her.

But why was a woman as talented and attractive as Kathryn volunteering at all? The fashion industry was wide open with jobs for women as talented as her. There had to be another reason.

"Have you any idea who murdered Gussie?"

Kathryn was looking at the portrait of Anthea Woodruff hanging on the wall. When she spoke, her words had nothing to do with Sonya's question.

"You know, Gussie was Anthea's best friend. She told me Anthea Woodruff was a great woman." She wiped away a tear with the back of her hand. "She would be horrified to know how Gussie died."

Sonya was about to ask another question when a police car came to a screaming stop outside. Kathryn stood up, searched in her bag for her sunglasses, and put them on.

"It's okay, just tell the police the truth," Sonya comforted her. "They can't arrest you for finding a body." She smiled at Kathryn. "And promise me an interview after this."

Kathryn nodded and then whispered, "Yes."

She led Kathryn to the door, opening it as Detective Keith Harris and his partner arrived. Sonya knew Harris. She had worked with him on the murder of socialite Harriet Franklin.

"I'm glad to see you again, Sonya. It took us a while to get here through the traffic," he said as he stepped toward her. "Did you find the body?"

"No, no," Sonya said, moving away. "This is Kathryn Petite. She found Gussie. I'm here by chance. The dead woman left a message on my voice mail last night. And I stopped by to see her on my way to work."

"Where is the body?"

"Over there, behind the counter."

"Another nice old lady killed for the sake of a few miserable dollars."

As he stepped toward the body, Harris added, "You two stay where you are." When he reached the counter he stood for a few moments studying Gussie's body, then spoke briefly into his handset.

"Forensics and backup are on the way," he said to his partner, who had stayed by the door. Harris pulled a notebook from his back trouser pocket. "Let's get the details from these ladies."

Chapter 13

Harris motioned to Kathryn and Sonya to sit on a brown leather sofa in a corner away from Gussie's body. He introduced his partner, Ian Campbell, and then the two detectives pulled up chairs and sat down in front of the women.

Harris tapped the notebook with his pen. "Let's hear the details," he said, adding to Kathryn, "Please take off your sunglasses. I want to see your face."

Kathryn hesitated and Sonya turned to her. "Kathryn, you must do what Detective Harris says." She gently slid the dark, tortoiseshell-rimmed glasses off Kathryn's nose and handed them to her. "Here, put them in your handbag." Kathryn sat blinking in the sunlight that streamed through the shop window, clutching her sunglasses tightly in her hands.

Harris said, "First, let's have your name."

"K-Kathryn," she stuttered, "but please, my mouth is so dry I can't speak. Could I have some water?"

Harris nodded. "Get it, please, Sonya." Sonya nodded and stood. In the kitchen, she saw an unwashed casserole dish in the sink. Gussie must have been disturbed as she was clearing up her dinner dishes. That would have been late; Gussie had told her she was so busy working on plans for the party, she didn't get around to eating until eight or nine. Sonya opened the fridge, took out a small bottle of Evian, and went back to the sofa. Kathryn sat, silently studying the sunglasses in her hand. Sonya unscrewed the cap and handed her the bottle. Kathryn took several slow sips. She's thinking hard, Sonya realized. She's working out what to say. She does have something to hide.

"Come on." Harris's voice was firm. "There's no reason not to tell me your name."

"It's Kathryn Petite. I work as a fashion stylist for magazines." She took another sip of water.

Harris gave her a hard look. "A fashion stylist?" he asked incredulously.

Kathryn nodded. Sonya could see why he found this hard to believe. Kathryn was dressed in an olive skirt and a loose beige blouse. On her feet were old brown loafers. She wore no makeup and had pulled her hair back from her face in a simple ponytail. Sonya understood his uncertainty. Kathryn was attractive but she'd dressed as if to hide this. As if she didn't want to be noticed.

Harris went on. "What's your address?"

Kathryn mumbled it, then pleaded, "Please don't release my name or address. I can't have any publicity about a murder. I only arrived in New York ten days ago, and I'm illegally subletting an apartment. The agent told me not to tell anyone. She could get into trouble with the owners."

Harris ignored her. "Tell me exactly what happened this morning."

"I had arranged with Gussie to come in early. I bought coffee from the café around the corner. Gussie likes it from there; it's her favorite coffee shop!"

"How did you get in?"

"I unlocked the door."

"Who gave you the key?"

"There are two keys." Her voice grew more confident. "Gussie gave them to me."

"And you opened both locks?"

"No, just the small lock. The dead bolt was already open."

"And when you came in you found the body?"

"Yes. I called the police and did what the sergeant told me. I was waiting by the door when Sonya buzzed. The sun was right in my eyes and I let her in because I thought she was the police."

"Do you know if Gussie usually closed both locks when she was alone?"

"Yes, I think so."

"So Gussie must have opened the door and let in the murderer?"

Kathryn closed her eyes and thought. "Yes, I suppose that is what must have happened. She said she always closed the dead bolt when she worked late. She said she had been mugged once and now wouldn't take any chances."

"Why did Gussie give you the keys?"

"I opened the shop for her yesterday. One of her cats was sick last week and she said if it didn't get better she would take it to the vet. On Monday she was really worried and asked me to open the shop so she could go to the vet before she came in. She hoped he would examine the cat and discover what was wrong right away. But he kept it overnight for tests."

"Why did she trust you with the keys? Weren't there other volunteers she could have asked?"

Kathryn flushed. "Gussie and I got on extremely well from the moment I arrived. She trusted me. And most of the volunteers are married and they're busy in the mornings. Gussie didn't want to inconvenience them."

"And you didn't give the keys back?"

"I tried. We had coffee at the café yesterday afternoon and I offered them to her, but she told me to keep them."

Campbell touched Harris on the shoulder. Harris nodded and Campbell left.

"I see." Harris turned a page of his notebook. Sonya could see he doubted some of Kathryn's story. "So, you've been volunteering for less than two weeks?"

Kathryn sighed. "Yes, I just arrived from Washington and I'm looking for work. I'd heard a lot about Woody's and the designer clothes they sell, so I decided to volunteer here until I got settled."

"You like working in a thrift shop?"

Kathryn looked around the shop and for the first time Sonya saw her smile.

"Yes, I do," she said. "It's fascinating. In my job I'm always looking for something different, to make a shoot stand out. To give it a special look. Here there is so much. The clothes, the objects, the furniture all interest me. Every day new things come in. We never know what we'll get." She turned and pointed. "See that huge black breakfront over there with the bands of silver? That came in last Thursday. It's pure art deco. I could use it for a whole series of photos. It would be perfect for models in slinky dresses."

For the first time she looked directly at Harris. "I wonder all the time about the different things we sell. Who owned it? Why did they buy it? Why did they give it away? Each piece here is connected to a life. Each piece has a story."

"Did you like Gussie?"

"Yes. More than that, I admired her. She was a real businesswoman and she also cared about people. I feel I got an education from her even though I only worked for her for a short time. Gussie was passionate about the shop and I caught some of her passion."

"Did she talk to you about the Woodruff sisters?"

Kathryn slumped back on the sofa. "Not really. They're having the anniversary party on Friday, so we discussed details about it that concerned them, but nothing about their private lives."

"Tell me a little about the details."

Kathryn started to get annoyed. "I can't remember, just things like who would speak at the party and when. Nothing important."

"Did you meet the sisters?"

"No. Julia and Ellin came into the shop, but Gussie didn't introduce them to me."

Harris turned his attention to Campbell, who had returned and whispered to him. Harris stood up and moved away to listen.

Then Campbell sat down and took over the questioning. "What did you talk about at the café with Gussie?"

Before Kathryn could answer, Harris signaled Sonya to come with him. "Now it's our turn to chat."

He walked to a sofa on the far wall. He motioned to Sonya to sit looking away from the forensic team that had arrived and were beginning to work around Gussie's body.

"I've been thinking of giving you a call," he said as he sat beside her on the sofa.

Sonya was pleased but only said, "Well, you have my number."

"And you have mine. Why didn't you call me?"

Sonya didn't know how to answer. Harris was attractive, but she wasn't sure it was a good idea for journalists and cops to get close. "Let's talk about the murder."

"Okay, if that's what you want. Who is this Kathryn Petite? How long have you known her?" he asked.

"I've only seen her here. She's shy, reserved, speaks softly. She told me the same story she told you."

"So what's with the stylist bit?" Harris asked. "She looks like that and yet she claims she puts together outfits for photographers?"

Sonya thought for a moment. "Yes, I believe she is. Perry and I were shooting here on Monday and she really knew her stuff. With her help we got the job done in half the time I expected. I gather she's spent most of her time volunteering here, which is strange for a woman as talented as she is." Sonya shook her head to clear her thoughts. "I may be way off, but I have the feeling Kathryn came here for something. And that it's connected with the Woodruff family. But whatever it is, she won't talk about it."

"What about this party?"

"It's scheduled for Friday night, to celebrate Woody's fortieth anniversary. Gussie was responsible for most of the planning. Apparently that's why she asked Kathryn to come in so frequently. She was short-staffed. It'll be interesting to see what the Woodruffs do now."

"Do you believe Kathryn's story?"

"Only about being a stylist."

"Did she tell you anything about the argument she had yesterday with Gussie in the café?"

Sonya looked at him, surprised. "An argument?"

"Yes."

"She told me that they went there; in fact that was the last time she saw Gussie alive. She said Gussie took her out to thank her for all the time she'd spent volunteering. She didn't mention an argument, but I had a feeling that their chat wasn't as pleasant as she made out."

"The manager told Campbell that Gussie called and asked to reserve a booth for her at the back. He said Gussie sounded worried and asked him to keep an eye on them."

"What happened?" Sonya didn't hide her interest.

"According to the manager, the conversation didn't go easily. He said Kathryn became upset. Gussie stayed calm. At one stage Kathryn appeared to get so angry that he thought she was about to walk out. Then Gussie managed to calm her down."

"Could the manager hear anything?"

"No, they were too far away."

Harris glanced up, and Sonya followed his gaze. He was watching the photographer, who was standing on tiptoe to get a different angle of Gussie's body.

"Whoever did that knew what they were doing," he said.

He looked back at Sonya. "You haven't changed, have you? Still the curious producer." Sonya felt uncomfortable under his gaze. This wasn't the time for the conversation to get personal. She said nothing.

After a moment he continued, "Well, what about the Woodruff sisters? Do you know them?"

"Yes, Hilda, the oldest one, had a small dinner party so I could meet them and discuss their plans for the party."

"Do you think they would have keys to the shop?"

Sonya considered. It was a difficult question to answer. She had no intimate knowledge of the sisters. She thought for a while, then said, "I really don't know, but Hilda might have keys. She has a small office at the back of the store, where apparently she goes to smoke and make calls on her cell phone. It's pretty dismal and I can't believe she'd go there when the shop is closed. Julia is the sister closest to Gussie, so she might. As for Ellin, she might have keys, but I doubt it."

Harris stood up, fumbled in his top pocket, and pulled out a card. Sonya knew she was being dismissed.

"Well, if you have any more ideas," the detective said, handing her the card, "my cell number is on the back."

Sonya looked across at Kathryn sitting with Campbell, her head bent and her dark glasses still clutched in her hand. Harris stood up and Sonya rose with him. He gave her a quick smile and waved her out the door.

Perry was waiting for her on the sidewalk, along with half a dozen other crews. The word was out. Gussie's murder would make the midday news.

"Anything happening?" he asked.

"Nothing much," she said softly. "Kathryn found the body and our favorite detective, Keith Harris, has been questioning her. I'll try for an interview when she comes out, but I don't think I'll get it. She didn't even want to give her name to the detectives. So just try for a shot of her leaving. It'll be any minute. She's wearing a beige blouse."

Perry gave Sonya the mike, put the camera on his shoulder, and stood beside her watching the door. It seemed an eternity until the policeman on guard quickly opened it to let a woman dressed in a black coat and hat slip out and hurry up the street.

Sonya did a double take. "That's her," she breathed to Perry. "She's grabbed some clothes from the shop as a disguise." Perry chased her up Madison Avenue, but before he reached her, Kathryn hailed a cab. Perry continued shooting as she climbed in and the cab pulled away.

He walked back to Sonya and said, "I got one shot of her, just as she climbed into the back seat and slammed the door. That's it."

Sonya wanted to see the tape. "Come on, Perry, let's go back to the office," she said.

As they walked to the van, Sonya decided Kathryn knew a lot more than she admitted. Maybe she had told Campbell something. She would call Harris and ask.

Chapter **14**

Madison Avenue
Wednesday, 9:30 A.M.

"Just go up Madison Avenue," Kathryn said to the taxi driver. "I have to check the address." She kept her head down as she fumbled in her handbag, pretending to look for a piece of paper. Then she told the cabbie to drop her off a block away from where she lived, pulled her hat down so he couldn't see her face, and sank against the seat.

"You've wasted a lot of money not knowing where you're going," he said as he turned the cab onto Ninety-fourth Street and headed toward the East River. "What were you doing? Trying to get away from that TV cameraman?"

Kathryn didn't answer. She told herself that she'd been fast, Perry couldn't have a usable shot of her. And, if he did, the chances were that Sonya wouldn't use it. As a producer, her only interest in Kathryn was that she had found Gussie's body. Sonya couldn't know she was Hilda's daughter.

When the detectives had finished questioning her, she'd seen the cameramen on the sidewalk. She must have looked shocked, because Harris told her to sit down and finish her water. "Don't be concerned about them," he'd said. "They just want to know who you are." She'd given him a grateful smile and then asked if she could get some things she'd left in Anthea's Room. He had nodded his consent.

She'd known exactly what she wanted. She'd gone straight to a black coat she'd put on a display stand for Sonya's shoot. Dressed in that and the matching wide-brimmed black hat pulled down to her eyebrows, she felt concealed. She waited until the detectives had their backs to her, then walked confidently past the officer guarding the door and quickly up the street.

This was the second time she'd run away from Woody's. But yesterday was different. She had been angry. So angry and upset she couldn't speak to Gussie as they left the café. Her gut told her the old woman was manipulating her and that she had no intention of helping her get to know Hilda or any of the Woodruffs. The anger stayed with her and, this morning, when she looked down at Gussie's body sprawled lifelessly on the floor, she had been amazed at how little it affected her. She had moved carefully around it and went into the office where she put on a pair of the thin rubber gloves the volunteers used to go through the bags of donated clothes. Seeing Gussie's phone lying on her desk, Kathryn instinctively moved to put it back in its cradle, then thought better of it.

She knew she had to call the police, but first, she would take a few minutes to see if Gussie had kept any information about her or her adoption. She checked the papers on the desk and in the small filing cabinet. She opened the bottom drawer of the desk and took out Gussie's handbag, where she found only the assortment of odds and ends an elderly woman would collect. She put it back.

Kathryn had left the office and reached for the phone on the counter, but Gussie's body had fallen close to it, and she knew she mustn't touch it. Her cell phone was the answer. She went to the back of the shop, near Hilda's office, and used her cell phone to make the call.

Then she waited by the door, preparing what she would say. She didn't want the police to know about Hilda being her birth mother or that she had argued with Gussie.

Her plan had worked, but only partially. Everyone seemed to suspect her of something—first, Sonya Iverson, then Detective Harris, and especially his partner, Detective Campbell. By the time he spoke with her, Campbell had been to the café, where the manager told him about her afternoon coffee with Gussie. Campbell knew they had argued and Kathryn had tried to return the keys to the shop. Luckily, she had been able to stick to the story that Gussie had taken her out to thank her for her work.

The taxi stopped; Kathryn paid the driver and got out quickly. At last she could breathe easily. She let herself into the building. Riding up in the elevator, she realized she was exhausted. She wanted to sleep, a long dreamless sleep.

Her apartment was as she had left it that morning. The scrapbooks on the dining table, the half-finished mug of coffee in the sink, the covers of her bed thrown back. It wasn't home, but it was a refuge.

The sight of Gussie's face staring lifelessly at the ceiling kept crowding into her mind. There was so much about the family that only Gussie knew, things that Kathryn would never learn. She began to sob as she moved toward the bed. She would get in, pull the covers over her head, and forget everything.

She reached for the bottle of tranquilizers, poured two into her hand, swallowed them dry, and buried her head in the pillow.

The shrill of the phone woke her from a fitful sleep. After her long nap, her mind was foggy. She couldn't remember where she was or what had happened. Her eyes were heavy and the dry sour taste in her mouth was practically unbearable. The phone rang again, and she stumbled out of bed into the living room. Who was it? No one had the number except Marta and Gussie.

She picked up the receiver and mumbled, "Yes."

"May I speak to Kathryn Petite?" a woman's voice said, then added tersely, "You certainly take a long time to answer the phone."

"I'm sorry. It's Kathryn speaking. Who is this?"

"Hilda Woodruff. I need your help." Her speech was crisp, almost sharp.

Kathryn sat down on the arm of the sofa. She was speaking to her birth mother. Almost unable to breathe, she gasped, "Yes."

Hilda went on in the same tone, "You must understand how shocked we are about Gussie's death. I am beside myself with horror and grief. It's impossible to believe a thug would break into Woody's and murder an old woman."

"What was taken?"

"That's for the police to announce." She took a deep breath, and Kathryn sensed that she was controlling her irritation at the question.

She wanted to cry out to Hilda that she was speaking to her daughter. She gripped the phone to control herself. But she feared that if she told Hilda now, it would ruin her chances of a reconciliation. She was silent for a moment and then said, "It will be hard to find out what is missing. Things come in and go out quickly. Each day several volunteers handle the sales, so there's no real record. Gussie was the only person who had a finger on everything."

"As I said, it's up to the police," Hilda went on. "They assure me that the forensic cleaning team will have finished their work this evening. Woody's can open whenever we want."

"That's good," Kathryn said.

"Yes. Well, I'm looking for someone to be in the shop every day and keep things going. To more or less take Gussie's place. I've asked several of our volunteers, and while they are willing to come in for a few hours each day, I need someone full-time. Several volunteers recommended you. I wonder if you would be available, say for two weeks."

Kathryn hesitated. "I'm not sure, I'll have to think."

"I'm quite willing to pay you, and pay you well."

"No, no, it's not a matter of money." Kathryn's mind raced. She wanted to meet Hilda, but not at the shop, with the volunteers watching. She swallowed. "I'm a private sort of person and I wouldn't want to deal with inquiries, especially from the press and the police."

"And there is no reason you should. The thrift shop is run by the Woodruff Foundation. Our PR director, Sara Watkins, is set to handle all the matters dealing with Gussie's death. All you would need to do is to refer callers to her."

"I understand. What about the party?"

"The party is another matter. I want it to go on, for Gussie's sake as much as anything. But I've not yet made a decision. You must understand how difficult this is."

"Yes," said Kathryn. "I do." She knew she had to accept Hilda's offer. "And I will help out. That is the least I can do for Gussie."

"That's good." Hilda sounded relieved. "I want Woody's to be back in business immediately. Do you think you could come in tomorrow?"

"Yes," Kathryn said, though she felt herself break out in a cold sweat at the thought of it.

"Ten o'clock then. I'll have Sara meet you. She'll spend the whole day with you, so you can learn what to say to curious customers. She's extremely competent, you need have no fear."

"Fine." Kathryn's voice was unsteady.

"I haven't met you, have I?" For the first time Hilda voiced some interest in her. "One of us will visit the shop tomorrow. I hope to, but you can imagine how busy I am. Anyway, Sara will call you."

With that Hilda said good-bye and hung up. Kathryn had been dismissed.

So that was her birth mother. Kathryn replayed the conversation in her mind. Hilda came through as a self-centered woman who relished the power the Woodruff name and money brought her. She would have her way, whatever the cost. Kathryn began to understand why Gussie feared her.

She glanced at her watch. She needed coffee; she had slept too long. It would help clear her mind if she talked to Marta. But she would have to be careful what she said.

Marta picked up on the first ring. "I was just about to call you; for some reason I've been worried about you."

"Oh, Marta," Kathryn said, "Gussie Ford, the woman who runs the thrift shop, was murdered. I found her body in the shop this morning when I let myself in."

"Murdered how?" Marta was shocked.

"She was stabbed. I found her lying on the floor near her office."

"Why didn't you call me?"

"It all seemed so unreal. I had to force myself to believe it was Gussie lying there. She looked so tiny and old. I called the police, and when they arrived they questioned me. I think the detective thought I was an idiot. He asked my name and I got confused. I didn't know whether to give him my real name, Pettibone, or the name I use at the shop, Petite."

"Which did you use?"

"Petite. If I'm questioned about it, I'll say that Petite is my professional name."

"Fair enough. After all, you went to New York to make a new start in fashion, and Pettibone is not a glamorous name. Did the detectives ask any questions about your family background?"

"No, just about how I let myself in and found the body. When they finished, I got home as fast as a taxi could take me, took a couple of tranquilizers, and went to sleep. I have to keep telling myself that it's true, that Gussie's dead."

Her heart began to thud. "Marta, Hilda called me and asked me to take Gussie's place in the shop for two weeks. She wants to keep it open and is even thinking of having the anniversary party. I'm frightened, but I want to do it. I want to meet all the members of my family."

"Wow," Marta replied. "You're taking a big risk there. You're doing exactly what Hilda's attorney warned you not to do."

"I know, but it may be the only chance I have. I feel so strange. When I spoke to Hilda I took an instant dislike to her. Gussie's death seems to be merely an inconvenience to her." She swallowed hard. "And while she was asking me to do her a favor, she made me feel like a servant. When I hesitated, she offered me money."

"Oh, Kathryn, don't judge her so harshly. The Woodruffs must be beside themselves. Imagine the press they'll get on this. They have all the money in the world and yet they let a faithful old employee work late and alone in a shop that wasn't secure."

"The press is already on the story," Kathryn replied. "When I left the shop there were TV cameramen and photographers outside."

"Well, that could work to your advantage. After this publicity, Hilda won't want more about the baby girl she put up for adoption. She may accept you."

Marta paused for a long moment. Finally she said, "Kathryn, do you ever think how hurt your mother, Zoe, might be if she knew how passionate you are to know your birth mother? After all, she raised you with love and care. You meant everything to her."

"Marta, I can't talk about that. I'm still bitter that she didn't tell me I was adopted. That I was the cause of her fights with Dad and the reason behind the divorce. She forced the only father I've ever known away from me. I can't forgive her. Maybe I'll change, but it will take time."

"Kathryn, move on. Stop thinking about it. Put on the DVD of one of your favorite old movies and watch it mindlessly. Or find something on TV."

"I'll try."

Kathryn hung up, made coffee, and sat on the sofa. It was time for the local TV news. She wanted to see what they said about Gussie's murder.

It was the lead story. She watched Gussie's body being taken from the shop, then stock footage of the three Woodruff sisters as the reporter explained how their mother started Woody's. Detective Harris said the police were investigating the murder and would issue a statement later. The story closed with a shot of Gussie taken Monday morning. In a medium shot Gussie was discussing clothes; Kathryn was standing beside her. The older woman took a silver lamé dress from a rack and held it up. The camera zoomed past it and onto Kathryn's smiling face. Kathryn was horrified.

"That was Woody's volunteer Kathryn Petite, who found the body," the reporter said. "And what a sad day it was for her and for all of those who had come to love this old lady."

Kathryn's throat tightened with fear. It was just what she had tried to avoid.

Chapter **15**

As soon as she walked in, Sonya knew that news of Gussie's murder had spread throughout the office. Her friend Sabrina, the makeup artist, was perched on the receptionist's desk, obviously waiting for Sonya. Sabrina stood up and grabbed Sonya by the arm. "What's going on? Don't tell me that one of the Woodruff sisters is involved in a murder?"

Sonya shook her off. "Not as far as I know. I'm sorry, Sabrina, I have to go. I'll talk to you later."

"But what happened?" She tugged Sonya's arm. "I thought you were doing a puff piece on the Woodruffs' thrift shop. Now you're investigating the murder of the old lady that ran it. You sure know how to find bodies. How did . . . ?"

Sonya looked at her friend's round, eager face, with clownlike spots of bright red rouge on her cheeks, and shook her head. "Sabrina," she said, "you know the games Matt has been playing with me since we got back from Hawaii. I know he's trying to get rid of me, but I'm fighting back. He just called and said he's holding a special meeting about the murder. I've got to get to it."

"Lunch then?" Sabrina said, dropping her hand.

"It's too early to say." Sonya moved away. As she walked along the corridor to the conference room she could hear the buzz of the staff. Gussie's murder was a breaking story. Anything could happen.

Rick Carlton, the show's other senior producer, was coming from the opposite direction. He stopped at the conference-room door to wait for her. "Did Perry get there in time to get a shot in the store?" he asked.

"No, the police arrived just after I called you. We waited on the sidewalk to get an interview with Kathryn Petite—the volunteer who found the body—but she was too fast. Perry chased her up the street and just managed to get a shot as she climbed into a cab. Of course, he shot the body being taken out, and we got the usual statement from the police."

"Bad luck."

"Is Donna coming to the meeting?"

"No, she was here for the eight thirty, but I hear she's on the nineteenth floor, meeting with the execs."

Rick walked her to a chair near the head of the table, and sat next to her. As she took her place, the room grew quiet.

As she expected, Matt wasn't there. He liked to keep the staff waiting.

"You want coffee?" Rick offered.

"No, thanks. I'm already too keyed up. And I want to be calm for Matt."

On cue, Matt came in, sat down without a word, and opened a file folder.

"Tell me, Sonya, what happened, what you know, what you did, and where things stand now."

Sonya gave them all a quick summary of the events at the shop, and concluded, "So the story now includes a murder. It is doubtful Gussie would have let in anyone unless she knew them. I plan to interview the family and several other people." She was careful not to be specific about Kathryn. She wanted to shape the story in her own way.

"Who do you mean specifically?"

His tone was more offensive than usual. Sonya fought her dislike of him, keeping her voice low and steady. "I mean the three Woodruff sisters, maybe some other members of the family, and, perhaps, some of the volunteers."

"I see," said Matt with derision. "So you have another murder story. You are getting quite a reputation. Anyone would think you are the star of the show, not Donna." He glared at her, as if daring her to answer.

She glared back for a moment, then looked away. He had treated her unprofessionally in Hawaii. Now he was punishing her for his own lack of judgment. He was rude and critical, but worse, he undermined her work. More than once he had suddenly sent Perry to shoot an assignment when he knew Sonya needed him.

In a quiet gesture of support, Rick moved his arm a few inches so that his elbow just touched her arm.

"Sonya," Matt said, "I think that you have too much on your plate right now. You have a full lineup of assignments to shoot and then to edit. This story is too much for you to handle, so I've decided to have Rick take over. Give him your notes and contacts." He laughed. "We don't need a detective on this story, we need a producer."

Sonya sat still for a moment, not believing what he had just said. She had originated the idea for the story, had done the research and the preliminary interviews. He had absolutely no right to take her off it.

She exploded. "You have no reason to do this. The work I have lined up will be completed on schedule—as always. You know that as well as I do."

She stood up, put her hands on the table, and leaned toward him.

"Your decision has nothing to do with my ability as a producer. It's about you and your need to control everything. You can't accept the idea that I can develop a story and make it into a ratings winner." Sonya knew she was out of control, but she couldn't stop.

"Ever since we got back from Hawaii you have been doing your best to undercut me. I've had enough. This story is mine and I'm doing it."

Matt's face went stiff with rage. He shouted at her, "You'll do what I say! I am the executive producer, and you work for me."

Sonya hadn't finished. "You're the one who thinks he's the star of the show. But Donna is, and I'll wait for her instructions."

Matt stood to face her. "You will hand over this story to Rick or give me your resignation. Your choice."

There was a gasp from those around the table.

Sonya was stung. The showdown between her and Matt had been long coming, but in that moment, she realized she would leave rather than put up with his arrogance. As much as she enjoyed working on *The Donna Fuller Show*, she had other options. With her reputation, she could move into a good job at another network. Still, if she left, she wanted to go on her own terms.

"I am doing this story, Matt. You can have my resignation when it's done." Sonya kept her voice ice-cold. Then she wheeled and walked out the door.

"Don't you leave!" Matt roared after her. "Come back here!"

But Sonya was already in the corridor, heading for Donna's office. If she was still at the meeting on the nineteenth floor, Sonya would just sit and wait.

Donna's assistant greeted her with a smile. "Hi, Sonya. I hear you're on another murder story. That's good news for the ratings. Donna's just come in. You need to see her?"

"Yes." Sonya took a deep breath, but before she could say another word, the door to Donna's office swung open.

Donna Fuller herself stood there. She didn't seem at all surprised to see Sonya, and her first words made it clear why.

"I've heard from Matt. You better come in," she said. Then turning to her assistant, Donna added, "I don't want to be disturbed."

Once inside, Donna offered Sonya a chair and sat opposite her on the sofa. Sonya knew that she would have a fair hearing.

"Now what is the problem?" Donna began. "Matt called and said he wanted to see me 'about Sonya.' I told him to wait. I thought I would first hear your side of the story."

Sonya let it all pour out. "Matt is vindictive. He sees me as some sort of competition. He's more than ambitious, he's paranoid. If he wants me out, then I am willing to leave the show—but not before I do this story. No way. You personally will have to fire me to get me off this story."

Donna leaned forward and patted her on the knee.

"Sonya, no one wants you to leave. You're an important part of my show. Despite what Matt may have said in anger, he values your work as much as I do." She paused. "But I don't want you to be stubborn about this story. I want you two to work this out."

"Donna, there is no way to work it out. I'll do this story either for your show or for the competition."

"I don't want any threats, Sonya."

"I mean it, Donna."

"I believe you, and I understand how you feel. This is your story and rightly so. I'll tell Matt. But it is imperative that you two work together. You can't be productive with this growing animosity between you. So, I want you to go to lunch with him today and come to an understanding."

"Today?" Sonya objected. But one look at Donna made her realize that she meant it. Donna couldn't have her executive and senior producer at loggerheads. She would overrule Matt's decision, but she had to find a way to let him save face.

"Sonya, remember the show is the most important thing. Not Matt's abusive behavior."

"Of course, Donna. I'll try."

"Fine. Now get back to work, and keep me up-to-date. I'll do the major interviews—Hilda Woodruff for a start. Pre-interview her for me as soon as you can."

Sonya left, relieved that she had Donna's support, but still furious about Matt. Sabrina was waiting for her. "Oh, Sabrina," Sonya said. "I'm sorry I didn't have time to talk to you when I came in, and now I'm in a rush again."

"Sonya, wait a minute. Perry's been looking all over for you. He heard about the business with Matt and you know how he feels about you." She paused and studied Sonya's face. "What should I tell Perry? Have you seen Donna?"

"Yes, and it's okay." It was all she could manage. She was close to tears and the last thing she wanted was anyone to see her crying. That could start a rumor that Matt had won the battle.

"I'll let Perry know. See you later."

"Okay, thanks."

Sonya went to her desk and checked her voice mail. The only message was from Perry, asking her to call him on his cell as soon as she could. Though Sonya knew Sabrina would find Perry eventually, Sonya felt she had to talk to Perry herself.

Perry sighed with relief when he heard her voice. He asked, "You okay?"

"More or less," she said. "I want to talk to you and I need to get out of the office. Can you join me in fifteen minutes at the coffee shop near the Franklin Building?"

"I'm on my way," he replied.

Sonya felt better just hearing his voice.

He was waiting when she arrived. She watched him give the waitress his wide, friendly smile. Then he glanced at the door, saw Sonya, and waved. She felt a rush of affection for him. Perry was not good-looking, with his droopy ginger mustache and heavy jowls, but he was strong and vital. And, most important, he was reliable.

"Oh, Perry, thanks for coming," she said as she sat in the chair opposite him. "I had to talk to you."

"I've ordered the usual coffee for you," he said. He touched her arm briefly. "I heard what happened at the meeting. You're not quitting, are you? We're a team. I want to stay with you."

"No, I am not quitting—not until we finish the Woodruff story anyway. Donna insists that I work things out with Matt. I'll try. I love working with Donna. And with you." She gave him a brilliant smile.

The waitress brought the coffees and a bran muffin for Perry. "Do you want some?" he asked. "I didn't order you anything because you never have anything but coffee in the morning."

Sonya nodded. "The last thing I want to do in the morning is eat. I've always been that way. Did you hear what happened after I left the meeting?"

"From what Rick Carlton told me," Perry responded, "Matt just stood there for a minute, then grabbed his file and left the room. Rick was sure that he went to see Donna. He'd want to cover himself by getting his story to her first."

"Oh, Perry," Sonya said, blinking away the tears. "I'm so fed up with him. Not just because of this story—he's been treating me like this ever since we got back from Hawaii. But I won't let him drive me out. Donna asked me to have lunch with him today. I hate the thought of it, but have no choice." She swallowed hard. "You, of all people, know this is ridiculous. I have no interest in his job."

"Everyone knows. The bastard is paranoid. The whole staff is angry about the way he treats you. It must have gotten through to Donna. And if Donna knows, then the nineteenth floor knows." He shook his head. "I can fix Matt for you; just one blow is all I'd need. He's an arrogant fuck who needs to be taught a lesson."

Sonya was taken aback by Perry's outburst. She had to calm him. "Thanks, pal," she said. "I'll do what Donna asked, I'll have lunch with Matt and see where we go from there. Let's plan the story. It's scheduled for Tuesday's show."

"Sonya, let me know immediately if he attacks you again."

She smiled her thanks. "Of course, Perry. Now about the murder. . . ."

At last he was able to bring his mind to it. "I gave our tapes to local news for the noon broadcast. You'll be able to view them this afternoon."

Sonya picked up her coffee mug and cradled it in her hands.

"I told you that I got a call last night from Gussie. She wanted to talk to me urgently. The more I think about it, the more I'm convinced it was about Kathryn Petite. Don't you think it strange that she suddenly showed up out of nowhere, devoted all her time to being a volunteer, made a great effort to be friendly with Gussie, and suddenly Gussie is murdered?"

"Could be a coincidence, Sonya."

"That's true, but at the back of my mind, when we were working together on Monday, I was thinking there was something not quite right about her. She worked well with you, but she hardly spoke to me and she got out of the way when she saw me coming. I had the feeling she was frightened of something."

"Well, I have to agree that there was something odd about her. She was so eager to please."

"Yes, and remember how she rushed to help Julia Woodruff when she came in? Kathryn raced to get her a glass of water, and then took it to her in Gussie's office, closed the door behind her, and stood nearby. I'd say she wanted to hear what was going on inside."

Sonya drained the last of her coffee and reached over to pick up the bill. Perry took it from her. "If you don't mind," he said.

"Perry," she said. "I'm the one who's been bending your ear."

"As usual." He grinned.

They got up and walked to the cashier. "I want to interview all the members of the family," Sonya said. "There's something going on that I can't figure out. Hilda dominates the sisters, that's for sure, and they don't like it. But I can't see how Gussie fits in."

"She's been running that shop for years, hasn't she?"

"Yes, and she knew a good deal about the Woodruff family. Maybe it wasn't all good."

"Yeah," Perry drawled. "So, what's next?"

"I'll set up interviews with them this afternoon. Donna wants to do Hilda, so I'll have to do a pre-interview with her. I want to interview Kathryn. I believe she may be the key to this murder."

"You really think she's capable of doing it?"

Sonya shrugged. "I don't know. Anything is possible."

"Well," Perry said, as he opened the coffee shop door for her. "Don't forget the most logical explanation is that someone off the street murdered Gussie for money."

"I doubt it. I was in the store before the police arrived and saw that the cash drawer hadn't been forced open. The whole place looked as neat as when we were shooting. I believe someone came to the store for the sole purpose of murdering Gussie."

They left the café together. Perry took Sonya's arm to guide her through the crowded street. Sonya looked into his eyes and smiled, then moved away from him. With his support the piece would be great, and bring in those elusive high ratings. Another feather in her cap.

"Thanks, Perry. For the coffee, for your support, for everything. When I called you, I felt so vulnerable. Now I'm fighting fit."

Chapter 16

Julia sighed as she laid out breakfast in the sunny kitchen at the back of the Upper East Side apartment. King was a finicky eater and she knew he would have skipped breakfast. Maybe he'd eat some yogurt and honey or a slice of toast with her. Orange juice was too acidic for him. Caffeine made him jittery, so the coffee had to be decaffeinated, and as his cholesterol tended to be high, the milk had to be skim.

Julia sometimes wondered if any drop of Woodruff blood flowed in King's veins. He was so like his father—his dark good looks, his wiry energy, his quick intelligence, and his even quicker temper.

"Did you demand Hilda give me back my job and my office?" he'd shouted at her last night. The phone had rung just as she came in, and she'd forced herself to pick it up.

"Please, King," she had said, trying not to let him upset her. "I'm too tired to discuss it tonight. All I'll say is that Hilda was as difficult as I expected her to be. Come for breakfast and let's talk about what's to be done."

He had agreed reluctantly, saying he had an early meeting with his attorney and would come when it finished. Now, he was about to arrive and she had to tell him that Hilda had laughed in her face. The thought of his reaction frightened her. Her palms were already slick with perspiration.

She heard his key in the door and then his call. "Mother, where are you?"

"I'm in the kitchen."

She went to greet him. He kissed her on the cheek. She closed her eyes and held on to him.

"Oh, King," she let it rush out, "Hilda was foul. Arrogant, rude, impossible. The way she's been since your grandfather died. I don't know what's to be done." She felt a wave of frustration. "Let's have coffee. It will make us feel better."

She poured coffee into two cups and topped them with milk. Then she pulled out a chair and sat down, picking up her cup and nursing it in both hands.

"Tell me every word she said," King demanded.

Julia tightened her grip on the cup. King banged his fist on the table.

"Every word."

"She said you weren't executive material. That Father had made a big mistake in bringing you into the company and promoting you the way he did. That you weren't doing the job of a senior vice president and it was time you were replaced." She thought for a moment, wondering if she should warn her son of Hilda's threat. Then she decided he should be prepared for what might happen. "Hilda said you were lucky that they hadn't fired you. And she didn't rule out that happening in the future."

"God, how I hate her. She's been plotting to get me out of the company since Grandfather died. And why? Because she wants Wells to head it. With me out, she thinks she'll get him in. And what's crazy about this is he doesn't want it. He's said time and time again he's not interested. He's happy in the hotel business. This is not about Wells or me. It's her power lust. But she won't get me out, I promise you."

Julia shook her head.

"I did what I could. You know that," she said. "Ellin came with me for support, and she agrees that Hilda has no right to demote you."

"I have never understood why the two of you put up with her."

"It's always been impossible for us to argue with her. It's the way the family works. She's our older sister. She bossed us around when we were kids. We accepted it then and we accept it now."

"Did you tell Ellin I've hired a team of lawyers?"

"Yes, and she's horrified. She doesn't want a scandal."

King sat silently by her side.

She put her hand over his. "When I first became pregnant, your father wanted me to run off with him and live in a commune. Perhaps I should have, it might have made life easier for you."

"No. I'm glad you didn't. I loved Grandfather and I know what he wanted from me. I'll follow his wishes. Hilda can't stop me."

Julia remembered her first meeting with King's father, Avery Jenkins, when she was twenty and a sophomore at Brown. She'd been to a civil rights rally where Avery was speaking. He was brilliant, a born leader. All the coeds were in love with him and he slept with many of them. But she was the one who got pregnant and she was the one who had money.

King interrupted her thoughts with an unexpected question. "Was my father in love with you?"

"I doubt it." She looked away. "I was in love with him; I took him home, introduced him to the family, and demanded that they let me marry him."

"Do you think he married you for your money?"

"King, it was so long ago. You know he came from a poor family; I only met them three or four times. Hilda was convinced he was a fortune hunter when she heard his father was a bus driver in Boston and his mother worked as a maid in a hotel."

"Hilda is a snob. But isn't it ironic that I will be the head of the family that she thought was too good for him?"

Julia ignored his question. She wasn't going back to that subject. She went on, "But money or not, it could never have worked out. Everything about your father and me, our interests, our lifestyles, just didn't fit." She smoothed the yellow tablecloth, wishing she could remove the problems as easily as the creases.

"I know the family rejected him. But in all these years, why didn't he try to reach me? Didn't he have any feelings for me?"

How many times had she heard that question? She was convinced Avery's disappearance was the reason King was so determined to be recognized as the head of the Woodruff family and the company. In his mind, he had to prove himself to a father he'd never known.

"King," she said impatiently, "I've told you before that he left you because he realized that you would have a better life with me and my family."

King shook his head and said nothing.

Julia poured fresh coffee for them both. She sat down and breathed on hers to cool it. How many times had she gone over this with him? How could she make him accept that his parents had simply had a fleeting affair, a quick wedding, and a quick divorce? She tried to make it sound painless, but it hadn't been easy. She had never told King about the nights Avery had come home late and beaten her in a drunken rage. Eventually she'd become so frightened for her baby that she'd called her father. He'd paid Avery to get out of her life and the life of her child.

"King, Avery was proud of you, but he wanted to go his way. And he went with my blessing."

"He could be dead for all we know."

"Yes," she said. But she thought it was more likely that he was in jail or on the run as a fugitive. Avery Jenkins had belonged to a radical group, and she'd heard he'd been arrested for manufacturing explosives. She wasn't surprised by the news of his arrest; he'd often told her that he believed violence was justified in the right cause. The last she heard of him, an attorney had gotten him off on a technicality and he had headed for Canada. An old college friend told her he had changed his name. She didn't want to know what it was.

But it would be useless telling King any of this. He had brooded about his father all his life.

"King, it's all in the past," Julia said. "Be happy you had a grandfather who gave you everything you needed. Be satisfied with that."

He looked at her with his dark, shadowed eyes. Avery's eyes. She couldn't escape the thought that King was as violent as his father. Julia shivered.

"Whether you like it or not, Hilda heads the family," she continued. When your grandfather set everything up, it was natural that he chose Hilda. She is the oldest daughter."

"She wormed her way into his affection when he was too ill to know what he was doing," King said bitterly.

Julia was growing weary of him. "You have two options," she said. "You can stay at the company and fight, or you can resign, get out, and do something that interests you. Run for office. Be like your grandmother and start a charity. The city is full of people who need help. You are blessed; you will never need money."

"My God, Mother, she's brainwashed you. Come on, out with it. You don't want me to sue."

"No, I don't. I believe the media will tear us down, and even if you get your position back, you'll be miserable. Hilda will see to that."

"You're frightened of Hilda, aren't you? That's why you expect me to bow out and do nothing?"

Julia shook her head. "I'm not afraid of her."

"Well, if you are not afraid, explain why she has the office at the shop and not you. You're there several times a week, discussing problems with Gussie. Hilda almost never goes there. Yet she has an office at Woody's and you don't."

"Oh, stop. Hilda has the office because she's head of the foundation."

"Don't you believe it; Gussie spies for Hilda. That old lady is as devious as they come."

King stood up and leaned against the sink. He pointed an accusing hand at her.

"You knew I was in anguish at the office on Monday, but where did you go? To Woody's, wasn't it? You gave Gussie an account of everything that happened. And you can bet that as soon as you left, she was on the phone to Hilda. That woman is my enemy."

"Please, King, you're being paranoid. Gussie is my friend and your friend too." Julia watched him closely. He was angrier than she'd ever seen him.

He put his hands on the table and leaned toward her. "I saw the lawyers this morning. You know, Mother, I'm looking forward to a hard fight."

She stood up, wanting to slap his face. The phone rang. "Take a message for me," she said. "I can't talk to anyone."

She turned away as King reached for the phone. She heard him answer, and then, in a sullen voice, say, "She's upset and doesn't want to talk to anyone." He listened for a moment and then said, loudly, to Julia, "It's your sister, Hilda. She doesn't trust me with a message. She wants to speak to you."

"Oh, no," she said. But she held out her hand for the phone.

"Oh, yes," he mimicked.

Julia took the phone from King, hoping he would leave the room. Instead, he sat down and pulled his chair closer to her so he could hear the conversation. She kept her voice low. "Yes, Hilda, what is it?"

"Oh, Julia, I have some terrible news, and I wish I could be there to tell you in person. But I think it's best you know before you hear it on the radio or TV."

"What news, Hilda? What is it?" Julia's heart began to beat faster as Hilda spoke.

"Julia, are you sitting down?"

"Yes, and King is beside me. For God's sake, tell me."

Hilda hesitated. "It's Gussie," she whispered. "Our Gussie is dead. She was murdered last night as she was working in the shop."

For a moment Julia sat paralyzed. Then she sucked in a harsh breath. "Gussie murdered? It's impossible. Who would do such a thing?"

"Some person from the street." Hilda paused for a long moment. "The police believe that Gussie let her killer in."

"Gussie let a stranger into the store? No, never. Gussie was mugged years ago, and she said she'd never let it happen again," Julia said. "I know Gussie better than anyone. She would only open the door to a person she knew and trusted."

She stopped, horrified at the implication of what she had said. King put his arm around her.

In her normal voice, Hilda said sharply, "Julia, pull yourself together. She could have been killed by a friend or any of the volunteers. You always thought of her as a gentle woman. But that wasn't the real Gussie. She was tough and she had a lot of enemies."

"No, that's not true."

"Of course it is. I only kept her on at the store because it was Mother's wish. Mother confided in her. She knew all about us. And she wasn't past using the knowledge for her own advantage."

"Did the . . . murderer"—Julia hesitated as she said the word—
"take anything?"

"No money. But it's hard to say, the shelves were packed with things
because of the big push for the party. Only Gussie knew what was there."

"Yes," Julia echoed, "only Gussie." A feeling of unreality swept
through her. She rested her head in her hand. It seemed too heavy to
hold up. "Who found her body?"

"One of the volunteers. Kathryn Petite. She's been coming in every
day to help. Gussie had given her a set of keys."

"I know her, she's that tall blonde. I met her on Monday. Is she all
right?"

"Yes, the police questioned her and told her to go home."

"What are we to do? What do the police say?"

"They're still working at the store and will be for a few more hours.
Detective Keith Harris is in charge. He said he'd call me later."

"And the party. What about it? Should we cancel it?"

"I don't know. I don't want to. But I have to wait until I hear what
Harris says. I have to call Ellin now, but I'll get back to you as soon as
I hear something more."

Julia handed King the phone. He stood and replaced it in its cradle
on the wall.

"Mother, I'm sorry, for your sake."

She nodded, too stunned to move. "Gussie would never have let
just anyone into the store."

"She let me in," he said defiantly.

"Let you in? When did you see her? Not last night?"

"Yes. Last night."

"My God, King, why?"

"I called her Monday afternoon and told her to stop questioning
you about me. What had happened at the company was my business
and she had no right to repeat it. She said she hadn't, and that if I were

a Woodruff I'd make my accusations to her face. That was too much for me."

Julia could hardly breathe. It was hard to understand what he was saying. All she could think was that Gussie had been murdered and that King had been with her just before she died.

He went on, almost nonchalantly. "I asked her how long she'd be in the store, and she said she usually stayed until ten, but that night she was going home early to care for her sick cat. I said I'd come on Tuesday about nine. When I arrived, I pressed the buzzer and she let me in."

"How could you treat her so badly? She's cared for us all. She's looked after you since you were a baby. I have photos of her holding you in her arms."

"You've always been blind to what she is really like. She latched on to Grandmother because Anthea married big money."

"Have you told anyone else about going to see her?"

"No. But I have nothing to hide." Despite his bravado, he was afraid. She could see the tension in his face.

"Tell me what happened in the store."

"We argued," he said bluntly. "You could say we had a flaming row. I was furious and I let her have it." He shrugged. "She told me how ungrateful I was. That I was the eldest grandson and I had a role to fulfill. I should do it with dignity. She went on and on, until I just wanted to escape from her."

"And you left?"

"Yes, Mother, I left."

"That's all?" Julia insisted.

"No." He jerked out a laugh. "I slammed the door behind me."

Julia looked at him. He was so like his father. How could she know if he was telling the truth? She shook her head. It didn't matter. She would never repeat what he had told her.

Chapter 17

Sonya left Perry outside the coffee shop and waved down a cab. It was better to return separately to the office. She didn't want to involve him in her struggle with Matt. Everyone in the office knew they were friendly, but having coffee with him after Matt had tried to fire her could make him seem to be an accomplice.

Anyway, she wanted to be alone. She sat, not seeing the crush of the traffic, as the cab turned onto Sixth Avenue. Her mind raced over the events of the morning.

Her chest tightened. Matt had been rude and abusive to her, and now she had to have lunch with him. Donna was wrong to insist on it. It would have been better to put it off for a day or two, to let them both cool down.

She was convinced that Matt had been showing off in the meeting. He couldn't fire her. She had a contract, and he'd have to prove that she was violating some clause. She could make a case right now with the human resources department about his behavior this morning. That would cause problems for him. But she knew she would never do it.

As the cab pulled up to the network entrance, her cell phone rang. Donna's assistant told Sonya she'd made a reservation at twelve thirty for lunch at Pescatore, a fish restaurant about a five-minute walk from the studio. She and Matt would walk over together. Sonya mumbled a low, "Thank you," and hung up. She looked down at her brown sweater and jeans. Too casual. She'd dressed down, expecting to spend the day in the editing room. But Pescatore was a fine restaurant with an up-market clientele.

Sabrina was the answer. Five minutes of her magic and she'd be transformed into a TV personality. She went straight to the makeup room and found Sabrina full of curiosity.

"Donna doesn't waste time, does she? Scheduling your lunch like that?" she said as she dipped her brush into blusher and smoothed the color onto Sonya's cheek. "Matt must be dreading it as much as you are."

"I'm to meet him at the reception desk at twelve fifteen." Sonya sighed.

"You'll be fine. I'm sure he got the word from Donna."

"You're sure or you know?" Sabrina's gossip was usually accurate.

"Well, the word is that Donna let him have it, and then, like the bully he is, he caved in and agreed to the kiss-and-make-up lunch. Anyway, for what it counts, we're all on your side."

Sonya bussed Sabrina on the cheek and walked to her office. Sabrina was right. It was time for Donna to deal with Matt.

Her voice mail light was flashing. She switched it on and heard Keith Harris asking for a favor. He wanted to view Perry's tapes from Monday morning. It was a long shot, he said, but maybe they showed some valuable item that was now missing. Who would kill an old woman for something they could buy for a few dollars? She called him back. "Detective Harris—," she began.

He interrupted her with a laugh. "I'm Keith. Why are you being so formal?"

She relaxed and laughed back. "Okay, Keith, I'll have dupes of the tapes made. They should be ready by midafternoon."

"I'll come over and get them from you."

"I'll leave them at the desk with the receptionist. I may not be here then."

"Sorry to hear that. But I'll see you another time."

"Good-bye." She tried to sound firm, but then changed her mind. "Keith, I do want to talk to you. I'm sorry to be so abrupt, but I'm having a rough day."

"Can I help?"

"Thanks for the offer, but I have to work this out myself. And I'm already running late."

She said good-bye again and hung up smiling. He was kind—considerate and caring.

She took a look at herself in her mirror. The makeup helped, and so did the comb Sabrina had tucked in her hair. She headed to the reception desk and found Matt, uncharacteristically early, waiting for her.

"Ready?" he asked.

She nodded, and they went through the door and down the street. Neither spoke. As they reached the restaurant entrance, Matt stopped.

"Sonya, this isn't easy for either of us. But we need to work out our problems for the good of the show and the network. So let's do that and then enjoy a good meal."

Sonya had to admire his mercurial style. He was an office politician of the first order. He'd do anything to get to the top.

"I understand, Matt, and I'm sure it's possible." He held the door open for her and she smiled. "I'm looking forward to the food. I love this place."

Matt was more subdued than he'd ever been. Sabrina was right, he was a bully. Just like those in the school yard back home in Minnesota. As soon as they were challenged, they backed down.

She ordered the fillet of sole and so did he. While they waited for their food, Sonya told him that she understood how tough the pressure was to constantly deliver high ratings. She added that he was a fine executive producer; the best she'd ever worked with. He accepted her flattery with a complacent smile.

Then she insisted that in the future it must be understood she would always complete stories that were clearly hers.

"Okay," he agreed. "But, as much as I like your work, I make the final decisions. The show is my responsibility."

Sonya told him she understood, and then let the discussion drop. They each had said what was expected, and neither had apologized for the flare-up.

"Right, let's move on," Matt said. But Sonya knew their problems weren't resolved. Matt would never forgive her victory. There were battles ahead and she had to be ready for them. The important thing was that she could continue working on the Woodruff story. She had won—for the time being.

They spent the rest of the lunch talking about the Woodruffs.

"Other than the obvious interviews," she summed up, "I have to wait and see what happens. The Woodruffs are undecided about the party on Friday, but my guess is that Hilda Woodruff will go on with it. I'll keep you posted, and if I get stuck I'll ask Rick to give me a hand."

"Sure," he said.

"Thanks, Matt. I have a lot to do. The story won't make tomorrow's show, but certainly Tuesday's."

"If you're sure about Tuesday, then I'll promote the hell out of it on tomorrow's show." He flashed his grin again.

Sonya took up his challenge. "You'll have it in time."

They walked to the studio in silence again, and parted with a quick good-bye.

Back in her office, Sonya set to work. She wanted to interview one of the sisters that afternoon. First she phoned Hilda to schedule a pre-interview that would enable her to prepare questions for Donna.

Her call was answered by a maid, who said she would check to see if Hilda was home. Sonya guessed Hilda was avoiding the press, but to her surprise the oldest Woodruff sister came on immediately.

"Yes, what do you want?"

"I know this is a bad time to call," Sonya said. She kept her voice soft. "But as Donna wants to continue with the story, could I come over and have a short chat with you this afternoon?"

"You want my reaction to Gussie's murder?" Hilda asked indignantly. "I've already released a press statement."

"Oh, no," Sonya said. "The story we are doing is the one we talked about. At dinner on Friday night we agreed that Donna would interview you about Woody's."

"Not now."

"Are you having the party?"

"I haven't decided."

"I hear from the newsroom that people are leaving flowers outside the shop. It's touching."

"I've heard that, and as you say, it's touching. As to the interview, I'm still considering it and I'll call Donna Fuller when I make up my mind. But believe me, I have no time for a chat with you."

Sonya put the phone down, wondering at Hilda's abruptness. On Friday they had a pleasant dinner at her home. Now Hilda treated her as if they had never met. Just because of the murder? Or was something else going on?

She called Donna's assistant to warn her about a possible callback, then decided to try Ellin. As the youngest Woodruff daughter, perhaps she wasn't as much involved with the family decisions as Hilda.

Ellin agreed without hesitation. She seemed eager to see Sonya. "I feel lonely," she said. "Derek was here for lunch but he had to go back to surgery. So come whenever you like. I'm here."

When they got to the apartment, Sonya realized why Ellin was so talkative. She opened the door with a martini glass in her hand.

Perry put down his tripod and gave Sonya a quick look. Sonya knew what he meant. "Yes, Perry," she said. "I'll be fast."

Ellin led them into the living room. Then she went to the bar, picked up a half-full pitcher and poured a glass for Sonya.

"I make excellent martinis, you must have one."

"No, thanks." Sonya kept her voice pleasant but firm. "Water will be just fine."

"Oh, I hate to drink alone."

"No, really, it's against network rules," Sonya insisted. Then seeing the disappointment on Ellin's face, she added, "Well, not now, but perhaps when we finish."

Why was Ellin drinking? Sonya thought back to dinner on Friday night. Ellin had hardly touched her wine. On Saturday afternoon she was sober. So she wasn't a habitual drinker. Something had happened, and it probably had to do with Gussie's murder. She looked quickly around the dimly lit room. Something was missing. Raj.

"Where's your beautiful Raj?" she asked. "He's the most extraordinary cat I've ever seen."

"Derek's got him. It's time for Raj's annual vaccinations so Derek took him to the clinic when he went back after lunch."

"I'm sorry, I was looking forward to seeing him."

Ellin gave a strange laugh. "That why I'm lonely. I thought you'd guess."

Perry set up quickly and Sonya watched the monitor as he focused on Ellin. The martinis had given the woman a glow. Her wide smile revealed perfect teeth and her high cheekbones gave her face a feline look.

At last they were ready to begin. Perry rolled the tape and Sonya said, "Tell me about Gussie."

"I never knew her really well. I am not sure anyone did, aside from my mother. Gussie was strong. Maybe that came from her Scottish heritage. She was a no-nonsense lady, for sure. Even with our father."

"What do you mean?"

"We were all a bit afraid of him, even Mother. But Gussie wasn't. She always held her point. I think he admired her for it."

"Did Gussie have enemies?"

Ellin sat back in shock. "Do you mean people who would want her dead?"

"That, or perhaps someone who disliked her?"

Ellin blinked. "Lots of people thought she was bossy. The volunteers, for instance. She'd get cross with them if they came in late or left early. She would give them a lecture on the importance of charity in a city full of immigrants like New York."

"And how about your family? Did Hilda like her?"

"We all liked her. Maybe Hilda a little less. Gussie knew everything about the three of us, and I think Hilda always resented that." She hesitated, and then rushed on. "But I don't mean that any of us would kill her. There were just differences."

"What differences?"

"Nothing much. Little things." Ellin stopped and looked at the pitcher of martinis on the bar. Sonya knew that it was useless to go any further with that line of questions.

"How about Derek?"

Ellin made a face. "You know what husbands are like. We hardly discussed her. Once in a while, he would say that she was a busybody.

But she liked cats, and he took care of hers. You know she brought one of them to him on Tuesday morning. It was old and it died that evening. He was worried about telling her; he knew how much she loved it."

Talking about the cats seemed to relax Ellin, so Sonya decided to press her.

"What were you and Derek doing Tuesday night?"

"You sound like the police." A hint of resentment crept into her voice.

"No. I am just setting the scene for my story. You know, what the family was doing while the murder was taking place."

"I see." Sonya doubted Ellin understood, but was relieved that the explanation satisfied her. "I was here at home until after dinner, and then I went with Julia to visit Hilda. Derek went to his surgery, as he often does. He likes to check on the animals he keeps overnight." Ellin looked up, shaking her head as if telling Perry to stop recording. "I don't want to say anything more, Sonya."

When Perry removed her mike, Ellin picked up her glass and asked Sonya to refill it. She took a long swallow, then turned to Sonya.

"I want you to do me a favor. A big favor."

Sonya was wary. "I'll try, of course I'll try, but you must remember I am a reporter and producer. I can't promise anything."

Ellin nodded. "I don't want your cameraman to hear, so please come to the dining room."

Sonya hadn't realized how drunk Ellin was until she got up and started for the door. She staggered as she walked past the camera and would have fallen if Perry hadn't caught her.

Sonya gave Perry a grateful glance and steered Ellin out of the room. Ellin pulled a chair from the dining-room table and sat heavily. She closed her eyes and for a time Sonya thought she'd forgotten what she meant to say. Then she realized the woman was struggling to find the right words.

She put out a hand and pulled Sonya close to her.

"You might hear some things about Hilda and Derek. But they're not true. Please believe me and please, don't repeat them. If you do, you'll cause me a lot of pain."

"What kinds of things?"

"I can't tell you. But when you hear them you'll understand."

"I won't use anything unless it's relevant to the story. That's all I can promise." Then, to reassure her, Sonya added, "Donna is a first-rate journalist and her program is not a tabloid show."

"Thank you."

Perry called that he was finished packing the gear. Sonya replied that she was coming and then turned to Ellin.

"Ellin," she said, "you may be interviewed by the police. If that happens, call me and tell me how things go. And if you want to talk some more, I'd be happy to come over. Here's my cell number."

As soon as they were on the sidewalk, Perry asked what the big secret was.

Sonya sighed. "She didn't say exactly. That last martini muddled her thinking. At first I thought she believes Hilda has a thing going with Derek. But I'm not sure."

She looked at him and grimaced.

"Right now the only thing I am sure about is that I wouldn't want Hilda Woodruff as a sister."

Chapter 18

Wells Fowler stood in the lobby of his hotel, pleased with what he saw. The lunch crowd had come and gone from the hotel's increasingly popular restaurant, George, and the staff quickly had it looking as fresh as it had after the morning's cleaning. Nearly all the rooms were booked for the night and two of the banquet rooms were being prepared for private functions. His father had had a specific customer in mind for the hotel, and he'd been dead right. The look was understated and the food and service excellent. It was a hotel just right for the businessperson who wanted the quiet, intimate comfort of a home, as well as the latest high-tech features. Wells, pleased with his success, smiled to himself, thinking of his plans to establish a chain of similar boutique hotels.

He walked over to the concierge's desk. "How's the day going, Joe?" he asked.

Joe looked up at him over his glasses. "Couldn't be better," he said. "The only bad news is the murder of old Gussie Ford. She was a New York character. We'll miss her coming in for an occasional early dinner."

"We will indeed," Wells said, careful to keep his tone sincere. He turned to the gleaming red apples that were piled in a brass bowl at the corner of the desk. With a cheerful wink at Joe, he took one and bit into it.

It was juicy and sweet. His father would have approved. Many of the old-timers said that, at twenty-six, he was too young to run a hotel. But the staff was behind him. It was working out the way his father had planned. Wells loved the hotel business, just as his father had wanted him to. He bit into the apple again, then turned as he heard the click of high heels on the marble steps leading down to the foyer.

"You know I am furious with you." His mother's voice trembled as she tilted her face for his kiss. "Why didn't you return my calls this morning? Why did I have to come here to speak to you?"

He gave Hilda a quick peck, took another bite of the apple, then leaned over the desk and threw it into the concierge's trash can.

When he turned back to his mother, he saw that she was shaking. He couldn't tell whether it was anger or nerves, but whatever it was, he didn't want to have a scene with her in the lobby of his hotel.

"Why don't we talk in private?" He took her elbow and walked her to the manager's office. She kept silent until the door closed behind them.

"Have you no feelings for me at all?" she demanded then, as she turned and faced him. "How do you think I feel after all I've been through? I had a horrific morning, the police, the press, questions about the party. Ellin weeping her eyes out. King listening to my conversation with Julia. I am devastated. I never dreamt anything could be as bad as this."

"Stop it. Get a grip on yourself." He pointed to one of the chairs in front of his desk. Hilda sat down and closed her eyes. She looked worn out. Gussie's murder had obviously upset her deeply, more than he would have thought possible.

"Do you want a drink?"

"Just water, I took a tranquilizer. Really, Wells, you should've returned my calls. I have no one else to rely on for advice."

He smiled to himself. She didn't accept anyone's advice. He opened the bar, dropped two cubes of ice into a glass, and filled it with mineral water. She took the glass and drank gratefully.

"What about your sisters? Don't tell me Julia and Ellin weren't ready with advice?"

"Of course we talked. But I am the oldest daughter and you are my son. At a time like this I need your support."

"Oh, Mother, let's get the facts straight once and for all. King is the person you should turn to for support. He was chosen by Grandpa to head the family. I'm a Fowler, and happy to be one."

Hilda shook her head. "How can my son be so cruel? Can't you for a moment think how dreadful Gussie's murder is to us? She tried to be a second mother to us all. Don't you remember anything she did for you? How she arranged for Professor Bernhardt to advise you when you first went to Harvard. You were full of praise for her then. You told me that meeting the Bernhardts was the best thing that happened to you and that you would be eternally grateful to Gussie."

Wells took a deep breath and let it out with a rush. He couldn't blame Gussie for his brief, secret marriage to Ruth Bernhardt. He was the one who had fallen in love with the frail young woman. But Gussie had known about Ruth's mental problems and could have warned him.

He gave his mother a hard look. She knew nothing about the marriage, and he was not about to discuss the Bernhardts with her. It was time for her to go.

"What could I have achieved if I'd obeyed your frantic calls and come running this morning? Would you have listened to my advice?

All you wanted me for was to hold your hand while you issued commands." He laughed. He felt like himself again. "I'd rather eat apples."

"When did you hear about Gussie's murder?" she asked, handing him the empty glass. He put it on the desk, deliberately not asking her if she wanted a refill.

"I guess it was late this morning. Joe heard it on the radio and told me."

"And you didn't think to return my calls?"

"Mother, I'm not getting into that again. What have you decided to do about the party?"

"I think we should hold it as planned. There's a lot of sympathy for Gussie in the neighborhood, people have been placing cheap flowers in front of Woody's. From all accounts, it looks terrible."

"Oh, Mother." Wells shook his head in disapproval.

Hilda ignored him. "I've asked for the body to be released as soon as possible and Detective Harris thinks it will be okay for Thursday morning. I've decided to hold a private service for Gussie at the John Stewart Funeral Home Friday morning. She had no family, so the foundation is arranging it."

"Who is invited?"

"Just the family, of course. Our PR, Sara Watkins, has sent an obituary notice to *The Times,* saying we will hold a public memorial service at a later date. We will have to arrange it, we've had so many calls from people."

Wells grunted. "We should invite the longtime volunteers to the funeral on Friday. They were closer to her than some of us Woodruffs. Julia would know who to call, perhaps half a dozen. They were her real family."

Hilda shook her head. "I don't think that's a good idea. The volunteers can wait to pay their respects at the memorial service."

Wells laughed. "You don't think it's a good idea because it's my idea."

"That's not true. Don't be so harsh with me. If you really believe we should have some of the volunteers there, I'll arrange it. One of them, Kathryn Petite, has agreed to work full time for a few weeks until we decide what to do. She could make the calls to the others."

His mother looked at him and smiled bleakly. "Wells, now that I've conceded that point, please won't you change your mind and make a small speech at the party? Just mention Gussie's contribution to Woody's, and how much it meant to the family."

"No way. I'll talk to the volunteers and nothing else."

"But, Wells, Gussie's dead, murdered in the most horrible way. How can you object?"

"I won't be two-faced. She tried to interfere with my life in ways that I won't go into. I still resent it."

"Then whom should I get to speak?"

"King, of course." His voice was hard. "You should start repairing the damage you caused by demoting him. Nothing can alter the fact that Grandpa believed in his ability. He was trained for the job and was doing well until you tried to fire him. He should speak."

"Never," she said. "To let him speak would indicate that I regretted what I'd done."

"You should regret it, Mother; it was totally unjustified."

Hilda closed her eyes and shook her head. "Wells, you are making things impossible for me."

"Ask Derek then," he said. "He's got a lot of charm, and although he's not a Woodruff, he's always wanted to be one. He'd whiz through it without a moment's thought."

He watched her face. At first her expression showed she disagreed with his suggestion but gradually her distaste faded.

"Derek," she repeated. "He didn't seem the right choice at first, but perhaps he is. He's known Gussie for more than twenty years, and he can certainly speak on behalf of the sisters."

Wells got up and opened the door. "There, you see, Mother, I've solved your problem. Now you'd better go home and set things in motion."

Hilda stood up. "Is that all you've got to say to me?"

He laughed, then kissed her on the cheek. "Is your car outside, or do you want one from the hotel?"

"I've got my car." He escorted her onto the street and signaled her driver to pull in to the curb at the entrance. Wells opened the car door and helped his mother into the back seat. "You'll come to the service?" she asked.

"Yes."

"Call me," was the last thing she said, as the black limousine turned into the traffic on Park Avenue.

He stood for a moment, watching the car pull away. He knew his mother disliked Gussie, and yet the news of her murder seemed to have crushed her. Was it all a maneuver to get him to make a speech? What was really going on with her? He shook his head. He didn't want to think about her or Gussie.

He went back into the lobby, but the pleasure he'd felt standing there before she'd arrived had gone. He wasn't surprised. Each time he saw his mother, she left him more determined to live his life the way he wanted.

He ran up the back stairs to the third floor and his small apartment. He opened the closet and got out his running gear. He had to get out into the air. It was the only way to ease the panic that was gripping him. Despite his outward strength, she still had the power to shake him.

He changed quickly, told his assistant manager that he'd be back in an hour, then headed for Central Park. A couple of times around the reservoir would calm him.

Gussie Ford is dead, he told himself. Case closed. No one now would ever know of his marriage to and divorce from Ruth Bernhardt. He was safe, and so was his inheritance.

He reached the park and started around the jogging path, but Ruth's pale face swam before his eyes. Gussie had arranged for him to meet the Bernhardts through Mrs. Bernhardt, who had been a volunteer at Woody's.

He had fallen in love with their daughter, Ruth, the first night he went to their home for dinner. She was eighteen, frail and beautiful, with wide glowing eyes, and dark hair that curled away from the delicate oval of her face. He realized now how frightened she'd been, but then he wanted her so badly that he persuaded her to marry him secretly. As the ceremony ended, Ruth had burst into sobs. He had comforted her, taking her to his apartment and holding her. They continued to live apart, spending as much time together as possible but concealing their marriage from their families and friends.

Wells soon realized that every time they made love, the periods of sobbing grew longer and more intense. He realized that if the marriage was to succeed, Ruth needed psychiatric help.

In despair, he went to Professor Bernhardt and confessed. Bernhardt was wild with fury, saying Wells had forced his daughter, a sick young woman, into the marriage. Wells had fought for her, saying he wanted to live openly with Ruth as his wife.

Then Gussie had intervened, summoned to battle by Ruth's mother.

"If you stay married to Ruth, you will be cut out of your grandfather Woodruff's estate. He strictly forbade his heirs to marry outside the Christian faith. You know the Bernhardts are Jewish, so accept the professor's offer of a quick divorce."

Last year, at his mother's Christmas party, Wells asked Gussie how Ruth was. Gussie had turned on him. "Her father died last year and she is near collapse. You ruined her life."

"Ruined her life? How? She was sick. I just didn't know."

"She was only eighteen, you must have realized how highly strung she was," she had said. "Forcing her into marriage without her parents' consent was too much, and you should have known that."

He had been astounded by her accusation. "I have no idea what you are talking about. I asked her to marry me and she accepted. I didn't take advantage of her. I didn't know she was unstable."

"I don't believe you. When I knew her she was a bright, happy girl who came to Woody's after school to help out. Now she is a disturbed woman who refuses to leave the house."

"Gussie," he said, "I'm sorry, but all this happened years ago. I can't be blamed if she hasn't been able to get on with her life. God knows her family is behind her. She's been given every chance in life."

"Except for the love and protection of a husband. You ruined that for her."

He had not known what to say and had walked away from her.

But the harassment had continued. Gussie called him and said that Ruth's doctor recommended that they meet, so that Ruth could obtain closure. He refused. "Gussie, there is nothing I can do for her."

Circling the reservoir, Wells picked up speed. Sweat poured down his body but the wind was cool in his face. It was time to forget about Gussie and all her threats.

She had called him on Sunday and said that unless he went to Cambridge and spent time with Ruth, she would tell the estate lawyers that he had been married to a Jew. There was no getting out of it. She would do her best to see that his inheritance from the Woodruff Trust was cut off.

She was well aware that he needed money from the trust to finance his hotel-chain dream.

He thought of her body lying in the shop. She was dead. He was safe. Nothing could go wrong now.

Chapter 19

Sonya stopped at the coffee machine on her way to her office, filled a mug to the top, and added two packets of sugar. She needed it. She was tired. The fight with Matt had taken more out of her than she was willing to admit, and her interview with Ellin Woodruff had puzzled her so much she'd had a restless night. Ellin had been so organized on Saturday afternoon, but yesterday, after the martinis, she had almost lost control.

Sonya had been so impatient she came back to the studio immediately and transcribed the tape. It was barely usable. To protect Ellin, Perry had taken mostly wide shots. But even so, anyone who knew Ellin would see she'd been drinking.

As she'd tossed and turned last night, Sonya thought about Ellin's whispered plea. It probably meant that Derek was having an affair with Hilda. Ellin's frequent comment that Raj, the Bengal cat, was the love of her life was really a cry for attention. She felt rejected and angry. Having a sister play around with your husband would be hard to take, and if true, Hilda had a lot to answer for.

But there could be other reasons. Derek was a gambler. Perhaps he was in debt and needed money. And Ellin's depression could have had something to do with Gussie's murder.

Sonya put the mug on her desk and clicked on her computer. She had to catch up with the office e-mail. Sipping her coffee, she scanned down the list, and saw one to the staff from Matt. It was terse and to the point.

Before a producer leaves with a cameraman, the assignment must be cleared by me.

She laughed. It was directed at her, and the fact that yesterday she had asked Rick to send Perry immediately to Woody's. The rule was difficult to obey, and Matt knew it, but he had to have a final dig at her.

The e-mail she wanted was there. It was from Sara Watkins, the Woodruff Foundation's PR director, confirming Donna's interview with Hilda Woodruff at two that afternoon. The e-mail also stated that a small, private funeral service for Gussie Ford would be held at the John Stewart Funeral Home on Friday morning at eleven.

Sonya called Perry and told him to meet her downstairs. She wanted to spend part of the morning at Woody's, shooting the piles of flowers that had been left there. "No rush," she said. "Woody's won't be open until ten and it'll only take a few minutes."

She smelled the bouquets before she saw them; a strong, unpleasant odor, a mixture of sweetness and decay. She knew people had started placing flowers outside the store almost immediately after Gussie's death. Even so, when Perry pulled into a parking spot outside the shop, Sonya was astonished by the number of offerings.

While Perry unloaded the gear, Sonya examined the display. Some bouquets had cards attached. One read, in arthritic script, "Dear Gussie, thank you for the years together." Sonya smiled. It must have been left by one of the volunteers. Several cards read, "We'll miss you, Gussie," while the one attached to the most expensive flowers, a spray of white orchids, said, "You did so much, you deserved better than this." Sonya shivered. Gussie had been a neighborhood treasure, and her friends were paying homage the only way they could.

"You'd think she was a celebrity, not a little old woman who spent her life sorting old clothes," Perry said as he unscrewed the legs of the tripod and set it down.

Sonya nodded in agreement. "Get wide shots of the sidewalk and the shop and then tights of the flowers. We'll shoot some of the notes too. Give me a minute and I'll tell you which ones I want." Sonya looked around. She also needed sound bites from bystanders. A number of curious onlookers were already watching Perry at work.

Sonya smiled at a slim, well-dressed woman in her sixties. The woman nodded and smiled back.

"You knew Gussie?" Sonya asked.

"Yes, for a long time," the woman answered. Sonya asked if she would talk on camera and she agreed.

Perry swung the camera around and Sonya began with, "Were you doing any buying at the shop?"

"Yes. I've come to Woody's for years. I collect china dogs, and Gussie would let me know when any came in. I got some exquisite pieces at bargain prices. She was a thoughtful woman and had an extraordinary memory. I hope they catch her murderer and put him away for life."

Perry went back to shooting flowers, and Sonya stood beside him, watching passersby stop and look. People, she mused, were always fascinated by a TV camera. She did a few more interviews, mostly hearing praise of the old woman.

She noticed a man in a gray tracksuit gazing at the flowers. It was impossible not to recognize the well-trained body of Steve Pendleton. He came over to her.

"Did you know Gussie Ford?" Sonya asked.

"I knew a lot about her from Hilda Woodruff," he said. "But I only knew her by sight."

"Do you live near here?"

"Yeah, I moved here about a year ago to be close to my clients. It makes life easier. I walk my dog every night about ten or ten thirty. On Tuesday I saw a light in the store."

"Was that unusual?"

"No, the old lady often worked late. As I looked, the light went off. I waited, thinking I'd say hello to her, and check if she was all right, but no one came out. I thought it was strange. Why would she stay in the shop in the dark? But then I thought she might have lain down for a nap. A quirky thing to do, but then after the stories Hilda told me, I guess that's the way she was."

"Did you see anyone else around?" Sonya asked.

"No, no one."

"Have you told the police?"

"No, I don't want to get involved. It might upset my relationship with Hilda."

"Oh, Steve, you've got to. I'll give you the number of Keith Harris, the detective in charge. Call him."

Steve sighed. "You don't know how temperamental Hilda can be. She's got a real temper."

"Okay, I'll let you off the hook. I'll call Harris and pass on the information. I've got your number and if he wants he can follow it up."

She thought for a moment. "And tell Hilda you talked to me. I don't want her mad at me."

"Okay," he said with a shrug, and walked away.

That helps pinpoint the time of the murder, Sonya thought. From what she'd seen in the kitchen, Gussie had been washing her dinner dishes when her murderer had pressed the buzzer. She was a thrifty woman and would have switched off the office light before going to the back of the shop. That's what Steve must have seen. And the murderer may have been there, watching. She was reaching for her phone to call Keith Harris when a cab pulled up. Kathryn Petite climbed out and behind her was Sara Watkins, carrying a briefcase. Kathryn had a set of keys in her hand and went straight to Woody's door.

"I'll try for an interview," Sonya whispered to Perry, and then walked toward them.

"I'm here to open the shop," Kathryn said. She looked at Sara, who had just paid the cab. "Please help me get these flowers off the step so we can get in." Sara bent down and began shifting some of the bunches onto neighboring piles, clearing the steps.

"Sara," Sonya called, "it's Sonya Iverson. I got your e-mail and want to thank you for your trouble."

Sara straightened up. "Sorry, Sonya, I didn't realize it was you."

"I'm just getting a few shots of the flowers. It's amazing how many there are."

Kathryn pushed the rest of the flowers off the step with her foot as she unlocked the door and went inside. Sara followed and Sonya quickly stepped in behind her, holding the door open for Perry.

"We aren't open." Kathryn didn't hide her annoyance.

Sonya flashed a smile. "I know this has been extremely difficult for you, Kathryn, but I hope you'll give me the interview you promised."

Kathryn shook her head.

"I just want to talk to you about finding Gussie's body. Nothing more."

Sara interjected, "I think it's clear she doesn't want to be interviewed."

"Sara." Sonya pitched her request in a firm voice. "Kathryn found the body. She gave a reluctant interview to the police. Then, when she left, she grabbed a disguise and scurried out as if she were terrified. I have that on tape." She paused to let her next words sink in. "She looked more than terrified, she looked guilty, and, as I said, I have it on tape."

The two women looked at each other. It was obvious they had talked about handling the press.

"I'm only going to ask a few questions," Sonya said.

Sara put her hand on Kathryn's arm. "I think you should do it if you want to. You know what to say."

Kathryn said, "All right, but just a few questions."

Perry set up two chairs opposite each other and placed his camera for a medium shot of Kathryn. For visual interest, he set up where a shelf of neatly arranged high-heeled evening shoes would fill the background. Sonya looked in the monitor. "Great, Perry," she said. "It's exactly what the shop is about. Secondhand luxury."

She sat down, clipped on her mike, and began.

"Tell me how you found Gussie's body."

Kathryn described how she had come in and seen Gussie's body on the floor. "You know, you saw it," she added irritably.

"You're right, but I needed to have your reaction on tape." Sonya kept her voice soft. "You knew she was dead?"

"Oh, yes, dead a long time. The blood was dry."

Sonya leaned forward and looked directly into her eyes.

"Why did you sneak out of the shop and run away from us like that?"

"I was distraught. I couldn't have said anything to anyone. I just had to get away from it all. Surely that's easy to understand."

"Yes, it's easy to understand," Sonya comforted her. "How did you get along with Gussie?"

Kathryn glanced at Sara, who shook her head, then walked to the camera and put her hand over the lens.

"Hey, what are you doing?" Perry called out.

"That's enough," Sara said. "Kathryn's agreed to take Gussie's place for a couple of weeks. You must see how difficult it is for her to come back here."

"It's all right, Sara," Kathryn said. "I have nothing to hide." Sara stepped back. Kathryn looked directly at Sonya.

"Gussie and I got on beautifully. She appreciated my being here, and I, in turn, learned a lot from her. She was a wonderful woman, as I'm sure everyone will tell you."

That's too pat, Sonya thought. Kathryn was clever. She had done the interview, but revealed little.

She thanked Kathryn for her time and signaled Perry to turn off the camera. Sara joined them, smiling. Sonya smiled back. "We want to get a few shots of the counter and Gussie's office. It's okay with Detective Harris, and it will only take a few minutes." She made it a statement, not a question, but Sara objected anyway. She was good at her job, Sonya thought.

"Do you have to do it this morning? Hilda Woodruff asked Kathryn to make certain phone calls. She has to get started."

"We must," Sonya replied. "The party is tomorrow night, and I'm sure the caterers will soon be here to set up their equipment. We'll do the office first, so Kathryn can get to the phone."

Sara nodded acceptance. Perry unplugged the lights and moved them into the office. Sonya followed him.

"Let's do the office quickly, but take your time when you move outside. I want to hang around for a while to see what happens."

Gussie's office was small. Sonya left Perry to light it and went back into the shop. Sara was in Anthea's Room and Kathryn was at the rear, talking on her cell phone. Sonya wandered around, looking at the merchandise. She'd been too busy working before to examine it.

She picked up a silver frame holding a photo of a woman in an evening dress. The frame was simple but beautifully crafted. Maybe she'd buy it. She had just turned it over to see the price when the buzzer went. Sara went to the door and opened it for Derek Shelby. He smiled at her, then caught Sonya's eye and walked straight to her.

"Hi," he said. "It's good to see you." He took the frame from her, then frowned. "That's not the one I'm looking for. Have you seen one with a photo of a Bengal cat?"

Sonya stared at him in astonishment. "No, but I wasn't really looking, just staying out of the way until Perry finishes shooting Gussie's office."

"Then help me out," Derek said. "I'm in serious trouble with Ellin; I think I must have wrapped her favorite photo of Raj. It must have ended up in one of her boxes with the other things, and it could be here."

Sonya glanced across the room. Kathryn was still on the phone. Sara was sitting at a table going through papers from her briefcase.

"Well, of course I'll help," Sonya said. "Was it big or small?"

"Medium, about five-by-seven, the sort of size you don't notice. When I picked it up, I probably didn't even check the photo."

Derek and Sonya walked along the wall, looking at the frames that were displayed among various objects.

"I had no idea of the variety of stuff that's here," he said. "I've been in and out of the store many times, but I've never stopped to look. I really know nothing about Woody's."

"I'm surprised—I thought the whole family was involved."

"Sonya," he said unexpectedly, "the frame's not the only thing I'm worried about. Hilda has asked me to speak about Gussie at the funeral and at the party on Friday night. I hate speaking in public and I don't know what to say. You write for a living, any suggestions will help."

"Then don't do it. Surely some other member of the family could step in."

"No," he replied. "Wells refuses to do it, and Hilda won't have King speak for the family. I'm the one she's chosen."

"Oh, Derek." Sonya almost laughed at him. "You must remember some anecdotes about the shop. Just string them together with praise about Gussie's work and what it meant to the family. And keep it short; believe me, no one wants to listen to a long speech."

"Sonya, I just can't do it. I didn't know Gussie at all. I always had the feeling she didn't like me."

Then the obvious solution flashed in her mind. "Why don't you ask Sara Watkins, the publicity director for the foundation, to write it? If she does, she'll make sure Hilda approves it."

He shook his head. "That's exactly what Hilda suggested. But I've had enough of the Woodruff Foundation. I don't want to deal with it."

"That was Sara who let you in," Sonya insisted. "She's extremely competent, and it's her job to help you."

He hesitated, looked away, and then smiled. "You're right, thanks. I'll ask her. But before I do, can you show me where Gussie's body was found? I promised Ellin I'd ask. She's very upset, you know."

"There," she said, "behind the counter."

They moved toward it in silence.

"How sad," Derek said softly. "She died without knowing that her cat had also gone. It's just as well I decided to wait until morning to tell her. I wonder if, in her last moments, she thought of that cat." He lowered his voice and then said, almost as if he were speaking to himself, "I know if I were dying, I would think about the animals I've treated. Caring for them is the best thing I've done in my life."

They stood in silence, looking down at the spot where Gussie's body had lain. Sonya was surprised to see tears in his eyes.

Chapter 20

Sonya left Perry to pack the gear in the van while she went into the café around the corner to buy them coffee. When she came back, Perry was waiting for her in the driver's seat. She handed him his cup and a muffin.

"Kathryn's a different person from the one we worked with on Monday," he said as she climbed into the van.

Sonya took a careful sip of her coffee. "How so?"

"On Monday morning, she was kind of hiding who she was. She told me she'd come to New York for a reason. She didn't say what it was, but she was nervous about it. Today she's ready to take over and run that shop. Think of the way she kicked those flowers off the steps and how she ignored Sara Watkins's advice."

Perry's observations were important to her. He spent so much time behind the camera looking through the viewfinder, he'd developed a keen eye for little signs of what people were hiding.

"Do you think Kathryn killed Gussie?" Sonya asked.

"No, I'm not saying that. But either Gussie's death, or something that happened after we left, has changed her."

"Yes?" Sonya wanted him to continue. But she could see he was embarrassed.

"I'm only guessing. You're the one who solves murders."

"Oh, come on, Perry, tell me what you think."

"Well, I don't know." He stuffed the last of the muffin into his mouth, chewed it, and took another swig of coffee.

Sonya put her coffee into the holder between their seats. "That gives me something to think about." She sighed. "Maybe Kathryn did kill Gussie, but what could be her motive?"

"They were getting along on Monday morning. I thought they really liked each other."

"Yes, so did I." Sonya glanced back at Woody's as they drove away. She thought about Monday morning. Gussie had been in good spirits except when they were in Anthea's Room. There, a flood of memories had brought on tears. As for what had happened later, Sonya could only guess. But they couldn't have had a serious disagreement, otherwise Gussie would have asked Kathryn to return the keys to the shop.

Sonya pushed Kathryn out of her mind and turned her thoughts to Donna's afternoon interview. Hilda Woodruff wanted to do it in the library of her apartment and had called in her decorator to style it. The Woodruff money had to be obvious on TV.

"What are you doing for lunch?" Perry asked.

"Eating at the desk while I check e-mail," Sonya said. "You're not offering to take me out twice in one week?"

"Yeah," he said. "I don't mind. You're a cheap date."

"And you're a generous guy," she said with an easy laugh. "But no, thanks. We have to get to Hilda's apartment early. I'll meet you at the garage, say at twelve thirty."

She was nervous about the setup and was sure Hilda would do her best to get the upper hand with Donna. But Donna could handle it. Sonya had seen her manipulate enough people to get what she wanted. But Hilda was used to getting her own way, with the power of great wealth. If something upset her, she could stop the interview and walk out. That mustn't happen. Since Hilda was the head of the Woodruff family, the interview with her was pivotal to the piece.

Sonya stopped at the makeup room first. "You're all set with Donna?" she asked Sabrina.

Sabrina rolled her eyes dramatically. "What do you think, honey?" she said. "Donna will look gorgeous and I'll be packed and ready to go, so that no light will shine on her perfect little nose."

"Oh, no, you'll be there too?" Sonya let out an exaggerated sigh. "It'll be as crowded as Times Square on New Year's Eve."

"What do you mean? I always go."

"Sabrina, I'm only joking, Hilda is a diva of the first order. She's got a decorator, a florist, her hairdresser, and her makeup artist all lined up. Her PR, Sara Watkins, who will also be there, told me she's on edge about this interview."

"Well, that's no reason for you to be." Sabrina rolled her eyes again. "So I'll get you lunch. What do you want? A sandwich? Coffee?"

"No coffee, I've just had one, but a sandwich would be great."

Sonya stopped by Donna's office and told her assistant that she would be at the Woodruff apartment by one, and would expect Donna at two. "Tell her the PR tipped me off that Hilda is likely to be difficult."

Sonya went back to her office, switched on the computer, and started to read her messages. As she checked them off, she called Keith Harris and left him the name and number of Steve Pendleton. She told Harris she'd be busy for the next few hours, but he could call her in the late afternoon. Sabrina brought her a chicken sandwich. Sonya blew her a kiss and put the sandwich in her bag. She'd eat it in the van.

Twenty answered e-mails and a short ride later, Sonya and Perry were shown into the library where Sara Watkins and the decorator were waiting for them.

"What a room," Perry said. "Beige and gold. The perfect combination for quick lighting. You couldn't have chosen a better spot."

The decorator, whom Sonya had recognized from an earlier story, stepped forward. "Mrs. Woodruff wants you to photograph her with the orchids behind her and the view of Central Park in the background. She thinks viewers will be interested in the way she lives."

Sonya's heart sank. Just as she had expected, Hilda had a firm idea of what would look good, and like most people who weren't in the business, she didn't really understand how television worked. It would be impossible to light Hilda's face and Central Park at the same time. There was too much contrast.

"I understand, but it's hard for us to decide on the final shot until we have both Hilda and Donna here." She flashed him a smile and asked if he knew what color Hilda was wearing.

"A light blue dress with gold earrings and a gold chain at her neck. We thought it would look feminine with the beige and gold of the room." He paused, giving her a smug look. "And sophisticated with the orchids in the background."

"Great," she said, and sighed with relief as he left the room. Donna never wore blue because too many of the women she interviewed did.

Donna arrived right on time, and to Sonya's amazement Hilda appeared and rushed to greet her. As they entered the library, Donna took both of Hilda's hands in hers and said, "I know I told you on the phone how much I appreciate your doing this interview. But let me say it again. I do appreciate it, especially when you have so many unpleasant arrangements to make."

Hilda smiled at her and sat in the seat Perry indicated. She was butter in Donna's hands. There would be no walkout.

Donna sat in the chair opposite and Sabrina quickly brushed her face with powder. She started the interview the moment Perry gave the signal he was rolling.

"The party will be held as planned. Was it hard to make that decision?"

"It was a hard decision. But I am sure that Gussie would want it that way. She was so proud of Woody's and its forty-year history."

"And the guest list is one hundred strong and full of celebrities?"

Hilda smiled proudly and listed some of the guests. Then she added, "And I hope they will all buy at least one piece to help the charities we support."

"Most of these people rarely stay long at a party," Donna asked. "Have you arranged for them to buy immediately if they find something?"

Hilda laughed. "We have. Of course, Woody's is a thrift shop. We're celebrating, but we're also raising money. We'll have a bevy of volunteers dressed in red T-shirts, ready to take payment at any time during the evening." She entwined her fingers in her first show of nerves. "I want it to be casual, Donna, and fun too. I brought in a design team to rearrange and decorate the shop. Our guests will be able to pick up a drink and then wander through wide aisles and see what we have. And there'll be an open space in the front with a podium, for a brief ceremony to honor Gussie."

Sonya was pleased to know that Gussie would be a part of the ceremony.

"Gussie Ford helped you plan all this?" Donna asked.

"Yes. Gussie was remarkable. Between us, we got companies to donate almost everything we need for the party. We want all the money from the sale to go to our charities."

"Why was Gussie Ford so close to your family?"

"Gussie's family came from Portland, as did ours. The families knew each other for generations. Gussie was my mother's childhood pal and remained as close as a sister. When her parents died, Mother made her a part of our family."

"So you've known Gussie all of your life?"

"Well, yes, a long time. I spent my early years in Maine, before Father moved us to New York. I still look on Portland as my hometown."

"You spent some time at school in Switzerland, didn't you?" Donna asked.

Hilda's face stiffened. "My goodness, how did you discover that?" she asked. She glanced at Sara Watkins, then relaxed and laughed. "That was a time I would rather forget. It was a dark period for me. I was in my early teens. I hated New York—the city, the teachers, the kids, the noise, everything. I begged to go to school in Switzerland, where one of my friends was enrolled."

Sonya was always astonished at Donna's success at getting the most unlikely people to pour their hearts out on camera. It wasn't just the questions she asked but her whole manner. No wonder she was a star.

"And your parents let you go?" Donna continued.

"Yes, after much weeping and wailing on my part. But I hated Switzerland as much as I hated New York. Mother came and stayed with me to help me settle down. The truth was I was homesick for Maine. So I went back there and enjoyed our glorious beach for the summer; then back to New York for school. Everything worked out fine."

"And that's when you first got interested in Woody's?"

"We all had to work to make it a success. Julia and I would stack books right-side up and keep everything as neat as possible. There was one job we really looked forward to and that was pairing the shoes and placing them, toes out, on the shelf. We both loved shoes, and when no one was looking we used to put them on and try to walk in them. The higher the heel, the better." She sighed. "Now looking back, I guess Gussie knew what we were up to, and let us have our fun."

Donna leaned forward. "Her murder must have been a great shock to you," she said in a low, soft voice.

Hilda bent her head, and rested it on her hand. Then she looked up at Donna and shook her head. "I can't believe she's dead. I've sat looking at the trees in Central Park, wondering where her spirit is and praying that she didn't suffer. It's hard to comprehend any death, let alone the violent killing of a gentle old lady."

Sonya was amazed. Hilda's words were poignant. But Sonya was suspicious. Either Hilda meant what she said, or she was an accomplished actress. She seemed to know what Sonya was thinking. Hilda turned and smiled at Sonya and asked for a glass of water.

Sonya handed her a glass. Hilda took several swallows, then the makeup artist she'd brought in for the shoot stepped forward and brushed more gloss on her lips.

"You look perfectly beautiful." Donna smiled. "Now tell me a little about your father, and his role in setting up Woody's."

"Father was a brilliant and busy businessman, with little time to spare for Woody's." Hilda gave a quick laugh. "Or for that matter, anything else."

"But he did help your mother start Woody's?"

"Oh, yes, Father loved Mother deeply. He gave her anything she wanted. She believed her role in life was to help the less fortunate. And what made her happiest was running Woody's."

"So she and Gussie really were a team?"

"As I said, more than that. Gussie was a part of the family. She was a great organizer and a great help to Mother."

Sonya noticed a bitter tone in Hilda's voice as she went on, "Sometimes we resented her being there. In a way, we felt she took our mother away from us."

Donna moved in quickly. "Did the resentment last? How do you three sisters feel about her now?"

Hilda realized she'd made a mistake. She took another quick look at Sara Watkins, then laughed to cover it up.

"I speak for all three of us when I say that we've nothing but love and admiration for Gussie."

"How would you describe her character?"

Hilda paused again. "That's a difficult question. It's not easy to sum up a person's character in a few words. Especially when you know them well."

Donna smiled encouragement.

"She was strong; I think that's what I admired most about her. She was devastated with grief when Mother died, but she kept Woody's going. She was faithful too. When we turned to her for advice, she echoed Mother's beliefs. Yes, those are the two words I'd use to describe her. Strong and faithful."

Donna thanked her, then accepted an offer of tea while Perry reset the lights for the reversal shots Sonya would need for editing. With a quick nod to Sonya, Donna followed Hilda out of the room. Sara Watkins went with them.

Sonya looked after Donna in admiration. "That was brilliant. What is it about her that gets people to talk?"

"She looks them straight in the eyes and makes them feel as if they are the most interesting person alive," Perry said. "That's what you do too."

"Yeah." Sabrina came forward and sank into Donna's chair. "But Hilda was coached. Did you see her giving those glances to that PR? She expected her to step in if she fouled up. It was a setup."

Perry agreed. "Yeah, Hilda eyeballed Sara all the time to make sure she was doing okay."

"But all that proves is that Hilda's a perfectionist," Sonya said. "We knew that already."

Sonya left them, saying she wanted to use the powder room. She glanced along the corridor and saw that only one door was closed. She opened it and saw Hilda's private sitting room with a TV camera and monitor set up. Sabrina was right. Hilda had rehearsed the interview.

It seemed ridiculous. Hilda was used to speaking to large audiences at functions as well as spur-of-the-moment interviews on TV. Gussie's murder had really put her on edge. Sonya closed the door and returned to the library.

Perry was still arranging the lights, with Sabrina sitting in for Donna.

"Donna's makeup looked okay, but I'm going to need a few moments to check it," she warned. "Don't rush me; you know what she's like. She'll be mad at me if she doesn't look good."

"When haven't I given you enough time?" Sonya joked. "She gets just as mad at me as she does at you."

Sara Watkins came in. "Are you ready? They're just finishing tea."

"Yep." Perry nodded. "Ready and waiting."

The two women came in and sat down, Sabrina checked Donna's makeup, and then Sonya fed her the re-ask questions. Perry worked quickly and in half an hour they were ready to leave.

Hilda took Donna to the entrance. "Thank you," she said. "You made it easy for me."

Donna smiled her thanks and stepped into the elevator. Sonya followed.

"Well, that went better than I expected," she said to Donna as the door closed.

"We got a lot of usable sound bites," Donna replied. "But I wonder how much of it was the truth, particularly the part about the loving bond between Gussie and the sisters."

"My guess is," Sonya answered, "that the sisters were jealous of their mother's relationship with Gussie and disliked her thoroughly."

Chapter 21

Wells's apartment
Thursday, 5:00 P.M.

The phone rang. Wells walked to the desk in his small living room and picked it up, expecting it to be the front desk announcing his cousin King's arrival.

Instead, the operator told him that a Kathryn Petite was on the line and wanted to speak to him. He knew the name, but couldn't recall why. He told the operator to put her through and then remembered that his mother had mentioned that she had taken over Gussie's job at Woody's.

"Hello," he said formally, "what can I do for you?"

She hesitated a moment and then, with a tremble in her voice, gave her name.

"Yes, I know who you are. How can I help you?" Hearing how upset she was, he spoke in a gentler tone.

"I would like to meet and talk with you. I have something important to tell you." As Kathryn talked, she grew more assured.

"What? Can't we discuss it over the phone?" he asked. He had a sudden thought, and before she could answer, he said, "Did my mother put you up to this call? Is it about my speaking or participating in some way in Gussie's funeral or at the party? Because, if it is, you are wasting your time . . . and mine."

"No, no, none of that," she rushed to say. "It's important to both of us."

"What could that possibly be?"

She hesitated, then said, "It's about Woody's. About the future."

What she said made no sense. Why call him? She knew he had no connection to the store. She must have an ulterior motive.

"Do you know something about Gussie's murder? Did she tell you something about me?"

"No, no, it's about something that happened in the past. I have to see you. I'll tell you then."

Perhaps it was the newly confident tone of her voice that made him agree to see her and find out what she had to say.

"All right, Kathryn, I will see you, but not until after the party. I don't want to discuss anything with you until that's over. Call me early next week."

"Can't I see you over the weekend?"

"No," he said with finality.

The beep on the phone line let him know that another call was waiting. It must be the signal that King is downstairs. It was the perfect excuse to end the conversation.

"I have another call coming in. I'll see you next week. Good-bye."

He didn't give her time to reply, just hung up.

He felt nervous about seeing King. His cousin had asked for a private meeting. He'd never done that before. What could he have to say that couldn't be said in the bar downstairs?

Maybe King knew what that call was all about. Perhaps Kathryn Petite had called him with the same mysterious request.

King was just a year older. Growing up, Wells often imagined what it would've been like to have King as an older brother. He'd always liked King, and knew it was his mother's fault they hadn't spent more time together. Many times Wells had heard his aunt Julia suggest that the boys visit each other, but Hilda had resisted. In fact, if it hadn't been for the vacations his father arranged for both of them, he wouldn't have gotten to know his cousin at all.

When he was ten, he remembered, he'd told Hilda he'd like to see King. She replied that she wouldn't tolerate a family conspiracy between them. At that age, he didn't know what the word *conspiracy* meant. But the way she said it, he was sure it was something bad.

Another time she had warned him that King, like his father Avery, wasn't to be trusted. He must be wary. She never said why.

Of one thing, he was sure: as the elder grandson, King had been their grandfather's favorite and occupied a special place in the family. Wells had heard how their proud grandfather had given Woodruff employees a holiday to celebrate King's birth. Hilda had told him to ignore the story. "No such thing happened," was all she would say.

It was always known that eventually King would take over the publishing business and run the foundation. Wells had heard his grandfather say that often.

It was a shock when the will was read and Hilda was given so much power. She'd managed to influence her father as he approached death. Now she was determined her son would move into what was meant to be King's place.

Wells had no interest in that. The hotel business was his life.

The phone rang again—King was on the way. Because Wells had been talking to Kathryn, the call came too late. As the operator disconnected, the door buzzer sounded.

Wells gave himself a quick glance in the mirror, ran his hands through his untidy hair, and opened the door for his cousin. King, as usual, looked like a suave, well-heeled investment banker in his dark, custom-made suit. Wells was always taken aback by King's resemblance to their grandfather. It was as if the old man had perpetuated himself by putting a stamp of ownership on his firstborn grandson. There could be no doubt they were related.

"Come in, King. I'm happy to see you," he said, offering his hand. King shook it without enthusiasm. "Can I get you a drink? Coffee, or something stronger?"

King took his time replying as he looked around the room and seated himself on the edge of the leather sofa. "Thanks, Wells. I guess I could use a whisky. A single malt if you have one."

"Sure." Wells could see he was ill at ease. It wasn't like King, who was usually strong and confident.

They said nothing as Wells poured the whisky. He poured himself a seltzer, and then sat in the chair opposite.

"You have a great place. I like it," King began. "I can see your taste in it. How did you keep your mother's hands off?"

Wells laughed. "Not easy, I assure you. Not easy. I just held my ground. In fact, she has never been up here, and never will be if I can help it."

"Your mother has a way of trying to run everything in sight. In fact, that's part of what I wanted to see you about. Maybe we can work something out." Wells saw his eyes narrow. "She's trying to run my life too, and I'm not going to stand by and let it happen."

King took a swig of the scotch.

"I came here because I want you to know that I'll do what I have to to get back my rightful position at the company. I'm not going to be demoted without a fight. For starters, I plan to sue. I've talked to my attorney, and I believe that I can find cause."

"That would be hard on the family, King. Think of what the media will do to us."

"I don't care, Wells. Goddamn it, my career is worth more than a few stories that make the family uncomfortable. I have a right to do what I'm doing." His voice got louder, and Wells saw that he was angry enough to carry out his threats.

He tried to calm him. "King, there must be another way. Let's talk it over. Tell me what happened as you see it."

King gave him the details of Hilda's campaign to undermine and demote him. How she had told Julia that she planned to get him out of the company—and the country.

Finally he said, "I guess you know she's made up her mind to put you in to run the company—"

"Wait, wait—," Wells interjected.

"No. You wait." King's jaw tightened and his voice was hoarse. "I have nothing against you up to this point, but I will get what Grandfather planned, and no one will stop me. Not your mother. Not you."

"Listen," Wells said in astonishment, "I don't want your job, or any job at the company."

"That's not what your mother says."

"Screw that. I'm happy where I am and I have plans for expansion. I just need the money to do it. I'm like you; I won't let anything stand in my way. And now's the time for my move."

"Yes, and for mine. Gussie was the only thing that stood in my way. She was making trouble for me, but that's over. And I can handle Hilda."

"What do you mean about Gussie?" Wells asked. "What trouble?"

"I'm not getting into that," King replied. "It's enough to say she's gone and won't cause any more problems. Let's get on with the future."

"I understand," Wells replied tentatively. He took a deep breath, then repeated, "I understand."

"Look," King continued, "if you mean what you say about staying in the hotel business, I want us to work together to get rid of whatever stands in our way."

"How?"

King stared at him. "Maybe we can go to the board. I think I can get my mother and Aunt Ellin to back us up and we can overrule Hilda. If that doesn't work out, then we can find another way. The important thing is getting what we want, however we have to do it."

"If I give you my support, you'll see that I get the money for my hotel expansion? I have gone too far with the plans to let anything interfere. I want the money, and I'm not going to wait too long to get it. So let's work together and we'll both get what we want."

Wells wondered where this bargain would take them, but the temptation to build his dream hotel empire was too great. He was more a Woodruff than he realized.

"I understand and I'll back you all the way." Then King added with a smile, "As I always have."

"Okay. Deal." Wells put out his hand and King shook it, this time with enthusiasm.

The tension in the room vanished. Wells offered his cousin another drink. This time he poured himself a vodka on the rocks.

As he handed the refilled glass to King, he asked, as casually as possible, "Do you know anything about this Kathryn Petite?"

"That she's working at Woody's and she discovered Gussie's body. Why?"

"Because she just called me out of the blue. She wants to see me privately. I put her off until next week. Now I wonder if she has something to say about Gussie's murder. Or if Gussie told her something about the family, and she wants to collect on it." He looked at King to see his reaction, but there was no change in his expression.

"All I know is that she called Mother, but Mother's been too busy to call her back." King leaned forward. "Do you really think she's trying to blackmail us?"

"I don't know what she's up to. For one thing, I can't imagine what she would know about us." Wells paused. "Do you?"

King shook his head. "No."

Wells kept his voice casual. "I just thought your mother might have said something about her."

King gave him a sharp look. "Not a word. But anyway, Hilda's taken over at Woody's. She called Kathryn Petite and asked her to work there full time."

They both sat in silence, finishing their drinks, and then, with a brief good-bye, King left.

Wells poured himself another vodka. When he had asked about Gussie, King held back. What was he hiding?

Wells was not sure they were on the same side.

Chapter 22

Julia felt herself stiffen with anger as three more extravagantly dressed women entered the chapel. She'd retreated to a side doorway when the first of them arrived, and now stood watching the group as they moved into the narrow pews. This must be Hilda's doing. They'd discussed the service and agreed that it should be small, just for the family. Typically, Hilda had then ignored their decision and invited these women, whoever they were.

As her mother, Anthea, would have done, Julia had filled the dignified, wood-paneled chapel with sweet-smelling bouquets of white lilies. Gussie's coffin lay on a velvet-covered bier under a wreath of white roses intertwined with pinecones from her native Maine.

As executor of Gussie's will, it had been Julia's call to decide when and where the service would take place. At first Hilda had dismissed her plan. "As far as I'm concerned there's no need for any service, especially on the same day as the party. She can be cremated quietly and we'll put an obituary in *The New York Times*. Sara Watkins can arrange for a memorial service at a convenient time."

"I don't care what you say," Julia had replied. "Gussie is going to have a service. You dismissed her in life. I won't let you do it in death."

Hilda had given her a hard look. "I see you've made up your mind, but I insist you keep it small. I don't want it to take attention away from the party. It's Woody's success we're promoting, not the death of one of our staff."

Julia had used the Woodruff influence to book the chapel at the John Stewart Funeral Home on short notice. For Julia, it seemed appropriate to say a quiet good-bye to Gussie in the morning and then celebrate her life and achievements at the Woody's party in the evening.

It was shortly after Anthea died that Gussie asked Julia to be the executor of her will. "It won't be difficult," Gussie had said. "I don't have much to leave, and one of the Woodruff Foundation attorneys is drawing it up. He assures me there will be little to do. He suggested I ask Hilda, but I think, dear Julia, she would be much too busy to be concerned about my few bequests. And so I appeal to you."

Julia had fought back tears. The death of her mother had been devastating; the thought of losing Gussie too was terrifying. "I don't want to talk about it. What would I do without you?" She had swallowed hard, then, seeing the pleading look in Gussie's eyes, added, "I'm sorry. Of course I'll do whatever you want."

Julia closed her eyes and rested her head against the smooth wood of the doorway as she thought back over the years. Hilda's change began when she came back from Switzerland. She withdrew from the family circle, her fits of rage became more frequent, she openly showed her disdain of Gussie, and indeed of all of them. Something happened there that had changed her. Julia often discussed it with Ellin, but they couldn't come up with an answer, and Hilda refused to acknowledge that she had in any way changed.

Once Julia had asked her mother about Hilda and received a worried reply. "You're too young. It's nothing you would understand. It's something Hilda has to work out for herself." Astonished at the sadness in her mother's voice, she'd dropped the subject.

Julia opened her eyes and saw Sonya Iverson, looking slim and efficient in a black pantsuit, as she helped her cameraman set up his tripod. She was here to shoot the service. This was another Hilda betrayal. The Woodruff family's farewell to Gussie was not something to be used to entertain millions of people. She would never forgive Hilda for this, but would not embarrass the family by asking Sonya to leave.

Sonya looked up, caught Julia's eye, and motioned that she would like to speak to her. Julia reluctantly nodded and watched Sonya come toward her. "The chapel looks beautiful," the newswoman said. "Did you plan the service?"

Julia ignored the question. "Who gave you permission to come here?" she demanded. "This is a service for prayer, not for publicity."

Sonya looked at her with genuine surprise. "I received an e-mail from Sara Watkins about the service. I took it to be an invitation." Sonya looked around the chapel and then said intuitively, "You mustn't be upset about that group of women who have on vintage clothes. One told me they bought them at Woody's and decided to wear them at the service as a tribute to Gussie."

So that was it. Hilda must have told Sara to invite these people for their publicity value. Julia wanted to scream in frustration, but controlled herself.

"I suppose you're right, Sonya," she said as evenly as she could manage. "Only Gussie would recognize the clothes, and she's not here to tell us."

"I just wanted to know if you would mind our getting a few shots of them, or even asking a few questions. But I'll leave if you want me to."

Julia hesitated. She didn't want Sonya there, and she didn't want the women either. But if she made a fuss it would upset the service.

She said, almost with a sob, "No, I didn't understand; anything that shows how much people loved Gussie is fine with me."

With a sigh of relief she watched Sonya move away. Then she turned and went into the room set aside for those participating in the service. Hilda was in a chair waiting for her.

"What were you and Sonya Iverson talking about?" Hilda demanded.

"Just the vintage dresses some of the women are wearing. That's all."

Hilda got up and closed the door. "I want to go on record that this service, this fuss over Gussie is too much. It's taking away from the publicity for the party."

Julia felt the blood rush to her head. The tension of the day overwhelmed her, but she forced herself to keep her voice low.

"Stop playing games with me, Hilda. I've had enough of them. You arranged for all those women to come. Don't deny it. I wanted the family to have a quiet moment in a beautiful chapel to say good-bye to Gussie. But you couldn't accept that. You had Sara Watkins invite these women. You deliberately spoiled something that should have been precious to the family."

Hilda tossed her head. "It may have been my idea to invite a few of Gussie's most faithful customers and Wells's idea to invite the volunteers, but it was your idea to have the service today."

"Hilda, Gussie deserved to be treated like family. This is what Mother would have wanted. Remember her, Hilda, our loving, generous mother, and how she valued Gussie as a friend?"

"Yes, I remember Mother. I remember her well. She shared more of her life with Gussie than she did with her daughters. To be perfectly honest, I'm glad Gussie's gone."

Julia tried to interrupt, but Hilda was not to be stopped.

"How do you think I felt growing up? Mother was ashamed of me and my problems. She'd rather be with Gussie than with her deformed daughter. Yes, that's the truth; Gussie gave Mother an excuse to get away from me. To leave me alone with a nurse."

Julia took a deep breath. She must stay calm on this day that belonged to the memory of Gussie. She lowered her voice and said, "The truth, Hilda, is that Mother was lonely. That's why she spent so much time with Gussie. Father neglected her. He had no time for anything but business."

Hilda shook her head violently. "You are so wrong. You never knew what was going on and you still don't. Father used to joke about you."

Her cruelty struck home. "One thing I know about Father is that he made a big mistake when he named you head of the trust and foundation. You think the money is yours, but it belongs to all of us."

"So you admit you resent me."

"Yes, and so does Ellin. And I'll never forgive you for what you did to King. I'll tell you now, that with Ellin's help I'm going to the board and see that King gets what he's entitled to. There's nothing you can do to stop me."

Hilda sneered. "I wouldn't count on Ellin if I were you."

"Stop it. I won't put up with you anymore and neither will Ellin. We've had enough of you."

Julia was shocked at the force of her own anger. She wanted to hit her sister. To beat her to the ground and get rid of her forever. Tears welled in her eyes but she wouldn't give in to them.

In a few moments she would have to stand up and speak about Gussie in front of her family and friends. She must concentrate on what she would say. She would deal with Hilda later.

Without another word Julia turned her back on Hilda and opened the door. The organist saw her and began playing the Bach piece she'd requested. Hilda pushed past Julia and went to the front pew reserved for the family. She bent and kissed Ellin and Derek but ignored King.

Julia looked toward Sonya and saw her standing next to Detective Harris. Seeing him alarmed her. Harris must have a reason to be there. He must suspect the murderer was with them in the chapel.

But she had to go on. She gathered herself together and walked down to the front pew. She ignored Hilda and sat between Ellin and Derek. Then, in a whisper, she asked Derek if he were ready.

"Yes, of course," he said, shifting his weight a little. "Julia, this request was so sudden; you must understand that I didn't have much of a chance to think about what to say." He glanced around the chapel. "And who are all these people? I thought this was just for the family. What happened?"

"Ask Hilda."

Julia looked at the organist, who nodded and allowed the music to fade away. Then, with a smile to Ellin, Julia got up and went to the lectern. She stood there for a moment, glancing from one face to another. She recognized some of them as volunteers from Woody's. They had a right to say a last good-bye to Gussie, she had to concede that. Her lips trembled and she reached for the glass of water and drank.

"I feel no need to hide my emotions from you. We are all devastated by the violent death of our friend Augusta Ford—our Gussie."

She took a tissue from her pocket and wiped her eyes. A murmur of sympathy ran through the audience.

"But I didn't come here to weep. I want to tell you about Gussie's goodness, and why we all treasured her so much. We three sisters looked on Gussie as a favorite aunt, the person to turn to when our mother was busy.

"I remember how she gave Ellin and me the thrill of our young lives. Mother was away with Hilda in Geneva. Ellin and I were left in New York with Gussie in charge. Gussie was determined to make us appreciate the city. She took us to the zoo, the top of the Empire State

Building, the Statue of Liberty, the Museum of Natural History. Everywhere. But there was one thing she didn't want to do. It took weeks of pleading before, one Saturday, she produced three tokens and we went off on our first subway ride.

"We were in seventh heaven . . . remember, Ellin?" She looked at Ellin and smiled. "For the first time we felt like New Yorkers. What's more, we had stolen a march on Hilda. That was one thing she couldn't do in Switzerland with Mother—take a ride on the New York City subway."

Julia knew she had the audience with her. She'd done what she set out to do. She stopped and looked around the chapel. "I don't have to tell you what a strong woman she was. You know from experience."

Several of the women murmured agreement and Julia smiled.

"We were blessed to have had Gussie. I give thanks for her love and care—love and care that extended far beyond our family. Thank you."

After prayers and hymns, Derek was next. Julia was sure Hilda had put pressure on him to speak. As he stood adjusting the microphone he looked directly at Hilda, as if seeking her approval.

Derek said he wanted to speak about Woody's and the important role it played in the city. He gave a list of charities the shop supported, and then said, unexpectedly, "It is hard to accept that Gussie died a violent death on the floor of Woody's, the place she was devoted to.

"But I think you will agree, her death in the shop was altogether fitting. If she had to die, I am sure she would have preferred to die there."

Julia shuddered. What an evil thing to say. To call Gussie's violent death a fitting end. The thought had to have come from Hilda.

Derek returned to his seat and the pastor led them in prayer. The organist began to play softly as the service ended. Julia set aside her dislike of Hilda and took Ellin's hand. "Let's go to the door and speak to some of the women as they come out. It's what Mother would want us to do."

Chapter 23

John Stewart Funeral Home
Friday, 12:30 P.M.

Perry removed the tape from the camera and handed it to Sonya. "What's this meeting with Harris about? I thought you had to get back to the studio."

Sonya accepted the tape and took her time writing the details of the funeral service on the label. "He just wants to talk to me."

"Then I'll wait for you."

Perry was becoming increasingly jealous of Harris. Most of the time, Sonya was flattered by his protective instincts, but this was irritating.

"No, Perry," she said. "He's invited me for a bite to eat. I'll get a cab back to the studio."

Perry shrugged and started to unscrew the legs of the tripod. "Okay, but I've plenty of time. I've nothing scheduled until the party tonight."

She looked at him as he bent over the tripod, and saw the resentment on his face. She was fond of Perry and was grateful for his work and his loyalty. She viewed him as a good friend, but that was it.

"I'll be in the editing room most of the afternoon. Give me a call there and we'll discuss tonight's work."

She looked around. Hilda had left but Julia was standing with Ellin, talking to several women. Sonya went to her and said how much she was moved by her eulogy.

"I feel pleased that it turned out so well." Julia gave her a weak smile, then put her hand on Ellin's elbow and led her to a waiting car.

Keith Harris was watching from the sidewalk as the few remaining people walked out. His gray suit and unprepossessing demeanor made him blend in with the crowd. If Sonya hadn't been looking for him, she would not have noticed him.

Perry stood nearby, tripod in one hand, camera in the other. As Sonya passed him to get to Harris, he said, "You know you haven't interviewed Julia, maybe you should try for it now."

"Perry, you're right, but we have the speech and that should be enough."

"Okay, just checking, see you later."

He walked away as she turned to Harris.

"I was just saying how good Julia's speech was. But then, of the three sisters, she was the most fond of Gussie."

"What makes you say that?"

Sonya hesitated. She didn't want to share too much. "I had dinner with the sisters and Gussie on Thursday night. Julia joked around with Gussie and even admitted that Gussie picked out clothes from the shop for Julia to wear. They seemed like good friends."

"Yes," he answered, "her speech was very moving. Come on, there's a deli around the corner. Let's eat."

Sonya had once read that the police were so unused to the high life, they were more scared of headwaiters than they were of hijackers. But even so, Harris's choice of a deli for lunch amazed her. It was crowded and noisy, not a table available.

"I'll get sandwiches and we'll eat in the park, that'll be quicker than waiting. What do you want?"

"A Swiss cheese sandwich with lettuce, tomato, and mustard, and a black coffee."

He pushed his way to the counter and gave their order. Sonya watched him as he waited. He was tall, but his rounded shoulders and a creased suit made him seem shorter. Even so, he had a quality of authority about him. It was the way he concentrated on what was happening. He gave the young Hispanic counterman his full attention as he smoothed mustard on the bread and piled on the cheese.

I trust him, she told herself. He's a good cop.

Finding a seat in the park was easy. He sat down at one end of the bench and with a grin, motioned her to sit at the other. "It's good to get some fresh air. It's not often I take this kind of break."

It was a beautiful day; the grass was fresh and green and the leaves on the trees shimmered in the sunlight.

He opened the bag and handed Sonya her sandwich, then took out his pastrami on rye. "That's what I call a treat," he said. "And delis aren't easy to find. Pizzerias are taking over."

Sonya unfolded the plastic wrap from her sandwich and bit into it. Not bad, but maybe it was just that food eaten outdoors always tasted better.

"So, what do you want from me?" she said.

He took a large bite, chewed thoroughly, and swallowed before answering. When he did, he leaned forward and looked at her with his gray eyes.

"I'm interested in what you know about this Kathryn Petite."

Sonya shrugged. "Practically nothing. I've checked the Washington phone book and asked our bureau there to do some research, but so far I've come up with nothing."

"Same here. The only Kathryn Petite I came up with is seventy-five and lives in Oklahoma."

"So our Kathryn's hiding under a false name."

Harris grinned at her, reached into the bag, and came up with a pickle. He examined it before biting in with obvious pleasure.

"You worked with Kathryn on Monday morning, the day before the murder. What was your impression?"

Sonya took a bite of her sandwich. "Well," she said, "I spent most of my time talking with Gussie, while Perry and Kathryn worked together. Kathryn told me she had worked as a stylist. She said it modestly, so I wasn't expecting much, but when she went into action she was fantastic. She and Perry got on famously; and she saved us a lot of time."

"How old do you think Kathryn is?" Harris asked.

She smiled. "She takes good care of herself, but I'd say about thirty-five."

"Married?"

"I don't know, but she could be divorced."

"Like you," he said.

Sonya felt herself flushing. She rarely talked about her short-lived marriage. She doubted that many people at the studio knew. She couldn't resist asking, "How do you know so much about me?"

He grinned again. "I've checked you out, thoroughly."

Sonya wasn't going to discuss it. "Well, I guess that's your job."

He gave her a quick look and said, "Don't be embarrassed. I've been that route too. I have an ex-wife and twin girls in college in California. My ex married a rich businessman. One of our problems was she wanted more out of life than a cop's salary could provide."

Sonya said nothing, and he went on, "What about you?"

"My story's for another time." She wasn't going to tell him too much about herself yet.

"Okay, back to the murder; did you notice any problems between Gussie and Kathryn that morning? Any difference of opinion?"

She thought back. "No, the only time Gussie was upset was when we were in Anthea's Room, and Gussie was saying how fond she was of Anthea and how much she missed her."

"Can you remember her exact words?"

Sonya recalled the old lady and how upset she had become when she looked at Anthea's portrait. "No." She shook her head. "She was close to tears. I wanted to keep her calm for the interview, so I changed the subject."

"No idea what could have upset her so much?"

"I put it down to the memories. She was preparing for the party and she must have been thinking a lot about Anthea. From what I hear, they were like sisters."

"And you don't think it was anything to do with Kathryn Petite?"

Sonya shook her head. "No. It didn't seem that way."

He rolled the plastic from his sandwich into a ball and dropped it in the bag, then leaned back and looked directly into her eyes. He was attractive but it was hard to decide why. She glanced away, embarrassed. But when she looked back, his eyes were still on her.

"What if I told you that when Gussie and Kathryn went out for coffee Tuesday afternoon, they quarreled about the keys to the store?" he said.

"How do you know that?" she asked.

"Ian, my partner, talked to the manager of the café where they went for coffee."

Sonya thought about it. Kathryn had been unfailingly polite and helpful. She doubted she would argue with Gussie. Anyway, what would they argue about?

"The manager didn't hear anything specific?" she asked.

"No, the booth was at the back."

"And Gussie wasn't upset?"

"Worried was the word the manager used. But Kathryn was another matter. She was crying when she left."

So there was a real problem between them. Gussie, who was extremely busy, had spared the time to take Kathryn out to talk in private. And she had made Kathryn cry.

Sonya looked down at the uneaten half of her sandwich. She'd lost her appetite. She went to put it in the bag, but Harris stopped her, grinning. "I'm still hungry; if you don't want it, I do." She watched him eat. It gave her a feeling of satisfaction to see him enjoying her sandwich. She was glad he was investigating the murder. But enough, she told herself, Harris is interviewing me. Just doing his job.

"Kathryn was crying," she repeated. "Well, that adds up. Perry was convinced that something happened to her after Monday morning."

Harris scratched his neck. "Why was that?"

"As I said, they got on extremely well Monday morning. When we arrived on Thursday, she barely spoke to him. Perry was convinced that it wasn't just finding Gussie's body, something else had upset her." She added quickly, "He doesn't think she murdered Gussie. But she does know something."

Harris pulled a notebook and pen out of his pocket and began to write. Sonya watched his fingers move over the page. His nails were short and well kept. He had good, strong hands.

"Do you think Kathryn killed Gussie?" she said.

"In my job, it's not a matter of thinking. I have to know. Kathryn has a sort of alibi. She says she was at home all evening, and we know she made a long phone call to a number in Washington. But she could have gone out to Woody's and back unnoticed."

"Her building doesn't have a doorman?"

"It does, and he says he didn't see her go out. But that doesn't mean a lot. He left the door unattended a couple of times."

Sonya put her hand on his arm. It felt natural. "So what motive could she have?"

"We need to determine the motive and whether she had the strength to stab Gussie with the fork. She's a tall woman, but a fragile one. Holding Gussie down while stabbing her wouldn't be easy. And Gussie was a fighter."

Sonya took her hand away. "You're right, but the murder is surely something to do with the sisters. They have all that money."

"Too much money for their own good. I've investigated enough murders to know the power of money. I'll tell you a lot of stories when you've got time."

"I'll take you up on that. But, right now, Keith, I've got to get back to the studio. I've got a pile of work before the party tonight."

"I'm planning to stop by there, but I have hours of paperwork waiting for me too." He put his notebook and pen back in his pocket, then picked up the paper bag and put it in a trash can.

As they walked to Fifth Avenue, Harris said, "Be careful. There's a murderer loose, and you may be poking into things that are threatening. If you're worried, call me." He hailed a cab and she got in. As it pulled away, she turned and saw him watching.

The traffic was grindingly slow, but it gave her time to think. She took out her own notebook and began to write. Was Kathryn Petite a murderer? Harris doubted she had the strength to stab Gussie, but he was wrong. He hadn't seen her with Perry, pushing the furniture into place for shots.

And her motive? With the Woodruff money it could be blackmail. Could it be that Kathryn knew some family secret and was planning to blackmail one of the sisters? If Gussie found out what she was doing, that would be motive enough to kill her.

Maybe Kathryn was the killer. She shrugged and put her notebook back in her bag.

When she walked into her office the phone was ringing. It was Perry.

"How did lunch go?" he asked.

"Fine," she said.

"He just phoned me," Perry said. "He wants to have a chat. I don't like the guy, so I put him off. I said I had to wait until you got back. What do you think he wants?"

Sonya wondered if she should have told Harris about Perry's observations. But it was done.

"I told him you said Kathryn's behavior changed drastically between Monday morning and Thursday."

"What did he say?"

"He didn't say anything, just made a note of it. He told me Kathryn had argued with Gussie Tuesday afternoon. He's just following a lead, so call him back."

She heard Perry take a deep breath. "Okay, I'll do it. What time do you want me to pick you up tonight?"

"Five thirty, that'll give us time to shoot what we want before the party starts at six thirty."

"It's a date," he said. He sounded happy. The resentment had gone from his voice. Sonya was relieved.

Chapter 24

Sonya unlocked her office closet, took out a sage-green top with a deep neckline, and put it on over her black pants. It was just right. It looked professional, but if she slipped it off her shoulders it was sexy. Sexy, she told herself, was what she wanted to be if Keith Harris stopped by the party.

She put on emerald-green earrings that deepened the color in her eyes, grabbed her jacket and bag, and headed out the door.

Perry was waiting for her in the van. "You look great," he said. "You'll be the sexiest woman at the party."

"You said the right thing," she said with a grin. She tossed her jacket into the back, and climbed into the passenger seat. "How'd it go with Keith?"

"You mean Harris? He hit me hard and fast with the questions. But I just told him what I knew about Kathryn. It's only my impression. I certainly wouldn't be called as a witness. Anyway, I don't like or trust him."

Sonya sighed. "I'm glad it went okay." She closed her eyes and leaned back.

———

Parking was easy. Sara Watkins had saved them a space near the shop and within minutes Perry had unloaded the gear. Woody's was ready for the party. The bouquets of flowers that paid tribute to Gussie were gone from the sidewalk. In their place were two klieg lights that lit up a fortieth anniversary banner stretched across the front of the shop. A red carpet lay across the sidewalk and six stanchions with velvet ropes stood ready to be put in place at six thirty when the guests would begin arriving. But already groups of spectators were waiting.

Sonya told Perry to get a quick exterior shot and then she went inside. Woody's had been transformed there too. A false wall, covered with blowups of photographs and news stories, stretched across the back of the shop. It concealed Hilda's office, the ugly back windows, and furniture that had to be temporarily stored.

Sara Watkins was waiting for her.

"You've worked magic," Sonya said. "It doesn't look like a thrift shop anymore. You've turned it into an I-want-to-buy-it boutique."

"It's Gussie's work, not mine. She spent months planning this. I'm glad you're early. Wells Fowler is here; he has thanked the volunteers and now he's ready to be interviewed. But I'd like to have a word with you before you start."

Sara looked worried and, Sonya thought, probably for a good reason. The Woodruff sisters couldn't be an easy trio to handle.

"Is there a problem?" she asked.

"Yes, to be honest, there is." Sara crossed her arms defensively. "I made a mistake letting you go to the service for Gussie this morning. It was meant to be private. So I must ask you, on behalf of the Woodruff sisters, not to use anything you shot there."

"You know I can't promise that. Anyway, I asked Julia if she wanted me to leave the service and she said it was okay to stay."

Sara put her hand on Sonya's arm.

"Sonya, it's not Julia, but Hilda who's upset." She sighed. "And she is really upset. She's in a dreadful mood, exaggerating it out of proportion." Sara shook her head. "It was a misunderstanding. But again, as I said, I've been instructed to ask you not to use the tape."

Sonya gave her a sympathetic look. "Come on, Sara. Tell me what happened."

Sara took a quick look around the room and then said in a low voice, "Wells persuaded his mother to invite some of the longtime volunteers. Kathryn and I called about half a dozen women, but apparently they called others. A few of the younger women came to pay tribute to Gussie dressed in outrageous vintage clothes. As you saw, it was well meant and perfectly harmless. But Julia felt it wasn't respectful and Hilda is afraid it makes the funeral look like a frivolous fashion show. That's not the image she wants for the piece on Woody's."

Sonya shook her head again. "I understand, but I can't promise anything. All I can say is that I'll keep your request in mind when I'm editing."

"Thanks, Sonya," Sara breathed with relief.

"I see Perry's come in, so let's do the interview with Wells."

Sonya walked to the tall, brown-haired young man who was standing with a split of champagne in his hand. "You're Sonya, I know." He grinned, revealing a set of perfect white teeth. "Drinking champagne out of a bottle isn't the Woodruff style, but I'm a Fowler, and I do what I like."

"That's okay with me, Wells. I was hoping to have a word with you at the service this morning, but I didn't see you."

"When you're in the hotel business, things sometimes crop up unexpectedly. I couldn't get away." He tilted his head and took a sip of champagne. "I'm sorry about the old lady. I wish Mother had, for once, followed my advice and made her retire years ago." He tilted his head again, drained the split, and put the bottle on a table beside him. Kathryn, who had been watching them, quickly took it away.

"Let's do your interview now. It won't take long."

"I have nothing to say about Gussie. I didn't know her well." He shrugged. "I saw her now and then at family functions, that's it."

"But you came to speak to the volunteers anyway?"

"I came because Mother insisted, and because I admire these women, who've given their time to help the charities that Woody's supports."

"Then let's talk about them. I've done several interviews about Woody's but no one has talked about the volunteers."

"All right, but that's all."

Sonya signaled to Perry to roll the tape. Wells, with his tanned face, was handsome. His quick mind and easy manner soon gave her the sound bites she wanted. When they finished he said, "Just so you know, I didn't make a speech. I thanked each woman personally. That's what my grandmother would have wanted."

"Were you close to Anthea?"

"Yeah, I knew her the whole time I was growing up. She died when I was sixteen. She was different from my mother. My mother is tough. When she wants something, she commands. My grandmother was the kind of woman who listened."

Sonya heard sorrow in his voice and thought of her own childhood. She was glad she'd had a loving relationship with her mother and grandmother.

Wells reached out and took another split from a waiter, tipped it up, and gulped it as he walked away. She stared at his back and wondered if he always drank so quickly.

She turned to Sara. "How many guests are you expecting?"

"Maybe a hundred. But with all the publicity, I'm worried about gate-crashers. There's a crowd outside already and in a few minutes

I'll have to go help my assistants at the door. I told Kathryn to look after you. So if there is anything you want later, let her know."

Together they went to the back of the shop to look at the display of blown-up photographs.

"Gussie went through our clippings and picked the photos that showed Anthea Woodruff working with different charities. You see her here with women in hospitals, kissing babies at clinics, and talking to patients in AIDS treatment centers."

Sonya was surprised to see Gussie featured prominently. At the center was a photo of Anthea standing with her arm around Gussie's shoulders at the opening of the shop.

"Did Hilda approve this shot?" she asked.

Sara smiled. "I fought for it. Gussie had to be on our wall of memories."

With that, Sara asked Kathryn to take over. Perry shot the photo display while Kathryn went to get King for an interview.

Like Wells, he said he barely knew Gussie. He was there because he was a Woodruff. He ended the interview by saying, "My aunt Hilda is tough. She doesn't ask, she commands."

Sonya realized that he and Wells were working together and had agreed on what they'd say.

Perry interrupted her thoughts. "I saw Julia, Ellin, and Derek arrive. Do you want to interview them?"

"No, that's enough interviews for now," she told Perry. "Let's go to the door, and get the guests arriving."

The shop was filling up fast. She could see Sara was in trouble handling the crowd. As Sonya and Perry neared the front of the shop, the impatient mob surged forward and pushed women through the door. Sonya watched them go straight to the shelves to look for bargains. She felt sorry for Sara, but knew the shots would give her story immediacy and energy. She guessed at least some of the women were gate-crashers.

Then Hilda arrived, flushed and disheveled after a struggle with the partygoers. Her face twisted in fury when she saw Sara. "Stop these people. They've no right to be here. None of them have invitations."

"I can't control the crowd," Sara said. "The best thing I can do is call the police. I don't want things to get nasty."

"No." Hilda raised her hand as if threatening her. "I don't want the police here. Do your job. Get these women out of here."

Sara looked at her blankly. "How? I don't have enough staff."

"You're an idiot!" Hilda shouted. "Consider yourself fired!"

Wells stepped forward and put his arm around Hilda, but she broke away from him and shook her fist at Sonya.

"And you, Miss Television, you mind your own business!" she screamed. "I know you were seen speaking to Steve Pendleton. Don't you dare interview him."

Wells grabbed her arm and pulled her away. "Go into your office and calm down. I'll handle this."

He went to the doorway and stood so that his body blocked the entrance. "Ladies, please!" he shouted to the crowd. "We're jammed up here, but if you'll give us a few moments, we'll sort things out. Please have your invitations ready so we can check you in quickly. This is an invitation-only party, so if you don't have one, come back tomorrow to shop. There'll be plenty for sale then."

Despite some determined "boos," he held his ground. Women with invitations stepped forward. Wells checked them and let them through.

"Isn't he fantastic? His mother must be proud," Kathryn said. Her eyes glowed with excitement, and, for the first time since they met, Sonya felt she was happy.

Perry was holding the camera above his head to get a wide shot of the crowd. After he lowered the camera she tapped him on the shoulder. "How's it going?"

"I have enough of this mob scene to fill the entire Donna Fuller show. And not one A-list celebrity has arrived yet."

"That's usual. It's not chic to arrive early. While we wait, we'll set up for the speeches. The podium's by Gussie's office."

Sonya said to Kathryn, "Hilda was scheduled to give a welcome at seven o'clock. That was twenty minutes ago. Can you find out what's going on?"

"Wells told her to go back to her office," Kathryn said, "where she can escape from the pandemonium for a bit, have a cigarette and calm her nerves."

"Right. After that scene at the door she'll need a cigarette. Please go and see if she's ready."

"Okay, but I'm afraid to go directly to Hilda. I'll have to check with Sara first."

Sonya nodded, then went to the podium. She looked around at the chaotic scene. Julia was with Sara near the front door. Julia had her hand on Sara's arm and seemed to be comforting her. Sonya watched Kathryn approach them, speak to Sara, then turn and make her way through the crowd toward the back of the shop. After a moment or two Sara followed her.

King was easy to spot; he had taken Wells's place at the door. Ellin appeared to be discussing a bag with a woman and Derek stood at the bar. Sonya surveyed the area but couldn't see Wells.

"I don't like this," she said to Perry. "Something's wrong. Hilda likes things to happen right on time." She hesitated, then added, "I'm going to check her out. Keep your eye on me in case I need you."

Getting past the crowd at the bar was the worst part. She slipped around one end, grabbing a bottle of water for Perry as she went. She edged into the narrow space between the false wall and Hilda's office.

Hilda's door was half-closed, but she could hear someone sobbing.

She pushed the door open and saw Sara standing with her arms around Kathryn, who was about to collapse.

Sonya went to them. "What's happened?"

Sara shook her head and pointed to the corner of the room. Hilda lay crumpled on the floor. Her chair was overturned beside her. At the back of her head Sonya saw pieces of crushed skull and bloody matted hair. Ugly streams of blood ran down her face and onto the manicured hand that lay under it.

Sonya stepped back in horror.

"She's dead," Sara said.

Sonya nodded. "I'll call the police. You stay with Kathryn."

She went to the edge of the wall and looked for Perry, but couldn't see him over people's heads. She grabbed a chair, stood on it, and waved to him frantically. He picked up the camera and started toward her through the crowd. Next, she took her cell phone from her bag and dialed Harris's number. He answered immediately.

"Harris."

She swallowed, then with her mouth still dry said, "You've got to come to Woody's. Hilda's been murdered."

"I'm on my way." She heard his phone click off.

"I called Detective Harris and he's on his way," she said to Sara, who had maneuvered Kathryn out of Hilda's office and was standing with her by the door.

"Please help me with her. She can't stand by herself. I must go and get Wells," Sara said.

Sonya took Kathryn from Sara and half carried her to a chair.

"Kathryn, pull yourself together," she said as she let the other woman collapse on the seat.

"This is all my fault," Kathryn said hoarsely. "I shouldn't have come here."

"What do you mean, it's your fault?"

Sonya looked up and saw the camera poke out at the end of the wall. Perry switched on the light and was ready to shoot.

She repeated her question, "What do you mean, your fault?"

"Not now, not now," Kathryn whispered. "Tomorrow. I have to tell someone."

"Yes, Kathryn, of course, tomorrow." Sonya thought quickly of the night's work ahead. "I'll see you tomorrow morning." Then she signaled Perry. He nodded his understanding and went to Hilda's office with the tape rolling.

Chapter 25

Network office
Saturday, 8:00 A.M.

Sonya picked up the stack of tapes she'd been viewing in the editing room, put her notebook on top, and headed for the conference room. Matt had called an eight o'clock meeting to go over plans for the story, and she had come in early to be prepared.

Perry had outdone himself. He had captured everything she needed to make a sensational piece. In a few minutes, he had taken both wide and tight shots of Hilda's body lying bloody and beaten in her tiny office. Beside her on the floor lay the murder weapon, a small, heavy brass vase, engraved with dancing women. Perry had zoomed in on its scarred bottom where Sonya could see an old Woody's price sticker. The murderer must have grabbed the vase by its narrow neck.

"What've you got?" Matt asked as Sonya put the tapes on the conference-room table. She hadn't expected him to be waiting for her. He made a habit of being the last to arrive. This must mean the Woodruff story would get most of the hour-long show.

Sonya had called Matt last night from the sidewalk after she finished shooting inside Woody's. From the background noise on his end she guessed he was at a party or at one of his gambling clubs.

She told him that she'd called the news department and it had sent a crew to cover Hilda's murder. Perry's tapes would be a scoop for the eleven o'clock local news.

"Okay," Matt had said. "I'll mobilize our troops. Let's meet at eight tomorrow."

"Good," Sonya replied. "There were so many people moving around, it was hard to get clean shots of the Woodruffs. I'll come in early and see what we have."

Since their argument, Sonya had felt a bit apprehensive about working with Matt, but now she pulled out a chair and sat next to him. "There's a lot here," she said in her most confident voice as she handed him a tape. "But you'll have to look at it. I've written down the time code for the murder scene. It's gruesome."

Matt picked up the tape, put it into the playback machine, and pressed the start button. He looked at Perry's shots of Hilda's body without saying a word. He rewound the tape and watched it again. Then he grunted. "You're right. It's awful."

She glanced at the clock on the conference-room wall. Five past eight. In a few minutes the rest of the staff would arrive.

"Who's coming in?" she asked Matt.

"Donna, Rick, and three of the associate producers," he said, keeping his eyes on the monitor as the shots of Hilda's body appeared once again.

Rick Carlton walked in, wearing his weekend jeans and an open-neck shirt. He gave Sonya his usual broad smile. "I saw the Woodruff murder story on the news this morning. I guess they used Perry's tape."

She smiled back at him. "Yes, they took about thirty seconds, mainly shots of Hilda as she arrived at the party. She was in a foul mood and it showed." She nodded her head in Matt's direction. "He's looking at the rest."

"So it didn't turn out to be much of a party."

"No," she said, "definitely not. It got completely out of control."

She thought back on the night. After Perry had got to the false wall and she'd sent him into Hilda's office, Sara had returned with a stunned Wells. His previously easy manner had been replaced by a shocked rigidity.

"Enough!" he'd shouted at Perry and put his hand over the camera lens. Then Wells went into the office for a long moment. When he emerged, he closed the door firmly behind him. He said stiffly to Sara, "I'll get the family together and tell them what's happened."

"Take them into Anthea's Room," Sara had said. "I'll clear the people out."

"Okay. After that, I'll get Derek or King to come guard this room. Then you go to the front door and wait for the police." He glared at Perry. "And you—get out of here!"

Sara had gone to Kathryn, who was still sitting on the chair next to Sonya. "Are you okay? I'm going to need all the help I can get."

When Kathryn stood up, Sonya saw that she was making a tremendous effort and put out a hand to steady her, but Kathryn shook her off. "I'll be all right. I'd like to help."

Sonya and Perry had followed Sara and Kathryn back around the false wall. Wells was pushing his way along the bar. Derek was leaning forward to take a drink, but Sonya had lost sight of him in the crowd.

Sonya had whirled around and grabbed the chair where Kathryn had been sitting. "Perry, stand on this. It's the only way you'll get a decent shot. Try to follow Wells as he talks to the members of the family."

She had held the chair steady while Perry got on. "Will you be all right? I want to get as close as possible to Anthea's Room and see what happens there."

Perry had murmured his assent.

"Okay," she said. "When you've got what you can, meet me there."

Keeping her eye on Perry, she moved to the entrance of Anthea's Room. Sara was inside. In a voice that amounted to a polite shout, the PR asked the partygoers to clear the room.

Many of the eager bargain hunters objected, but Sara stood firm. "I'm sorry, but this is a Woodruff family request and you must leave. You can come back later and get what you want." At the mention of the Woodruff name, the women slowly left, most of them carrying armloads of clothes.

"Thank you all so much," Sara said with forced lightness. Sonya could hear the anxiety in her voice.

Derek Shelby came up to her then and touched her arm. "Sonya, what's going on? Why is Sara clearing Anthea's Room?" he asked. "And where's Hilda? We were supposed to start the speeches half an hour ago."

It wasn't her place to break the news, so she merely shrugged. "I don't know."

Derek persisted, holding her arm so tightly it hurt. "It's something to do with Hilda, isn't it? That's why Wells is rounding up the family."

She shook her head. "Please let go of my arm."

Derek dropped his hand and gave her a nervous smile. As he went into Anthea's Room, he said, "I'm sorry. I don't like mysteries."

Sonya watched the other family members go into the room. Then she moved near the entrance to watch. They had gathered in a close group around Wells.

Standing between Ellin and Julia, Wells put his arms around their shoulders before he began to speak. Sonya had strained to hear. "I have to tell you that my mother . . ." Then he lowered his voice and she couldn't hear the rest. She moved closer to the entrance.

No one spoke. Ellin gave a low moan and began to sway as if she were about to faint. "No, it can't be true. Not Hilda," she cried. Derek went to her, but she pushed him away and reached for Julia. Julia held her for a moment, then looked at Wells.

"Who found her?" Julia asked.

"Kathryn. She had gone to ask if Mother wanted to begin the speeches."

"Do the police know?"

"They're on their way."

Now Sonya tried to remember the reactions of each of the family members. But it was all a blur.

Matt broke into her thoughts. "Donna will say the murder scene is too upsetting to use, and I agree. I see there's a shot of Hilda's body being carried out of Woody's. Let's go with that." He hadn't said much, but Sonya knew he felt good about the story and her work.

"I see Wells went to Derek Shelby first. Did you talk to Shelby? What sort of a guy is he?"

"It's hard to say, but I get the feeling he resents the Woodruff family."

"Well, I'm sure he doesn't resent their money."

Rick pulled up a chair and sat next to Matt as he reached for another tape.

"Sonya, what made you decide to go to Hilda's office?" Rick asked.

She sighed. "When Hilda arrived at the party she was angry at Sara. She went to her office to calm down but didn't come back to make her speech. I needed it for the story. I asked Kathryn to find out what was happening, then I got impatient and followed her."

"And found Hilda's body. You have a knack for that, don't you." He laughed.

"No, it was Kathryn," she replied, ignoring his attitude. "I didn't see the body at first, but when I did, I was horrified. I didn't know what to do."

"You panicked?" Matt asked with what amounted to a sneer. "You were certain she was dead?"

"Replay that tight shot of her, Matt. You can see there was no way that she was alive."

Matt grunted. "Did you get any information from the detective in charge?"

"No," she said. "He was flat-out busy, supervising it all."

Harris had been all business when he arrived at Woody's. Sonya had waited for him, knowing he would want to interview her.

When at last Harris had approached, he said, "I told you to watch out. You know too much about this, Sonya, and you have tapes. Be careful."

"I have Perry with me."

"Then stick with him. I'd feel better if you both left." He glanced over his shoulder at the people still searching for bargains. "This will keep me busy all night. I'll catch up with you tomorrow." She saw the anxiety in his face and touched his hand in agreement.

Perry had been watching them. "What did Harris want?"

"He told me to be careful and to stick with you."

Perry had grinned with pleasure.

"That's the first sensible thing that man has said."

"Okay, but we have to leave. Wait for me outside. I won't be long."

Perry left while Sonya watched the medical and the forensic teams go to Hilda's office. Under Harris's direction the police organized the crowd, getting names and addresses. Harris spoke briefly to Kathryn, who was driven home in a squad car.

After Kathryn left, Sonya joined Perry and the group of press who had gathered on the sidewalk. She met with the reporter from the news department, briefed her on what had happened, and gave her Perry's tapes. Then she went home to a restless night.

Now Sonya looked up as Donna walked into the conference room and gave her a brilliant smile. Donna's presence on a weekend morning was another sign of the importance of the story.

"I'm sorry to bring you in on a Saturday," Donna said as she took a chair near Matt. "But I think we should give the story the whole show. That means I want to do some of the interviews myself. Julia, as soon as you can get her. Maybe Wells or King, and Kathryn. She found Hilda and Gussie. She could be pivotal to the story."

"Wells is the best choice," Sonya said quickly. "He's Hilda's son. He's arrogant but articulate. You'll get some good bites. And with those gleaming white teeth and tanned skin he comes across as an attractive hunk."

"Kathryn?"

Sonya shook her head. "I don't know. She's hard to pin down. I have a pre-interview set for ten this morning. She said she has something to tell me. But I have no idea what. When I'm there, I'll do my best to set up an interview for you."

"Do we have any shots of her?"

"Yes." Sonya thought back. "I interviewed her and Perry got quite a lot of her with Gussie."

"What about King?"

"I don't know how much he'll say. One thing's for sure, he hated Hilda. She pushed him out of his job and his office. But he may be scared to say too much about it. He's sure to be one of the suspects."

Donna nodded. "Okay, set up interviews for me with Julia and Wells as soon as you can. When you've finished with Kathryn, call and let me know when I can interview her."

Donna left the room and Sonya huddled with the assistant producers around the monitor, identifying the members of the Woodruff family so they could log the tapes.

"You certainly shot enough," Rick said, pulling a face. "We'll be at this all day."

"Sorry." Sonya grinned at him. "You know I'd do the same for you."

She left them at it and went back to her office. First she tried Julia and was told she was not taking calls. Getting hold of Wells was difficult too. The operator at the hotel said he wasn't in, and it was only after sweet-talking an assistant manager that she discovered that Wells was spending the night at his mother's apartment. She called that number and got voice mail, so she called the hotel again, and talked the assistant manager into giving her Wells's cell number.

She woke Wells from what sounded like a deep sleep, and set the appointment for noon at Hilda's apartment. She was sure he would go back to sleep after she spoke to him and wondered if he would even remember her call. It didn't matter. She knew he was there, and if they had to wait for him to dress, so be it.

Yet it was strange. Why had he gone to his mother's apartment instead of his own? Was it sentiment or was it something to do with her murder? What did he hope to find?

She had no time to think about it. First she had to talk to Kathryn.

Chapter 26

Network building
Saturday, 10:00 A.M.

Sonya walked down the steps of the network building and looked for the car and driver she had booked to take her to Kathryn's apartment. It had been raining on and off all morning and the sky was a ceiling of gray that promised more rain at any moment. And it was cold. She buttoned her jacket and reached into her bag for her scarf. After the midweek burst of sunshine, *spring* had disappeared and *fall* was back.

Her car drew up to the curb with a splash of muddy water that sent her scurrying back. She wanted to shout at the driver for not being more careful, then she realized she was tired, and getting angry would only cost her energy. She gave the driver Kathryn's address and settled back to consider what she knew about her.

Leaving Woody's the previous night, Kathryn had run when she saw the photographers. Heading straight for the squad car, she climbed in, keeping her head down to hide her face.

Kathryn had had the time and the opportunity to murder both Gussie and Hilda. It was no accident that she had come to New York and volunteered at Woody's. Kathryn knew something about the Woodruff family, something she was using for her own purpose. Perhaps Gussie had tried to stop her and then Hilda discovered what was going on.

Yes, Kathryn Petite was a prime suspect. But it was hard for Sonya to imagine she had the strength of will to commit even one murder. She often withdrew into herself, avoiding confrontations. Perry had commented on that; the café manager said she'd left in tears after the argument with Gussie. Harris said he had doubts about her motive and strength as a killer, and he was an experienced detective. Sonya sighed. Kathryn was a mystery.

It was raining hard when she got to Kathryn's apartment. The apartment was in a prewar building in the nineties, close to the East River. Sonya told the driver to wait for her. The doorman was off-duty, so Kathryn buzzed her in. Four floors up, Sonya found Kathryn waiting in the doorway of her apartment. She looked fragile standing in the dim light of the hallway. She wore no makeup, and her hair, pulled back from her face, made her look ten years older.

"You'll have to excuse the place," she said as she ushered Sonya in. "It was all I could get when I decided to move here. It belongs to two sisters who are on a six-week vacation in Europe."

The door opened straight into the main room, which served as a living and dining area. A sofa in a faded chintz print was at one end, a dining table with four chairs at the other. Kathryn led Sonya to the sofa, pushing the coffee table out of the way. "I've made fresh coffee. Would you like some?" Sonya nodded and Kathryn went into the kitchen. She came back with two mugs and a carafe on a tray.

"So, Sonya, do you think I'm a murderer?" she said as she put the tray on the table.

"No, I don't. But I'm not the police."

Kathryn started to speak but Sonya put up her hand to stop her. "Before you say anything, you must understand that I am a journalist, and I may use anything you tell me."

"I understand." Kathryn sat down and poured coffee into the mugs. "It's hard for me to talk about why I came to New York. I know Hilda's dead, I saw her body lying there, but I'm still frightened of her." She hesitated. Sonya realized she was having second thoughts about telling her secret. That mustn't happen.

Sonya picked up a mug and held it to warm her hands. In a low, casual tone, she said, "Why are you frightened of her? Tell me about it."

Kathryn shook her head. "It's difficult. Everything has happened so fast."

Sonya put down the mug and caught one of Kathryn's hands in hers. "Start from the beginning. Tell me what happened in Washington."

Kathryn sat still for a moment and then began. "My mother died a little more than a month ago, after having a series of strokes. My father is dead, and as she had no other family, I took care of her alone. It wasn't easy. In the end, even with nurses around the clock—" She stopped. "I just wish I could have made life easier for her."

"I'm sorry," Sonya murmured. "Were you close?"

Kathryn started, then looked at her blankly. "Close?" she repeated. "I don't know what you mean by that."

"Well, most mothers and daughters share a strong bond."

"No, my mother and I weren't like that. I often felt that I didn't belong to her. She was an angry woman. Angry about her life. When I look back, I realize she felt as if she'd been cheated." She sighed. "And perhaps she was."

"It must have been difficult for you, Kathryn."

"Yes, it was. I shouldn't say this, but when Mother died, the first thing I felt was relief. After her first stroke she complained about everything; the nurses, the doctors, the food. If she didn't like a meal, she threw the plate on the floor. There was nothing anyone could do to please her."

She sat for a while without speaking. Sonya waited. "My godmother, Marta, was my saving grace. I couldn't have gotten through it without her. But then, after the funeral, she said she had something to tell me."

Kathryn swallowed hard, then picked up her coffee and, with closed eyes, took a sip.

"Kathryn, tell me what it was."

Kathryn lifted her head. "She told me that I was adopted and that Hilda Woodruff Fowler was my birth mother."

Sonya was stunned.

Kathryn took a deep breath and let it out in a rush. "It was a terrible shock. But in a way, I sensed all along that I was adopted. To tell the truth, I was thankful that at last I knew the truth. It explained so much." Sonya saw the relief in her face. "I felt an overwhelming need to find my birth family. And Sonya, perhaps that was the biggest mistake I made."

Sonya said quickly, "But it was a natural one. Most adopted kids want to know about their birth parents. Not only for emotional reasons, but for medical ones too."

"I didn't have to look far. Marta had all the details. I was born in Geneva and adopted in Paris. Marta's husband was an officer at the U.S. Consulate and he arranged it. She was sworn to secrecy then, but with my mother gone, she was free to tell me who my birth mother was."

"Did you contact Hilda?"

"Yes, I tried. I foolishly thought she would be as happy as I was. Not for a moment did I think she would reject me. But she had her attorney send me a letter saying that she had put the incident—me—out of her life, and was determined to keep it there."

"Do you have the letter?"

Kathryn put down her mug without answering and went into the bedroom. She came back with the letter and handed it to Sonya.

"Here it is. You see, she rejected me totally. I feel she must have thought I was after some of the Woodruff money, but it's not true."

Sonya took the letter and examined it. It was on heavy water-marked paper with the letterhead of a prominent New York law firm. More important, it stated exactly what Kathryn had said.

Sonya handed the letter back. "So you aren't interested in the Woodruff billions?"

Kathryn's voice was firm. "No. I don't need money. My adoptive father worked for the government during the day, but at night he played bridge and won a lot."

"He was a gambler?"

"No. He was brilliant at the game, and he was a shrewd investor. For my birthday and Christmas he gave me shares. I had quite a substantial portfolio by the time I went to college and when he died, he left me enough to live on comfortably for the rest of my life. My mother also left me everything she had."

"And you work, don't you?"

"Yes. As I told you and Perry I'm a photographic stylist. I stopped working when my mother had her first stroke. Before that I earned top dollar. I don't want for anything."

"So if Hilda rejected you and you don't need money, why did you come to New York?"

Kathryn sighed. She got up and went to the window, looking out into the rain. "I wanted a family. Please try to understand. If you don't have a family, you feel so alone. I was desperate." She turned and faced Sonya. "That's why I came here. I hoped to become one of the Woodruffs."

"That's why you volunteered to work at Woody's."

"Yes, it seemed the best thing to do. I used Petite rather than Pettibone so no one could find out who I was. I hoped to get to know them. To become friendly. If not with my mother, then one of my aunts."

"What went wrong?"

Kathryn came back and sat on the sofa. She leaned forward and said in a hard voice, "Gussie. That's what went wrong." She put her hands over her face as if to hide. "Gussie recognized me. She said I'm the spitting image of Anthea Woodruff, my grandmother. There's a portrait of her in the store. We have the same coloring, but Gussie said it wasn't only my looks, it was the way I moved, the tone of my voice. She called me the living reincarnation of Anthea."

"Did you admit that you are Hilda's daughter?"

"Yes, eventually. Gussie forced the confession out of me. I liked her, and I thought she'd understand and help me get to know the Woodruff family. But she didn't."

"Why not?"

"I think maybe Gussie was frightened that Hilda would find out that she had hired me and accuse her of helping me. She said Hilda would never accept me and told me to go back to Washington."

"Do you think she was scared Hilda would force her to retire?"

"Yes. She said she would help me but I would have to be patient. I didn't believe her."

"And she agreed to that?"

"Yes. We'd been arguing, but I convinced her. Then, when I let myself in the next morning, she was dead."

Sonya felt compassion for Kathryn. Still, if Kathryn's story were true, only Gussie knew who she really was. That could be a motive for murder.

"And now what will you do?" Now that your birth mother is dead, Sonya wanted to add.

"I don't know. I had a long talk with Marta last night and we both think it is too soon to decide."

"Have you told the police who you are?"

"No, I couldn't bring myself to do it." Kathryn shook her head. "I'll tell Detective Harris when he comes to interview me this morning, and then I'm going to call the family members and tell them."

"It's bound to be a shock. Don't expect too much from them, so soon after Hilda's death. Especially since some of them at least are sure to think you killed her." Sonya glanced at her watch. "Unfortunately, I have to go. Donna's interviewing Wells at noon and I have to prepare the questions."

As she got up, Kathryn reached out and took her hand. "Do you think Wells will believe Hilda was my mother?"

"I can't say. I interviewed Wells for five minutes. He seemed a reasonable young man."

Kathryn looked at Sonya. "I swear to you, I didn't harm Gussie or Hilda. I don't fight back. I've learned to cope with everything life hands me. That's my problem."

Sonya pulled her hand away. Kathryn's description of herself no longer rang true. She was much tougher than she pretended, stronger than Sonya had thought. She said, "I'll let you get ready for the police."

Kathryn walked with her to the elevator. Sonya got in and pushed the lobby button. She believed Kathryn's story. But perhaps killing Hilda had solved a problem for her. Hilda would never have accepted her. Now that she was dead, Kathryn could appeal to the rest of the Woodruff family.

Sonya sighed. As she walked through the foyer she buttoned her jacket against the chill of early spring. She hoped the interview with Wells would give her some insight into the murders.

Chapter 27

The heavy rain had stopped, but traffic was still gridlocked. Sonya looked at the clock on the limo dashboard. It would take another twenty minutes to get across town to the office. She opened her bag, got out her notebook, and started working on questions for Donna's interview with Wells.

She usually finished such lists quickly, but now she had to add questions centered on Kathryn's confession that she was Hilda's daughter. If Kathryn hadn't yet called Wells, Donna could tell him while the tape was rolling. His reaction would undoubtedly be dramatic, fantastic for the show.

She opened her cell phone and dialed Donna's number. Busy. She dialed again. Still busy. Well, a message would have to do. She waited for the beep, summarized what had happened, and snapped the cell shut. She picked up her notebook and resumed writing.

When Sonya arrived, Donna was waiting at her desk. She had been made-up, but her hair was still in rollers. Matt was sprawled on the sofa.

"How can you believe this woman's story? What proof do you have that she's Hilda Woodruff's daughter?" he snarled as she walked in.

"Yes, Sonya, what proof do we have?" Donna asked, more quietly.

Sonya sat in the chair farthest from Matt. "I believe her story because she does have proof." She took a deep breath to control her irritation. Then turning to Donna, she continued, "Kathryn showed me a letter from Hilda's attorney saying Kathryn was not to contact her about something that happened years ago."

Donna put her elbows on the table, locked her fingers, and rested her chin on them. Sonya knew the position. Donna was worried.

"Why is Kathryn so desperate to connect with the Woodruff family? Their money?"

"Apparently not. She's quite definite about that. She says she inherited enough money to last her a lifetime."

Matt burst out laughing. "I don't believe that. The sisters must be worth billions."

Sonya ignored him. "Donna," she continued, "Kathryn says she's an only child of divorced parents. Both are dead. She has no family. She came here hoping to find a new one in the Woodruffs."

"Do you think she is capable of murder?"

"I don't know. She's stronger than I thought when I first met her at Woody's. She had motive and opportunity to kill both Gussie and Hilda. Yet there is something about her." Sonya paused. "It's hard to describe, but my gut feeling is that she's innocent."

"Your gut feeling," Matt snorted. "Whatever that is, it won't stand up in court."

Matt was right. Sonya knew he was trying to put her down, but she still felt embarrassed about having rushed to defend Kathryn. Was it because she believed her innocent, or was it a snap reaction to Matt's challenge?

Their eyes locked. She looked straight at him until he turned away.

"Matt, I trust my instincts and they rarely let me down."

"Let's see what the police investigation has to say. That's what I call journalism. I'm not prepared to expose *The Donna Fuller Show* on your gut feeling alone."

Donna shot Matt a warning look and then said to Sonya, "What about setting up an interview? Do you think Kathryn will say all this on camera?"

"Yeah, that's more to the point," Matt broke in. "That would give us an exclusive for the show. I could promote the hell out of it. I'm sure nothing is too much for you to arrange."

Sonya moved her chair closer to Donna's desk. "Donna, it was a coup getting her to talk this morning. But I'm not sure she would be willing to repeat everything on camera. Several times I thought she was about to freeze and tell me to get out—"

"So why did she talk to you?" Matt interrupted.

"I guess I was in the right place at the right time—and she wasn't staring into a camera lens. Kathryn is lonely, she needed to talk to someone. But Donna, she's clever and she'll only do what she thinks is good for her. I'll do my best to get her for an interview."

Donna smiled. "I know you will. Has Kathryn told her story to the police?"

"Detective Harris was coming to take her statement this morning. He could be there now."

"So he might ask Wells about his new half sister before I get to him?" Donna frowned and looked at her watch. "Our interview is at noon. Sonya, I think you'd better get over there with Perry and set up right now. Forget the questions. Give me your notes and go. I'll get there as soon as Sabrina does my hair. I don't want Wells canceling at the last moment." She asked her assistant to tell Perry to meet Sonya at the van.

"I'm coming too," Matt said.

Donna shook her head. "No, it's not wise. The fewer of us the better."

Matt started to protest, but Donna held up her hand in dismissal. Sonya tore the pages from her notebook and gave them to Donna. She walked to the door and then looked back. "Donna, remember to go to Hilda's apartment. Wells stayed there last night instead of the hotel. I think he doesn't want to have it associated with the Woodruff family."

Donna smiled at her. "Hilda's apartment will be perfect. Set up in the library . . . the same place we did his mother's interview."

Matt, as usual, had to have the last word. As Sonya walked out she heard him say, "But I bet Wells won't mind being associated with Woodruff money."

Matt was probably wrong. One of the first things Wells had said to her last night was that he was a Fowler, not a Woodruff. And yet he was friendly with his cousin King. Perhaps that was because both of them hated Hilda. Could that be the basis of their relationship? Could that relationship have led to a double murder?

Perry was sitting in the van, waiting for her. "What's the rush?" he asked as she climbed in beside him.

"Perry, I had a wild session with Kathryn this morning. Turns out she's Hilda's daughter." As he nosed the van into the traffic, she told him the story.

He gave a low whistle. "That explains a lot. Is Donna planning on interviewing her?"

"Donna wants to, but I'll need all the charm I've got to persuade Kathryn to do it."

The maid who let them into the apartment was the same woman who had been there when they interviewed Hilda. This time, instead of her black uniform, she wore jeans and a T-shirt. Her eyes were red and swollen and her hair disheveled. She ushered them into the library, explaining that Wells had not told her about the interview until a few minutes ago.

"He doesn't live here and he never stays here," she said. "But he came in late last night and went to his old room. He just woke up," she added. "He said he won't be long."

Perry set up the lights quickly and Sonya arranged flowers and ornaments to make the background more attractive. Within minutes Donna arrived with Sabrina.

"Tell Wells we're ready when he is," Donna said to the maid. "We know this is a difficult time for him, and we want to be out of his way as quickly as we can."

Sabrina moved in and did the final touch-ups on Donna's hair and makeup. Then they waited for Wells.

Fifteen minutes later he walked in, looking as if he was about to pose for an ad in a fashion magazine. He had topped his gray flannel slacks with a bright blue sweater over a yellow checked shirt. The bright yellow showed off his tan and the golden highlights in his hair. It was a surprising outfit for an interview about the murder of his mother.

He shook Donna's hand and thanked her for her condolences. Then he said, "I want to be quite sure that you address me as Wells Fowler. My mother changed her name back to Woodruff, but I am a Fowler, and I will remain so."

Donna nodded. "Of course." She motioned to him to sit down.

Wells smiled confidently at Donna while Perry adjusted his mike and started rolling tape. "I know you'll ask me questions about my mother," he said. "The truth is that we didn't get along. We had different ideas about life. I spoke to her about once a week and we met for Sunday brunch once a month. And that's it."

"I see." Donna hid her surprise at his sudden statement. "Was there something you quarreled about?"

"Yes," he said. "You'll find it reported in every gossip column. I decided to work in my father's hotel business, not in Woodruff Publishing. I have great admiration for my grandfather, who founded the publishing company, but I'm not interested in women's magazines. I like dealing with people's needs on a day-to-day basis."

"Wells, were you fond of your mother?"

He hesitated. Sonya watched a nerve twitch in his cheek. He was an arrogant man, but an honest one.

"Of course I was. But she was disappointed in my decision. In fact, I don't think she ever really accepted it."

Donna kept her voice low. "Tell me when you last saw your mother."

"At the party. She was upset with the crowd at the door and I told her to go to her office while I sorted things out."

"Did you see her again after that?"

"No, she went to her office and stayed there. I was concerned about the crowd, so I stayed near the door to make sure things remained under control."

"Did you stay there the whole time?"

"No, my cousin King relieved me so I could mingle with the guests. When things calmed down, Sara Watkins took over from him."

"From what I see on our tapes, the party became chaotic."

"Yes, unfortunately. The word got out that Woody's had great bargains, and uninvited women pushed their way in."

"Wells, do you have any idea who might have killed your mother?"

He drew himself up. "Why are you asking me? Of course I have no idea."

"She never discussed her problems with you?"

"No." His voice was firm. "At our last brunch we discussed the party at Woody's, that's all."

Sonya saw Donna's face soften with sympathy. "Wells, tell me, how are you holding up?"

For the first time he let his sorrow show. He leaned back and closed his eyes. "I can't believe it's true. She was such a disciplined, powerful woman. She made things happen. She didn't let anyone interfere with her life."

He shuddered, struggling to control himself.

"It was a dreadful night," he said in a low voice. "I came back here, to her apartment, to be close to her. I wandered from room to room, trying to understand what had happened. Eventually I crawled into my old bed and went to sleep."

He fell silent. Donna waited until he looked at her.

"Wells," she said slowly, "do you know that your mother had a daughter before she married your father? That you have a half sister?"

"What?" he exploded. "What are you talking about?" He stopped to let the news sink in. "A half sister? How do you know?"

He stood up, then felt the tug of the mike on his sweater and sat down again.

"I don't believe it." He glared at Donna as he went on. "My father would have known, and he would have told me. We had no secrets."

"Wells," Donna's voice was conciliatory, "we only found out an hour or so ago."

"An hour or so ago!" His voice rose. "What do you mean?"

"Wells, please, let me tell you what we know."

He was silent, but anger still showed in his eyes.

"Your half sister is Kathryn Petite, or Kathryn Pettibone."

"That woman at the shop?"

"Yes. She was born in Switzerland while your mother was at school there. She was adopted by an American couple, the Pettibones. They were in the diplomatic service and eventually moved to Washington. Kathryn only found out Hilda was her mother a few weeks ago."

"What proof does she have?" he retorted.

"As I said, Wells, this just happened, but Kathryn showed my producer a letter from Hilda's attorney that admitted Hilda was Kathryn's birth mother." Donna paused. "The letter also said Hilda wanted to have nothing to do with her."

"What did she want from Mother? Money, I suppose."

"She says it's not money. She wants a family."

"What a joke. The Woodruffs are hardly your average loving family. No, I'd say she doesn't want us. She wants our money."

Donna shook her head. "Wells, it's not unusual for adopted children to want to know their birth parents."

He shrugged off her comment. "Kathryn Petite called me a day or so ago and asked to see me. She said she was volunteering at Woody's and wanted to talk to me about some ideas she had for its future. She's got to be up to something."

"What did you say to her?"

"I put her off."

Donna leaned forward. "Kathryn told us she was frightened Hilda would find out who she really was and forbid her to have any contact with the family. That's the reason she changed her name when she went to volunteer at Woody's."

Wells closed his eyes as he tried to control his growing anger. Then he gave Donna a scathing look.

"I'll see my attorney," he said slowly. "Donna Fuller, how dare you force your way into my mother's home just to expose her past on your show? It's a cheap and trashy thing to do."

He ripped the microphone from his sweater and pushed past Perry to get to the door. "Just get out of here!" he shouted. "Leave my mother in peace!" With that he left, slamming the door behind him.

Sonya went to Donna. "I'm glad we got that on tape, but I do feel sorry for him."

"You're right. He has every reason to be angry at being ambushed. He had no idea about his half sister and no matter how cool he seemed about his mother's death, he must be in shock."

"Unless he murdered her," Sonya said.

"He made no secret of the fact that they didn't get along."

Sonya nodded. "That could be a motive. But what about Gussie, why would he want to kill her?"

Why indeed? she thought to herself. But then, if Gussie knew the family secrets, she might well have known something about Wells. Wells had wanted her out of the thrift shop; he'd told his mother it was time she retired.

She rode back to the office in Donna's car, checking her cell phone for messages. There was one. Keith Harris asked her to call back. She wanted to speak to him. She had questions to ask. But not now, not in front of Donna.

Chapter 28

East Eighty-second Street
Saturday, 1:30 P.M.

"I'll do a 'Detective Harris' and buy you a sandwich for lunch. I suppose you want coffee as well?" Perry grinned as he turned off the engine of the van.

Sonya teased, "Yes, but you don't have to buy me lunch."

"Well, I make more money than Harris, so I can afford to be generous." Perry patted his wallet in his back pocket. "You want the usual?"

"Yes. And please, loads of mustard. I need it to clear my head."

"Okay." Perry got out of the van. She watched him stride along the street toward Lexington Avenue. Good, reliable Perry. He'd gone back to the studio after the interview with Wells, picked up fresh batteries, and was waiting for her when she finished working with Donna.

Now they were parked under a tree around the corner from Julia's Fifth Avenue apartment. When Sonya called after the morning meeting, King answered the phone. He said his mother was resting and couldn't be disturbed. At first he refused to be interviewed, but when she told him that Wells had agreed to go on camera, he backed down.

"I can do it about two, two thirty. But it has to be brief," he said.

"I'm going to the foundation office this morning, and I'll probably go back there this afternoon."

"That's fine. We'll be there at two. How's your mother?"

"Better than I expected. I didn't want to leave her alone this morning but she's adamant that I go to work. She's determined that the transition goes smoothly."

"Great. I'm glad she's doing so well."

"Yes, but don't count on seeing her this afternoon. There are things that have to be done, including a visit to the funeral home."

Sonya had offered her condolences and hung up. So, Julia was taking Hilda's place as head of the Woodruff family, and was moving to see that King shared her power. What a change. Last week he had been pushed off the executive floor and now, it seemed, he would occupy Hilda's office. How would Wells like that? Despite what he'd said about wanting to stay in the hotel business, would he resent King taking over the Woodruff empire?

Or had they reached some sort of agreement? She'd suspected that at the party. She looked up, saw Perry approaching with their lunch in a cardboard box, and rolled down her window to take it.

"I'm thinking about King and how he's setting himself up as head of the Woodruff interests," she said as Perry joined her. "There's the possibility that he murdered Hilda to do it."

Perry opened a packet of ketchup and squirted it over his french fries. "Yeah, he sure had the opportunity."

"I'm talking about motive. Of all of the Woodruffs, King has the strongest. Not just money, but power."

Sonya slit open the plastic wrapping on her sandwich and lifted the top slice of bread. There was a slathering of mustard on it. She picked up half the sandwich and bit into it.

"He must have been crazed at the way Hilda treated him," she said.

"I didn't see any comment about that from him in the press. He's kept his cool."

"His mother knew how he felt, and so did Gussie."

Perry was right. On Monday Julia had come to Woody's in tears and blurted out the story. Was she angry enough to have helped King plan to murder Hilda? Perhaps. She knew the layout of Woody's. She certainly knew the brass vase that Hilda used as an ashtray. Did she tell King to use it to kill Hilda? Sonya shook her head. Gussie had been murdered too and probably by the same person. Julia was no murderer. If King killed those women, he acted by himself.

At Julia's apartment, King opened the door. He was dressed formally, in flannels and a well-tailored jacket. She wondered if he had chosen the outfit to impress the Woodruff Foundation executives. But his nervous movements as he ushered them into the living room belied his apparent confidence. The room was large, with windows overlooking Central Park, and was pleasantly crowded with books, magazines, and photos. It was comfortable. Like Julia.

"I can only give you five minutes," King said. "I have to go back to the office. Mother is needed there as well, so I've sent her on ahead."

Sonya nodded her understanding. "Have you spoken to Wells this morning?"

"No, why?"

Sonya deliberately ignored his question. She motioned to Perry to set up with the bookcases in the background, then smiled at King. "I'm surprised to hear that Julia went to the foundation."

"The foundation's chief accountant called fifteen minutes ago and said he'd like to see Mother and me." His eyes rested on Sonya and she knew he was wondering if he could trust her. Then he gave a little laugh and went on, "He said he had uncovered something that we should both know about."

He hesitated, glancing at Perry, who was setting up a light stand.

"I can't say this on camera, but Hilda took two hundred thousand dollars from the foundation last week and he can't find out what she did with it," he exclaimed with enthusiasm.

Sonya was amazed at his lack of discretion. Why was he telling her this?

"That's a lot of money."

"Yes, it is!" He was gleeful. King was in a dangerous mood. His dislike of his aunt was venomous. He clearly wanted to see her reputation ruined.

Sonya hesitated. He had placed her in an awkward position. He said he wouldn't talk about the money on camera, but she was a journalist and she had the right to use what he told her. Maybe that was what he intended.

Perry interrupted. "If you'll come and sit here, I'll put on your mike and we can start."

King sat upright in the chair, eyes glinting, hands grasping the armrests.

Sonya smiled at him, then nodded at Perry, and began.

"Let's start by talking about what it's like to be a member of the Woodruff family," she said, and watched King's face as he struggled to frame a suitable answer.

"It's impossible to say. Two people have been brutally murdered in less than a week. The police are investigating, and we're supporting them in every way we can. The Woodruff family is devastated by our losses."

"Let's start at the beginning. How close were you to Gussie?"

"When I was a kid, Gussie was my mother's sounding board. Mother told her everything about me and Gussie often scolded me for upsetting her. I knew Gussie wanted to make sure I did the right thing, as a Woodruff. But as I grew older, I got tired of her interfering in my life. So, I saw her less often, and our relationship changed."

"What do you mean, to do the right thing as a Woodruff?"

"I was the oldest grandchild. You might say I was spoiled, but, at the same time, a lot was expected of me. Gussie lectured me about my responsibilities all the time. I used to say I didn't care."

"You were your grandfather's favorite?"

"Yes. I'm sure everyone recognized that. He treated me like a son. I think his love was mixed with guilt. He didn't approve of my father, and I believe he paid him to divorce my mother and get out of our lives." He covered his mouth with his hand as if to stop the words from coming. He knew he had gone too far. "I wish he hadn't. It was cruel to cut me off from my father."

Sonya realized he was telling the truth and looked at him with sympathy, but King glanced away.

She said softly, "I hear Hilda was close to your grandfather."

"So she was, after my grandmother Anthea died. Grandfather was desperately lonely. Hilda wormed her way into his favor and gradually got more power over his affairs. Mother and Ellin were helpless against her."

"And now, everything has changed?"

He closed his eyes and paused. "We'll see. The first thing is to find the murderer. Then we can start to undo the harm that my aunt Hilda did."

Sonya leaned forward. "And Wells?" she said. "Do you have a good relationship with him?"

King didn't seem to have understood her question. "What about Wells?"

Sonya let him sit for a while before speaking. Then she said, "I wonder about your feelings for him."

King looked at her bleakly. "I don't know why you would ask that question. We were kids together. Wells's dad was a great, generous guy. When Hilda would allow us to be together he'd take us out on his sailboat in the summer and to Aspen to ski over our winter break. We'll stand by each other no matter what happens. If Wells ever decides to give up the hotel business and come to work with me in publishing, I'll welcome him with open arms."

"Do you think that's likely?"

"No. Wells wants to expand the hotels. All he has to do is raise the capital, and now Mother and I can help him with that." He put his hand up. "That's all. I want to stop."

Sonya shook her head. "Just one last question."

He was annoyed. "Just one."

She paused, waiting to get his full attention. "Do you know Wells has a sister? A daughter who was born to Hilda when she was at school in Switzerland?"

King stiffened. "I don't know what you're talking about."

Sonya told him Kathryn's story and watched as first fear, then anger, crossed his face.

"This woman has definite proof of her birth?" he asked.

"Yes, as I said, I saw the letter from Hilda's attorneys."

"What does she want from us?"

"I can't say. All I know is what I've told you."

His voice rose. "She's a fraud, she's got to be. She's got no claim on us. If she had, my grandfather would have told me about her." He lifted his fist and banged it down on the arm of his chair. "No, she has no claim. My mother now heads the Woodruff family trust and business, and through her, control goes to me."

Sonya signaled Perry to stop the tape. She sighed. "I'm sorry to have to tell you about Kathryn," she said.

He shook his head. "I'll talk to Wells this afternoon. Mother has arranged to meet him at the funeral home and I'll go with her. Right now I'm worried about what she must be going through with the accountant. Mother loved Hilda and she'll be horrified at this Kathryn woman's claim. I've got to get to her."

He took out his cell phone. As he dialed, he walked to the far end of the room. Sonya waited until he returned, then looked at him expectantly.

"The accountant still can't find any trace of the two hundred thousand dollars," King said.

He left them outside the apartment building, jumping into a cab the doorman hailed for him.

"There goes a guy with a problem or two to solve," Perry said as he picked up the tripod and camera and started for the van.

"And what problems they are," Sonya agreed. "I think he told the truth."

"Why would Hilda want to steal money from the foundation? She was a rich woman, worth millions."

"She may have been cash-poor. Two hundred thousand is a lot of money to have on hand even if you are rich. Her fortune is probably locked up in investments. To get that amount quickly, she'd have to get a loan or sell something."

Sonya climbed into her seat, while Perry stowed the gear in the back of the van. Yes, she told herself, Hilda needed money in a hurry and didn't want anyone to know about it. Not the family, the accountants, or the attorneys. It all pointed to blackmail. And Kathryn was the obvious choice. She'd demanded money, gotten it, and then killed Hilda. Sonya shook her head. No, it didn't make sense. Why kill? If Hilda paid up once, she'd do it again.

Then there was Gussie. How did her murder fit in?

Sonya reached into her bag and took out the other half of the sandwich she'd taken from the studio.

Perry opened his door and asked, "Do you want coffee with that?"

Sonya nodded, "I sure do, and make it black as usual." She reached in her bag for money. "Forget it," he said and slammed the door. He came back with two cups. She took one and sipped cautiously as she ate.

"I rule out King as a suspect," she said. "What about you?"

"I'm with you. He seemed okay under the circumstances. He was loved by his grandfather; he loves his mother and his cousin. And he wants to know what happened to his father. He can't be all that bad. But what about his mother?"

"Julia had plenty of reason to get rid of Hilda, but not Gussie."

Perry started the van and pulled into the street.

"Back to the office?" he asked, and Sonya nodded.

"Thanks, and that's it as far as I'm scheduled. But hang around, and if anything else happens, I'll call you."

Rick Carlton would have her tapes logged in by now, but she still had to view them. She also had to report to Matt and tell him about the $200,000 that Hilda had taken from the foundation.

But more important, she wanted to call Ellin. Of the two sisters, Ellin was the more vulnerable, and the easier to get to talk.

As soon as she was finished with Matt, she dialed the Shelbys' number. Derek picked up. She offered her condolences and asked if she could speak with Ellin.

"No, she's too upset to talk to anyone. I've had to give her a sedative to calm her." His voice was low, tentative.

"I understand. You can't be feeling too great yourself."

"No. It's impossible to understand what has happened. I've gone over and over it in my mind, and come up with nothing. I can't believe any member of the family is involved."

"Of course not," Sonya said smoothly. She wanted to keep the conversation going, but she could hear the reluctance in Derek's voice and decided to change the subject. "How are the beautiful Bengal cats?"

"The cats? They're fine. At least they will be a comfort for Ellin when all this is over."

Sonya heard a click and then a slurred, "Hello. Is that you, Sonya?"

Derek broke in. "If you two are going to talk, I'm leaving. Good-bye." Sonya thought she heard the rattle of his phone being placed in the cradle.

"Ellin," she said in surprise, "how are you?"

"Oh, Sonya, I feel terrible. I don't know which way to turn. I need someone to talk to," she whispered. "Will you come see me?"

"Yes, of course. I'm on my way."

Sonya hung up, picked up her bag, and went downstairs. The pieces were falling into place.

Why was Ellin whispering? Why had Derek left so abruptly? Did he really hang up? Sonya had a good idea of what the answers would be.

Chapter 29

Derek and Ellin's apartment
Saturday, 3:00 P.M.

"Go straight up. Mrs. Shelby is expecting you." The doorman at the Shelbys' apartment house greeted Sonya as she shook the rain from her umbrella and stepped inside.

Sonya gave him a quick smile. "Thanks."

"You're becoming a regular. You must be a cat lover."

"You're right, I am." Sonya slipped the umbrella into its plastic case and headed quickly to the elevators.

Ellin, the most fragile of the Woodruff sisters, was in trouble and Derek was sedating her—perhaps to stop her from talking.

Last week, when Sonya had visited the Shelby apartment to see the Bengals, she'd sensed Ellin's resentment toward Derek. As far as Sonya could see, their only common interest was the cats. And there Derek had the upper hand. Ellin made the date to show Sonya the Bengals, but Derek had taken over. Ellin doted on Raj, the dominant male, but Derek had trained Raj to come to him.

Derek Shelby was a manipulator.

Sonya pressed the doorbell of the Shelby penthouse. No answer. She pressed again. It was too soon to worry. In the twenty minutes it took her to get there, Ellin could have fallen asleep. Sonya pressed again, keeping her thumb on the button for a good thirty seconds. Still no answer. She pulled out her cell phone. No signal. The only thing to do was go down and ask the doorman to call.

When Sonya got back to the penthouse, Ellin was holding the front door open. Her face was haggard. Dark circles under her eyes emphasized smudges of last night's mascara. Deeply etched crease marks lined the flushed cheek she'd rested on as she slept. Her crushed pink robe lay open over a cosmetic-stained nightdress, revealing her sagging breasts.

"Forgive me, Sonya," she said. "I didn't hear the bell. It rings in the kitchen and Derek had closed the bedroom door. He didn't want me to be disturbed." As she spoke she swayed toward Sonya. Frightened that she would fall, Sonya put an arm around her and walked her into the apartment.

"You look as if you could do with a strong cup of coffee," she said. "Shall I make it for you?"

Ellin said in a slurred voice, "There's a coffee machine in the kitchen, Derek made some at lunch. There should be some left."

Sonya led her to the living room and sat her on the sofa.

"Where's my Raj?" Ellin asked.

"Raj?" Sonya looked around for him.

"Oh, Derek's taken him to the clinic. I miss my Raj."

The coffeepot was almost empty. Sonya checked to see if it was still warm, then poured the dark liquid into a mug. She put the mug, along with milk and sugar, on a tray and took it to the living room.

Ellin was lying on the sofa, her head resting on an arm, her mouth open as she breathed heavily. Sonya put the tray on the coffee table and shook Ellin's shoulder.

"Ellin," she said, "here's your coffee. Wake up and drink."

Ellin opened her eyes and struggled to sit up. "All I want to do is sleep. I guess it must be the pills Derek gave me to help me get over the shock of Hilda's murder."

"Yes." Sonya kept her voice firm. "But you said you wanted to talk to me about something. What was it?"

Ellin reached for the mug.

"Drink it." Sonya sat down beside her. "You must stay awake."

Ellin sipped and made a face. "It's bitter." But she raised the mug and took a swallow.

"Just drink it down. I'll make some fresh in a minute. Just tell me, what are you worried about?"

"Derek," Ellin said. "I heard that he was having an affair with Hilda. But it's not true. It was just a malicious lie."

"How do you know?"

"He told me this morning. He said he'd never been unfaithful to me. He loves me and always will. I know he has his faults . . ." She lifted the mug and took another swallow.

"What faults? What do you mean?" Sonya kept her voice easy.

Ellin's laugh turned into a snort. "You must know my husband is a gambler. Everyone does."

"I know he plays poker. I heard that from someone at the network."

"Poker." She shook her head and continued slowly, "That's only for openers. Name a game and he's into it." She leaned toward Sonya to emphasize what she was saying. "He takes every penny I get. This apartment is mortgaged and so is his clinic. The only reason he's still in business is that he's married to a Woodruff. I can't remember how many times he's told me he'll have to declare bankruptcy unless I go to Hilda and get an advance on my share of the trust. It's degrading, but I do it to keep us together."

Sonya looked at her pitiful face. "Addiction to gambling's a disease. Did you try to get him help?"

"I tried, but he refused."

"Some women would have left him."

Ellin drew back. "I can't. I can't blame him when it's my father's fault. He encouraged Derek to gamble when we were first married. Derek got hooked and couldn't stop. To him, the next throw of the dice will always be the winning one."

"Was your father a compulsive gambler?"

"Dad was too good a businessman to risk losing much. But Derek lives for the excitement."

"But he wasn't like that when you married him?"

"No. Maybe he'd have an occasional bet on a football game. But that's it. Dad wanted a son and Derek was the nearest thing to it, so when Derek began to get in too deep, Dad would rescue him."

"He never recognized that Derek had a serious problem?"

The bitterness of the memories brought Ellin out of her stupor. "Eventually he did. I believe Derek's gambling was the reason Dad made our trust fund so tight. He wanted to protect me . . . but now . . ." She picked up her mug, drained it, and held it out to Sonya. "Is there any more?"

Sonya took the mug. She hesitated for a moment, then decided to take a chance on her next question. "Ellin, do you know that Hilda took two hundred thousand dollars out of the trust last week, and that the accountants can't trace it?"

Ellin sat quite still, and for a moment Sonya thought she hadn't heard her.

Then she said in a dull, flat voice, "I didn't know." She closed her eyes as she absorbed the meaning of it.

"Derek knew I couldn't get more money from Hilda, so I guess he went to her himself. That's what all the rumors were about." With the realization came anger. "He was in trouble and everyone knew it but me."

Sonya swallowed. "I'm sorry, perhaps I shouldn't have told you."

Ellin nodded. "Thank you for telling me. Now I know exactly what was going on." She was deadly calm. "Please get me some more coffee. I want to think about what I should do. One thing is certain, Hilda wouldn't have given Derek any money without demanding something in exchange."

"I'll make fresh coffee for you. It won't take long." Sonya got up and went into the kitchen. She emptied the dregs of the coffee down the sink and started to make a new pot.

She frowned as she worked. Derek and his need for money might well be the connection between the two murders.

Sonya refilled Ellin's mug with coffee and returned to the living room. "Here, this is fresh and hot," she said as she put it on the table. "It'll help you think clearly."

"My thinking is clear," Ellin replied. "I just called Derek and told him what a bastard he is. That I know about the two hundred thousand dollars he got from Hilda, and that he'll never get another cent from me."

Sonya was astounded at her courage. "What did he say?"

"He said what he always does—he admitted it, said he's sorry, and that this time he has learned his lesson." Ellin looked away, then said, slowly and clearly, "He told me he got in too far this time, and had done things that I could never understand or forgive. He said it would be better for both of us if he swallowed some pills and took a long sleep. I agreed and said good-bye."

Sonya grabbed her by the shoulders. "Ellin, do you know what that means?"

"Yes, I know what it means. In a few hours he'll be dead. And I'm glad—for his sake and for mine."

"My God, Ellin!" Sonya picked up her cell phone and dialed Keith Harris.

He picked up immediately. "What's up, Sonya?"

"Keith, Derek Shelby is trying to commit suicide. He's at his clinic."

"How do you know?"

"I'm with Ellin. He just told her he had no other way out."

"Okay, I'll call EMS and go straight over there. Talk to you later."

Ellin picked up her mug and cradled it in her hands. "You think I'm hard, don't you? But you know nothing. Nothing about my life and what I've dealt with. Everyone thought Derek was a great, compassionate man, and maybe he was in some ways. But underneath he was a demon who lived to throw my money away. I grew to hate him, and the hatred was consuming my life."

Sonya looked hard into her eyes. "Ellin, I had to call the police. I have to try and save him."

Ellin stood up, her coffee still in her hands. "I know. You did the right thing. But for me it's all over. I can begin a new life. I'm going into my bedroom to lie down and think about it."

Sonya watched her go, then called Perry.

"What's up, redhead?" He answered on the second ring.

"Perry," she said, "I believe Derek Shelby is the murderer."

"What?"

"He's at his clinic, and according to Ellin, he has swallowed a handful of pills. Get there as fast as you can. I'll call Matt." She gave him directions and said she'd meet him as soon as she could.

Matt wasn't as easy. "Why do you think he's the one?"

"Matt, I'm with Ellin Shelby. She told me that Derek is a compulsive gambler and is desperate for money. The only reason no one knew about it is because he had Ellin pay off his debts," she said. "It's a complicated story, but I believe his gambling debts could be the motive for both crimes."

"Why didn't you tell me you were going to see Ellin Shelby? I suppose you have Perry with you?"

Sonya took a deep breath. "No, Matt. I just called him and told him to go to the clinic."

Matt was quiet for a moment. She knew he was considering tearing into her for not telling him what she was doing. But the story was more important. "What's Ellin doing now?" he snapped in his most sarcastic tone. "Rushing to her husband's side?"

Sonya stayed calm. "No, she said she had enough of him and was glad it was over. I think she would be happy to see him dead."

"So you assigned Perry to this without my authorization?"

She was firm. "Yes, now drop it, Matt. I also called the police and they're on their way, along with the medics."

Matt paused. "Okay, I'll let it go this time. I'll notify local news; you had better know what you're doing before you accuse Shelby of murder."

Sonya hung up. She had to join Perry at the clinic. But what about Ellin? Should she be left alone?

She dialed Julia's number, but it was busy. She dialed Harris again. He was in his car now. She heard the high scream of the police siren as he spoke.

"We're almost there and the medics should be too."

"Keith, I'm afraid to leave Ellin alone and I have to get to work. I'd never forgive myself if I left and something happened. I'm not sure what she'll do. I can't reach Julia. Can you send someone?"

"I'll send an officer. Stay there till one arrives."

"Okay. In the meantime, I'll keep calling Julia. Keith, I think Derek Shelby is the murderer. I'll tell you why when I see you."

"Okay. We're here. Gotta go."

She hung up and tried Julia again. This time King answered. She told him what had happened.

"I'll be right over with Mother," he said. Sonya took a deep breath. She was convinced Derek had committed the murders and she knew why and how. It would make a great story.

Chapter **30**

When Sonya arrived at the clinic, reporters and cameramen were already camped outside the brownstone. Perry was easy to spot. He had set up near the entrance. She squeezed between his tripod and the black railing that edged the garden. "Where have you been?" he asked.

"With Ellin. I couldn't leave her by herself so I waited until Julia and King came. They were there in minutes."

"How is she?"

"It's hard to tell. Julia is the best person to be with her right now. What's happening here?"

"The paramedics went in about fifteen minutes ago."

Sonya looked at the clinic's front door with its discreet brass plate that read DEREK SHELBY, D.V.M. What a contrast the calm, elegant exterior was to the drama that must be going on inside. If Derek survived, how would Ellin react to the trial and all the publicity?

The door opened and Harris appeared at the top of the steps.

"Derek Shelby is alive, but in need of hospital treatment right away. Please stand back so the EMTs can get him to the ambulance," he said.

He looked over the crowd. When he spotted her, he raised an eyebrow and tilted his head.

She nodded, and mouthed, "Ellin is okay." Harris nodded in return. Sonya moved back to give Perry room to shoot Derek Shelby being carried out of his clinic, unconscious on a stretcher.

With the camera on his shoulder, Perry followed the stretcher to the ambulance. Then he came back to Sonya. "Why don't you ask your pal Harris to let us inside for a few shots of the office?"

"Perry, you know I can't ask, not with these other reporters here. I'll talk to him later."

"I thought your buddy would do anything for you."

"Perry, stop it. Let's get back to the studio."

When they arrived at the network office, Rick Carlton was waiting for Sonya. She gave him a quick summary of the action and then asked how logging the tapes had gone.

"They're done, you can start checking them as soon as you like. But you'd better call Matt first. He's been trying to get you on your cell phone."

Sonya sighed. "I must have been in a dead spot. I got his message and called him back, but his line was busy."

She noticed a couple of cartons of Chinese takeout on Rick's desk. "What's that?"

"I ordered takeout for the guys, there's some left if you want it."

She picked up one carton and looked inside; it was untouched. "Shrimp and scallops in black bean sauce. My favorite, thanks. You're the best. Now that I smell it, I'm ravenously hungry." She grinned. "I hope your wife appreciates you."

He grinned back. "Go call Matt before you microwave that. He wants to have a conference. I'll stick around for an hour or so."

Sonya picked up the food, blew Rick a kiss, and left. In her office, she threw her bag on a chair, and then dialed Matt's number. He answered immediately; she told him Derek was alive, but not conscious.

"How do you know?"

"Harris told us. I'll call the hospital in a little while to see if he's made it."

"Okay. Donna wants a conference call to discuss an outline for the show. Be ready in fifteen minutes. Have Rick listen in so he can work with you tomorrow."

"Fine." She put down the receiver. The shape of the story depended on Derek's survival and whether the police had proof of his guilt.

Sonya took the food to the staff kitchen. In three minutes she'd have something hot to eat and a break from the confusion of the long day. She pulled out a chair and watched the countdown on the microwave clock.

What worried her was that she hadn't interviewed Derek, and she wasn't sure how much B-roll they had of him at the party. The shot of him being carried out on the stretcher just had to be good enough to use. The microwave dinged. Sonya took the carton back to her office, then reached in her bag for her cell phone.

There were two messages from Harris. She sat down to return the calls.

"Where are you?" he asked.

"At the office."

"I thought I told you to take your phone with you everywhere?"

"You did, I just went to the kitchen to heat up some Chinese takeout."

"You don't follow orders, do you?"

"Please. You're not my boss." She was annoyed.

"Did it ever cross your mind that I might be anxious about you?"

"No, it didn't," she snapped. "You're not my husband either."

He laughed. "Not yet."

She was about to make a quip in return, then realized he was half-serious. She changed the subject. "How's Derek Shelby?"

"It's too early to say. He made himself a sophisticated cocktail of drugs. He's likely to end up in a coma."

"Poor Ellin."

"Yes. He left a note confessing to the murders and asking for forgiveness for what he did to her and her family. Maybe that'll be some comfort."

Sonya sighed. Her instincts had been right. But however sincere the gambling vet's confession, it couldn't make up for what Derek had done.

She glanced at her watch. "I've got to go. I have a conference call in a few minutes."

"I want to see you tonight. How long will you be?"

"I'll have to keep going for another two or three hours," she said. "What about you?"

"The same. Why don't we meet at that wine bar, The Grape Vine, on Third Avenue and Sixty-fifth Street? At nine."

"Okay," she said.

"If you're late, I'll wait."

Sonya clicked off the phone. What was she letting herself in for? He insisted on seeing her now, after an exhausting day, when he could easily come to the office and interview her in the morning. She had no information that wouldn't keep.

She suspected Harris wanted more than an interview, and attractive though he was, she wasn't prepared to get heavily involved. She'd been that route before, married to a man with a demanding ex-wife and two kids. Once was enough.

She went into the conference room, put Perry's last tape into the deck, and hit the Start button. It was playing as Rick appeared at the door. She told him about Derek's confession, then fast-forwarded until Harris appeared.

"I know Keith Harris," Rick said. "I worked with him when I was doing police roundups for the local news. He's a good cop. You're lucky you have him on the case."

"Yes. I know him from other stories too." She fast-forwarded the tape to the shot of Derek being carried out of the brownstone. She breathed a sigh of relief. It was everything she needed.

Rick agreed. "Sonya, you've come up with another winner."

"Thanks to Perry," she replied. "What would we do without him?"

"What would he do without you? You know he's crazy about you."

The phone rang. Sonya was pleased to hear Donna's calm voice. "Sonya, Matt's on the line too."

"You're sure that Derek Shelby is the killer?" was his first question.

"Yes, I'm sure," she answered. "He left a note asking Ellin's forgiveness for both murders."

"Will he survive?"

"Maybe. But he may be in a coma."

"Let me get it straight," Donna said. "Matt told me that you think Hilda paid Derek two hundred thousand dollars to murder Gussie. Why?"

Sonya paused for a moment. "Donna, foolish as it seems, I believe Hilda was dominated by her need to be in control of the business and her family. And people's opinion of her mattered, so when she received Kathryn's letter she was overcome with fear. It brought back all the unhappy memories. Gussie knew the truth about her having a daughter, so Gussie had to go."

"I'm sure you're right. Hilda had a reputation as a controlling woman, but an insecure one. And Derek Shelby was so desperate to pay off his gambling debts he was willing to commit murder? It's sad."

"Yes. There was nowhere else he could turn. Everything the Shelbys owned was mortgaged. The Woodruff Trust is tight, and Ellin had withdrawn her limit. The only way he could see to get money was through Hilda. They were seen together around town and that led to rumors that they were having an affair."

"Was that true?" Matt asked.

"It's possible but Ellin doesn't think so."

"So Ellin knew about it?" asked Donna.

"She'd heard the rumors, but refused to believe them. She didn't want to face Derek's problems any longer."

"So why did he kill Hilda?" Matt broke in again.

"That we'll only find out if he comes out of the coma. Hilda may have promised him more money but failed to give it to him. Or perhaps she wanted him to kill Kathryn as well. He refused and they quarreled. Then, too, Hilda was the only person who knew he killed Gussie."

Donna agreed. "Hilda was easy to quarrel with. Women were reluctant to have her on their charity committees. She was arrogant and wanted the last word on every detail." Donna paused for a moment, and then changed the subject. "So, Sonya, you're saying that our show's final outline depends on Shelby's survival?"

"Yes, Donna. We'll have to wait until the morning's medical report. We can't do any more interviews until we know how he is."

Matt broke in, his voice loud with excitement. "I think we've got a great angle for the story no matter what. It's one you haven't even touched."

"What's that?"

"You remember, I was the one who told you about Shelby's gambling. That got you on the track to solve the murders. Well, let's focus on his habit."

"What do you mean?" Donna asked.

"I'll get some guys to talk about how Shelby hung out at the clubs and got himself in trouble. You know, we can make this a real 'doctor ruins himself' story. I'll start on calls right away."

"Matt," Sonya said, "this story is not an exposé of gambling addiction. It's about a woman who wanted to find her place in a family. It's about an adopted child who wanted to be reunited with her birth mother, and the sequence of events that it set off."

"No way," said Matt. "My idea has more guts to it."

Beside Sonya, Rick nodded vigorously. She took a deep breath and spoke forcefully. "I see an interview with Wells, King, and Kathryn together. I think we need to end on a positive note."

"Sonya—," Matt said warningly.

Donna stopped him. "I agree. We should have something more about Shelby's gambling, but Sonya is right about ending on the reunion of Kathryn and her family. So let's do the interviews we need to wrap it up that way.

"Now everyone go home and get some rest. We'll have a staff meeting at ten tomorrow to decide on our next step." She hung up.

Matt briefly discussed possible shoots for the morning, then he hung up without saying good night. Sonya stood, stacked the tapes, and set the carton of cold uneaten Chinese food on top. "Go home," she said to Rick. "I'll stay a while, check tapes, and do some rough outlines for the show."

She looked at the food and realized she had lost her appetite. The argument with Matt had drained her last bit of energy.

After a quick glass of wine with Harris, her day would finally end. She could be in bed and asleep by ten.

Chapter 31

Sonya arrived twenty minutes late at the Grape Vine. The thought of meeting Harris made her nervous. She fussed, putting on makeup and combing her hair, and when she was ready to go it was raining again and she had to wait for a taxi.

Harris was at a small table at the side of the bar. He stood when he saw her, and then they sat facing each other. The detective loosened his tie and unbuttoned his collar. A tuft of silky black hair appeared at the base of his throat.

"I'm sorry this place is so crowded," he said.

Sonya gave him a quick pat on the arm. "We're only having a glass of wine," she said. "Any news on Shelby?"

He shrugged. "He owes you his life, but don't expect thanks. He knew what he was doing when he counted out the pills." He paused. "Our real trouble was with the cat."

"You mean Raj?"

"Whatever. It leaped around the room and ended up on top of a cabinet."

"That sounds like Raj. Ellin told me Derek often took him to the clinic. He is a Bengal; they breed them."

"I'll see that Raj gets back to her."

"Thanks. She'll appreciate it. Raj means a lot to Ellin."

Sonya picked up the menu and looked at the wine list. "Shelby ruined her life and she just put up with it. I don't know why she didn't walk out."

"I've given up wondering why people do crazy things," he said. "Tell me, when did you first think Derek could be the murderer?"

"I was suspicious after Gussie's body was found. He came into Woody's with a phony excuse of looking for a missing silver frame. He said he'd packed the frame, but I remembered that Ellin was angry with him because he hadn't done a thing. Then, he seemed to forget all about his errand. He just stared at the spot where Gussie died. He had a strange look on his face and it made me wonder what he was thinking."

"From the beginning he was on my suspect list. He didn't have much of alibi. Told us he was at his clinic by himself."

"That's only a dozen blocks from Woody's. He must have walked there, murdered Gussie, and walked back. That would have matched the time Steve Pendleton saw the lights go out. And another thing, Keith, after you examined Gussie's body, you said the murderer knew what he was doing. Of all of the suspects, he was the one with medical knowledge. It had to be Shelby."

"Thanks, Sonya, I'm glad I was of some help." He laughed.

Sonya grinned back. "Derek knew just where to put that fork under Gussie's ribs—and just where to strike Hilda's head to kill her quietly and efficiently."

"Sounds right, Sonya. Did you notice where Shelby was during the party around the time of Hilda's murder?"

"It was pretty hard to see anyone in that crowd, but when we started to shoot after the murder, he was at the bar near the fake wall by Hilda's office. We have a shot of him there having a drink."

"Great, I'll want to see that."

Harris leaned forward and looked directly at Sonya. "I'm so glad you turned up. I began to think you weren't coming."

Sonya glanced away quickly. The waiter caught her eye and came to the table. Sonya asked for a glass of chardonnay and a slice of seed cake. Harris ordered the same.

"Why were you late?" he asked. She frowned and shrugged her shoulders. "I'm pushing you too fast, right?"

Sonya looked at his eager face. She closed her eyes and forced herself to resist him.

"Keith, let's keep it cool," she said. "I have an hour-long show to produce for Tuesday night. It has to be completed by noon on Monday. I'm here because I need to check a few facts with you. For instance, did you know Derek was in debt?"

He sighed and leaned away from her. "Yeah, it's common knowledge that he was a high-stakes gambler and not a lucky one. He always owed money, but usually managed to stay one step ahead of the game. This time it caught up with him."

"And Kathryn? Do you believe her story?"

"Yes. We checked her identity. She is Kathryn Pettibone, and her mother, Zoe, died recently. What I can't work out is how Gussie recognized her so quickly."

"Apparently she's the spitting image of her grandmother Anthea. There's a painting of her at Woody's. Kathryn has the same bone structure. I think Gussie knew it immediately."

The waiter brought their wine and cake.

Harris picked up his glass and said, "You don't remember when we first met, do you?"

Sonya shook her head and took a sip of wine.

"It was at the public library, when Harriet Franklin was murdered. I asked you a few questions that night and then you put me off for a couple of days. I was a fool to agree to wait to talk to you. You were almost strangled," he said intently. "Do you remember my visiting you in the hospital?"

Sonya was silent. She picked up her fork, cut a bite of cake, and ate it. She had a vague recollection of seeing him at the hospital, but so many people—and police officers—had been there that no one stood out. Uncomfortable, she decided to change the subject.

"You know, it was only after I talked to Ellin this afternoon that I was sure who the murderer was."

"Do you believe she thought Derek was guilty?"

"Perhaps, but she couldn't admit it to herself. And, like the rest of us, she couldn't see a connection between the two murders."

"Neither one of Hilda's sisters knew about her child?"

"No, they were told she had to stay in Switzerland because she was too sick to come home. I'm sure only Gussie knew about the pregnancy."

"So Ellin and Julia still don't know that they have a niece?"

"By now, I'm sure they do know. They won't turn their backs on Kathryn, and I don't think King and Wells will either. But it will take time. The Woodruff family has lots of changes to face."

Sonya finished her glass of wine.

"Will you have another?" he asked.

Sonya shook her head. "No, I mustn't. I have to get a good night's sleep. Work starts early and it'll be a no-end day."

"What will happen if you're late?"

"I'm never late." She laughed. "Except, of course, tonight."

"I didn't mind the wait. You're worth it." Harris raised his hand and summoned the waiter to bring the check.

"Let me get this," Sonya said. "I can expense it." The minute she said it she realized she had offended him. Harris ignored her and handed the waiter his credit card. They sat in silence until the waiter returned. Harris signed the slip and then stood up. "Let's go. It's time we both got to bed."

Sonya walked out ahead of him and stood on the pavement. The rain had stopped and the wide avenue glistened like silver under the headlights of the cars. She took a deep breath. The air smelled damp but fresh. Tomorrow should be a fine day.

She turned to him. "Thanks. It was great talking to you. And thanks for the wine. I'll catch a cab home."

"I'll walk you home," he replied. "I know where you live. It's only a few blocks from here."

Sonya hesitated. "I'm tired," she said.

"A little walk will help you relax."

She looked at him for a long moment, then said, "Okay, let's walk."

He put his arm around her shoulders and she let him lead her. "I don't want to leave you while you're feeling down."

They walked in silence toward her apartment house. He stopped a few yards before the door and turned to face her.

"How about you fix a cup of coffee to help a weary cop get home?"

Sonya was tired of resisting. She rested her head on his shoulder and sank into the warmth of his strong, lean body.

He bent his head and whispered in her ear. "Sonya, why can't you admit you need me as much as I need you?"

He held her tightly, stroking her hair. Then he lifted her face.

"Come on, Red, let's go in," he said. "I'll make the coffee."